A
FRENCH
COUNTRY
MURDER

A FRENCH COUNTRY MURDER

Peter Steiner

THOMAS DUNNE BOOKS
ST. MARTIN'S MINOTAUR ✿ NEW YORK

THOMAS DUNNE BOOKS.
An imprint of St. Martin's Press.

www.minotaurbooks.com

Design by Susan Yang

Library of Congress Cataloging-in-Publication Data

Steiner, Peter.
    A French country murder : a novel / Peter Steiner.—1st ed.
        p. cm.
    ISBN 0-312-30687-3
        1. Americans—France—Fiction. 2. Police—France—Fiction. 3. Country life—Fiction. 4. France—Fiction. I. Title.

PS3619.T4763 F74 2003
813'.6—dc21

                                                                                    2002032514

First Edition: March 2003

10   9   8   7   6   5   4   3   2   1

Except for the point, the still point,
There would be no dance, and there is only the dance.
— T. S. ELIOT

Charles the great has come at last,
Come at last to stay.
He knows not where he's going, though
He thinks he knows the way.

He thinks he knows the way to love,
Through flowered fields and highways.
He does not know what love is or
That I will love him always.

A pretty girl there waits for Charles,
To ease his pain and kiss his eyes,
To circle him with chains of love,
To show him love and make him wise.

Charles the great might disappear
while thinking you can see him.
But life is short and art is long,
And she can live without him.
— HENRI KADUSCO

A
FRENCH
COUNTRY
MURDER

I

*E*VERY MORNING, AS THE BELLS OF THE CHURCH IN SAINT LEON SUR
Dême were clanging eight o'clock, Louis Morgon set the two pitch-
ers, one of hot milk, the other of coffee, along with a cup and a
knife, a baguette, the white and blue butter dish, and the little
cracked marmalade pot on the battered metal tray and carried them
all out to the terrace. If the day was cold, he put on a gray wool overcoat and wrapped an old plaid shawl around his neck. When it
rained, he sat contentedly under the faded umbrella as it flapped and
rattled in the wind and the rain dripped around him. When it was
hot, he wore a T-shirt and a pair of shorts. From the little table
between house and barn, he could gaze over the gravel driveway,
across the descending garden at the field running up the opposite
hill. What he saw changed with the weather and the seasons. But,
however it changed, it always pleased him as though he were seeing
it for the first time.

This year, as it happened, the fields were planted in sunflowers, which were in full bloom now, their massive heads sagging under the weight of their seed. And this particular Tuesday morning, the sun was brilliant. Its brilliance was refracted in the thousands of drops of dew that still clung to the grass, the hedge, the roses, the herbs and vegetables, the ivy and trumpet vine which climbed the stone barn. The sky was that particular blue which endures right down to the horizon, a color so intense and deep that you can feel the blackness of outer space behind it.

As Louis opened the door with his right hand, balancing the tray with his left, something fell lightly against his leg. He looked down to see that it was the arm of a dead man who lay across his doorstep, having been deposited there sometime during the night. Louis pulled his leg back, and the dead arm settled on the floor. Louis did not drop the tray. To an observer it might almost have appeared as though he had expected to find the dead man there.

Louis carried the tray back to the kitchen. Then, after steadying himself against the table for a moment, he returned to look at the body. It had belonged to a black man although by now the skin had taken on that peculiar gray pallor the dead share, no matter what race they may have been. The dead man wore blue jeans and running shoes without socks, and a polo shirt not tucked in. There was a red, green, and black embroidered skullcap sitting on the front of his head.

The man's throat had been slit from ear to ear. But, aside from the blood crusted black along the edges of the wound, there was no blood anywhere else, not on the ground and not on the man's clothes. The eyes were closed. The mouth was closed. The man seemed perfectly tranquil, but for the gaping smile which had been cut into his neck.

Louis was not entirely undone by the grim sight of this corpse, even though this was his first face-to-face encounter with violent death. Nor was he worried that the man's murderer or murderers might still be lurking about, although he perhaps should have been. Louis walked to the top of the driveway and peered down the hill. He came back, crouched down, and studied the man. After some hesitation, he lifted the hands, first one then the other, more to feel the weight of the dead arms than anything else. He looked at the fingernails, although he did not know what he expected to see. The arms were hard and heavy. They no longer had the feeling of human flesh.

Louis examined the clothes. The dead man's pants and shirt were clean and looked to be new. There was nothing in his pockets. The cap had the word *Liberté* embroidered on it.

Louis stood and looked at the dead man for a long time. Then he went inside, closed the door, and dialed the number of the police. When, a short time later, the police car came up the drive followed by the ambulance, Louis was seated at his outdoor table, his back to the corpse. He rose as though to greet invited visitors. The men shook hands all around. After a quick exchange of friendly words, Louis and Renard, who was the Saint Leon gendarme, went over to look at the dead man. Renard crouched down to look at the man. This was not Renard's first corpse by any means, but it was his first murder—at least, as he said with a slight smile, as far as he knew. The ambulance men had edged up behind Louis and Renard and were peering at the body.

"He was killed elsewhere," said Renard to no one in particular and stood up. He gazed for a few moments at the body from this vantage and then turned his gaze on Louis. At just over forty-five, Renard was probably fifteen years younger than Louis. He stood half a head taller than the older man. Louis's thin white hair riffled in the breeze. He felt the policeman looking at him. "Coffee?" he offered. Without waiting for an answer, he went inside to make a pot.

After Renard had finished with the dead man, he nodded to the ambulance men, and they lifted the corpse onto a stretcher. The skullcap fell off. One of the men picked it up and put it on the stretcher. They loaded the body into the ambulance and shut the door. Then they all stood in the bright sun and drank coffee. They drank in silence.

"A warning from 'the sordid world'?" asked the gendarme finally. "The sordid world" was one of those phrases which old married couples and old friends have as a sort of code for ancient and familiar arguments. It reminds them why they like and dislike one another. Louis did not answer.

The ambulance men waited. The gendarme motioned with his head. They took a last sip of coffee and set their cups on the edge of the table. They shook hands with Louis, got in the ambulance, and backed down the driveway. They did not turn on the blue lights. The ambulance disappeared backward over the rim of the hill. Louis and the gendarme listened while the driver changed gears at the bottom of the drive and drove off toward town.

"We are so far from Washington. How did they find you? And why?" Louis did not answer. "He looks North African. There will probably be a big investigation. It will get political."

"It already is political," said Louis and turned his face into the wind. He appeared to regret having said even that.

Then the two men made small talk. Renard promised to let Louis know if he discovered anything about the dead man. But neither man expected that he would discover very much. They stood in silence for a while, listening to the wind shake the leaves of the linden trees, listening to the birds. Then they shook hands and Renard left.

Louis returned to the kitchen with the empty coffee cups. He refilled the coffeepot, picked up his breakfast tray, and carried it back outside to the table. He sat down facing the field of sunflowers. The butter had gotten soft. The marmalade was sweet and bitter as good marmalade is. He ate his breakfast with relish and sorrow. When Dominique Brisard came clattering up the drive on her moped, he had just finished eating. She came every Tuesday morning to clean his house.

"Bonjour, monsieur," she said. "It is a beautiful day." She smiled broadly and swept her arms about her. Her gesture took in the garden, the roses climbing the front of the house, the fields, the sky, the whole world.

"It is a beautiful day, Dominique," Louis responded, and she thought in that moment that Monsieur Morgon was surely the most contented man she had ever known.

II

*B*ACK IN HIS OFFICE IN THE TOWN HALL, RENARD LIT A CIGARETTE.
The bright day spilled into his office through tall windows. The
Hotel de France across the square was bathed in sunlight. Its flower
boxes were overflowing with geraniums. Renard turned his attention to the small stack of forms he had assembled. Though he had
been a policeman for nearly twenty years, a murder is a milestone. A
murder is a big event. It must be reported in great detail. And not
only the murder itself, but what came before and after.

Renard was certain that this murder in particular would be scru-
tinized all the way up the line, through the prefecture, through the
department, until it landed in Paris. Just the thought of it made him
light another cigarette while the first was still burning. Although
Renard knew very little about Louis Morgon's past before he had
come to Saint Leon, he knew enough to recognize that the case
probably had international and—who knew—maybe even national

security ramifications. Yet there was so little he could report. Name of the victim: Unknown. Place of the murder: Unknown. And so on. Louis could perhaps be of help, but he wouldn't be. Renard was sure of that. Years before, Louis Morgon had turned his back finally and completely on his past, whatever it had been, in Washington, D.C., what he now referred to as "the sordid world." Renard surmised he had been connected somehow with espionage or politics, but he never asked. Washington was, however, the capital of the United States and as such, the center of all kinds of intrigue. Renard also knew that Louis had once been married and that he had two children. But, given that the two men were friends, that was very little.

In their conversations over afternoon coffee at the Hotel de France, Louis could be eloquent about the new wines, about a recipe for rabbit stew. He would talk on at great length about literature or about his painting. Louis would lay down imaginary fields of color with his hands on the white tablecloth. As far as Renard understood, Louis began his painting with colors that were not even meant to be seen in the finished work. These colors would somehow affect subsequent layers of color so that you would only sense their presence in the finished work. Renard had the tantalizing sense that Louis's discourses on underpainting were coded clues about his life. If he just heard them the right way, he was sure they would give him insights into his friend's past. But this understanding always seemed to remain just beyond his reach.

"Did you paint when you lived in Washington?" Louis would look at Renard as if to say, "Have I overestimated you? How can you be so direct and obvious?" Louis had been experimenting, he explained, with dark reds and umbers he had borrowed from the Italians. "Our light is more delicate than the Italian light, and so the reds come up wrong." They showed through too fiercely and suggested a more intense, a hotter landscape than he was painting here. "I am trying a lighter, yellower red, but it isn't quite right either. Not strong enough. You see, Renard . . ."

Sometimes, Louis dragged the protesting policeman into the barn whose downstairs had become his painting studio. There was the one dusty window in the garage door which even on the brightest days only dimly illuminated the old Peugeot parked there. But, entering the small door that had once been one of three stall doors and switching on the bright lights, one saw an ancient workbench, a jumble of tables and easels, and a bewildering arrangement of jars stuffed with brushes, of boxes and cans, of crushed and twisted tubes of color. There were stacks of partially built wooden stretchers, other stacks of stretched canvases, and a storage rack for paintings that covered one wall and reached to the ceiling. The cement floor was spattered with paint. A tall roll of canvas leaned in the corner. The smells of linseed oil and turpentine filled the room, a sensation which Renard had to admit he found pleasant.

Renard showered the forms with curses and cigarette ash as he labored over them. He scribbled diagrams of the crime scene and the position of the body. He described the wound as best he remembered it. He tried to make it all sound scientific and routine. When he was finished, he scrawled his signature across the bottom of the page.

He was supposed to report the murder to the authorities by telephone and to telefax them the reports. Instead he jammed the required copies into envelopes which he addressed to the regional prefect and the national gendarmerie. He walked them across to the post office and handed them to Madeleine Picard, the clerk. "Take your time with them," he told her.

Louis was certainly right about the case being political. Just involving foreigners as it did, this case would be passed up the line until it found its way into the hands of someone determined to make political hay. Then there would be loud cries for action, for solutions. Everyone would be nervous about it being an African who had been murdered, what with the bombings that had been going on in Paris and the heat that was coming just now from the smoldering Islamic revolt in Algeria. Before too many days, detectives and forensics experts and journalists would begin arriving from Paris. The journalists would concoct international political implications. The politicians would make pronouncements on television.

Renard walked to the hospital to have a closer look at the corpse. He pulled aside the sheet that covered the dead man. But the ashen figure, though he was now naked, revealed no more about himself than he had earlier. He lay on a stainless steel table, his arms at his sides, his hands palm up. Under the fluorescent light, he looked even grayer than before. His skin was hard and dry. His lips were opened slightly to reveal large teeth. "He lost a great deal of blood," said Boudin, the doctor. "The wound is deep. It was made with one cut of a very sharp, long blade, from left to right."

"My left or his?" asked Renard, feeling vaguely that he ought to ask something.

"His. There is very little blood on his clothing, as if whoever killed him changed his clothes. There is some bruising on his arms. His blood had a significant alcohol level. He was intoxicated when he was killed. I have sent samples out to be tested further. He was dead less than twelve hours when I first saw him at about eleven thirty. And there is this: Some back teeth were pulled after he was dead. Probably to make it more difficult to identify him."

"Where are his belongings?"

"There are only his clothes. His pockets were empty."

"Let me look at them." Renard did not want to appear less than thorough in front of the doctor.

"Did you call the prefecture?" asked Boudin.

Renard did not answer. The clothes did not tell him anything. He set the cap on the dead man's head. It slid off onto the steel table.

"What should I do with him?" asked Boudin impatiently, taking the cap and putting it with the other belongings.

"Keep him," said Renard.

"For how long?" asked Boudin.

"I'll let you know," said Renard.

"Our morgue is small," said Boudin.

"Anybody who wasn't murdered you can bury. You have my permission," said Renard and left.

Renard found Louis at the foot of his driveway.

"They must have carried him up the hill beside the driveway. I would have heard the gravel if they had been driving or walking on the driveway. Like you said, he wasn't killed here. There isn't any blood. There aren't any tire tracks."

"An elaborate way to deliver a message. Listen," said Renard with a great sigh. He knew already what the response would be, but he continued anyway. "In a few days there will be national police, detectives, reporters, and your tranquility will be gone. 'The sordid world,' as you call it, will reenter your life with a vengeance. Tell me what this is about or what you think this is about, anything you know, and maybe we can sort it out before they get here. I have delayed reporting it to my superiors. But it is only a matter of time."

"Solving the murder will solve nothing," said Louis, and started walking slowly up the drive. The gendarme walked beside him. The heavy heads of the sunflowers scraped against each other in the breeze. "Solving the murder will uncover things that should not be uncovered. It will raise questions which can never be answered, but which people—once the questions are asked—will not let go of."

"I have no choice but to investigate the murder," said Renard helplessly. He stopped and lit a cigarette.

"I know," said Louis. Renard walked back down the driveway. Louis watched as he reached the bottom. Renard walked back and forth, moving the gravel from time to time with his toe, looking at the grass, at the edge of the roadside. At one point, he stooped beside the road and picked up something. It was only a faded scrap of paper with nothing on it, but he stuck it in his pocket. He wanted to worry Louis, and he didn't know what else to do.

Renard walked slowly up the driveway again, watching the ground as he walked. Louis was sitting at his little table on the terrace.

"I have to look around," said Renard.

"Of course," said Louis.

"You didn't find anything, did you?" asked Renard.

"Nothing," said Louis. Renard knew that Louis would have already gone around the house, centimeter by centimeter, and that he, Renard, was now searching in vain.

III

At the base of the driveway, Louis had found a business card from the Hotel du Chateau and its restaurant called La Rilletterie. They were located, as the card said, just two hundred meters from the chateau on the main road in the village of Villandry. Closed Mondays. Someone had drawn circles on the back of the card, trying to get the ink started in a ballpoint pen. Louis had gone all the way around the house and barn and up and down the driveway several times by the time Renard had arrived. But there was nothing else to be found.

Louis spent the rest of the day painting. Then he drove into town as he did every evening before supper. He bought a trout at the fish market. At the bakery he got a baguette. He stopped at Madame Picard's house to buy eggs and butter. At home he picked some green beans and got some potatoes from the barn. The sun was still high as he sat down at the small metal table to eat the trout, slicing it carefully down the middle, lifting the tender flesh away from the bones, lifting the skeleton out and putting it aside. He gave the head to Zorro, the cat. The beans were firm, the potatoes sprinkled lightly with pepper and dill. Everything glistened under a film of Madame Picard's fat golden butter. He mopped up the butter with a piece of baguette.

He usually lingered after supper while the sun set behind the hill. But tonight he quickly carried the dishes inside and put them in the sink. He backed the car out of the barn and drove off south toward Villandry. It was late July, and the days were already growing shorter. The weather had begun to shift ever so slightly. It was still hot during the day, but days of such extreme clarity, as today, had become rarer. And even today, a slight haze built into the air as evening fell. Some nights there was fog on the rivers. Faint clouds trailed across the sky. A pheasant shouted.

Louis put on dark glasses and drove into the sun. He kept to back roads. If anyone was following, he did not want to make things too easy for them. Besides, he liked the back roads, and his car was no longer suited for highway speeds. No one followed him. The drive took just over an hour.

La Rilletterie was a tourist restaurant connected to the small Hotel du Chateau. They sat snug against the road which ran past the chateau and through the edge of the village of Villandry. The restaurant's small terrace was filled with diners. Directly across the road on the banks of the Cher was a campground filled, as it always was at this time of year, with vacation caravans. Lights flickered in the caravans, and the sounds of laughter and television drifted across to Louis as he left his car.

Inside, the restaurant was filled with diners too. A young woman greeted him. She was pretty. She had a quick smile and an appealing gap between her front teeth. Her brown hair was pulled back, but a few strands had come loose at the sides.

"I only want to ask you a few questions," he said as she began to show him to a table.

"We are very busy," she said, gesturing toward the tables with both hands.

"Just two questions."

"Quickly then." She picked up her pen and looked into her reservation book.

"Do you have a black man working here?"

"No," she said, and then as an afterthought, "are you from the police?"

"No," he said. "Have you seen a black man in the company of some white men?"

"No."

"They could be Americans, perhaps, or North Africans. They would have been here yesterday or the day before."

"We were closed yesterday. We're closed on Mondays."

"Or the day before."

"We get people from all over the world. Americans and Africans, Japanese. Please excuse me now. I'm sorry, I'm very busy." She picked up some soup bowls at a table and went into the kitchen. She returned carrying two plates with steak and *frites*. The people she was serving looked at Louis curiously. He walked to the bar and sat down. The young woman waited on him. He drank a kir.

He left the restaurant and walked across the street. The sun had set. Reflections of the first stars were dancing in the water. At the campground, everyone had gone into their caravans. The hotel was brightly lit. He went inside and asked the young man at the desk the same questions he had asked in the restaurant. The answers were the same. He asked for a room for the night, but none was available.

Louis was not so much looking for anything or anyone in particular, as he was trying to attract the attention of anyone who might have been interested in him. It was probably a futile thing for him to do, but it was all he could think of. As he had told Renard, he had no interest in solving the murder. In fact, the possibility that the life he had carefully and meticulously built for himself here could be disrupted and ruined in the course of a murder investigation was nearly as frightening to him as the likelihood that he was an intended victim himself.

He did not harbor any secrets that might be of importance to anyone else, at least, as far as he knew. He had kept his past to himself simply to keep it at bay, and he clung to this secret in a superstitious way, as though it were the key to his continued tranquility. But he saw now that his tranquility was probably lost, gone forever. Moreover, he felt certain—he did not know why, but how could it be otherwise—that when the killer, or killers had finished playing with him, they meant to kill him too.

The magnificent gardens of Villandry were closed and deserted. The last gardener had locked away his tools and gone home. The chateau had been closed up, and the people of Villandry were closing and shuttering their shops and homes for the night. The day's heat had lifted, and it was getting chilly. Here and there, a thin shaft of light shone through curtains that were not quite closed. The sound of cutlery on china escaped into the narrow streets. Dogs barked behind ancient wooden doors and in courtyards as they heard Louis pass, his steps echoing against the high stone walls. He wandered from street to street, uphill, away from the river, behind the castle gardens.

As he walked along the high garden walls, he came to an enormous wooden gate. In the middle of the gate was a door with a small sign that read: NO ENTRY. BY ORDER OF THE ADMINISTRATION, VILLANDRY CHATEAU AND GARDENS. The door was unlocked. He slowly pushed it open and stepped through. He found himself overlooking the darkening chateau gardens from above. He could still make out the great square plots below, with their rows of flowers and vegetables, and their patterns of exquisitely carved hedges. The trellises of roses, the precise curlicues of box sent their fragrance into the night air. Stars and a wisp of moon, which seemed to have suddenly appeared, were reflected in the great still pool.

It seemed impossible that whoever had dumped the murdered man at Louis's door the night before could have left the card from the Rilletterie intending for Louis to pick it up, come to Villandry, and then come up the winding streets and through the gate to this very spot. Still, Louis was suddenly on his guard as he realized in what a completely vulnerable position he found himself. He stepped back against the wall and looked around himself in every direction.

He saw something move in the bushes, not ten meters to his side. He moved soundlessly across the short grass. He leaned across a low hedge of boxwood, only to find himself peering into the upturned faces of startled lovers. "My God," they said, terror in their voices, "who are you?" "What do you want?"

Louis muttered an apology and quickly stepped back through the gate into the street. He leaned against the wall while his heart pounded. His earlier life, a life he had thought long buried, a life where deception and treachery were the norm, this life that he had finally loathed and wanted to be completely and absolutely rid of, had resurfaced and taken him over again, in the instant it takes to slice someone's throat. Changing your life, escaping to rural France, to Timbuktu, for that matter, would not make any difference. It was like a spiritual virus that, once contracted, lived on in you until it became virulent and broke out all over again.

His car stood bathed in light beneath a street lamp. It appeared not to have been tampered with. But, as he was leaving Villandry, a car followed him at a close distance. They crossed the Cher, then the Loire, then drove through Langeais, then left off the main highway at Cinq-Mars, up the hill and out into the country. The car behind him did not make any effort to conceal itself. They drove along deserted country roads and through darkened towns. In the Bois de la Barre, the road was straight and narrow, barely wide enough for one car. The dark pines flashed by on both sides and formed a tunnel overhead. Two deer leapt across the road ahead.

At Neuille Pont Pierre, Louis stopped at the traffic light. The street was deserted. The other car pulled slowly up beside him. It was a large late-model BMW. A man was driving, his face completely in shadow. The woman in the passenger seat talked to the driver, then laughed silently at something he said and turned to look in Louis's direction. The top of her face was in shadow. She continued her conversation with the driver as she gazed toward Louis. Was there a gap between her front teeth? Louis could not be sure.

As the light changed, the BMW turned left. It had a white oval decal beside the license plate with the initials CD, which stood for *corps diplomatique.* Louis memorized the license number. Then he drove on to Saint Leon, which was only a few kilometers further on. The next morning he called the Hotel du Chateau in Villandry and reserved a room for that night.

IV

$\mathscr{I}$T TURNED OUT THAT SOLESME LEFOURIER, LOUIS'S NEAREST NEIGH-
bor, had seen something. She greeted Renard pleasantly and inquired
after his wife and his mother. Renard tried to press ahead with his
inquiry. Of course, she had seen the ambulance leave. She was glad
Monsieur Morgon was all right, she said. She did not ask what the
ambulance had been doing there. Nor did she ask why Renard was
asking her questions. Renard concluded from this that Louis had
already spoken with her and had told her about the dead man.

"This is only a routine police investigation," said Renard nonetheless, hoping to make their interview as brief as possible. He spoke
in what he thought sounded like an official voice. "I regret, madame,
I cannot say any more."

Solesme Lefourier lived with her husband in the small cottage a
few hundred meters below Louis Morgon's driveway. She had inherited the house, along with its modest barn and garden, its wine cave

cut into the hillside, from her parents while still a young woman. Every day she tended her garden or sat at the window with a book, in either case, rarely out of sight of the road which passed in front of her house. Very little escaped her notice. Even after her ancient husband Pierre—he was nearly forty years her senior—was long asleep, Solesme Lefourier sat in her chair at the window and looked into the night. Solesme Lefourier had been crippled since childhood. Her spine was fused and twisted, so that lying down for any length of time caused her pain. So she sat at the window night after night, waiting for sleep to come. She heard the high barking of foxes that sounded like a child crying. She heard the wavering call of an owl and the shrill scream of a rabbit being killed. And she saw the few vehicles that passed up and down the narrow road.

The night in question had been cool. But she had had the window open. It was not surprising that she had noticed the passing of an unfamiliar car. She could see the bottom of Louis's driveway and the very top of his house above the crest of the hill, she explained. Renard turned around to look. Years before, she continued, she had watched from here while the roofers, the Lagrande brothers, took off the old slate tiles, repaired the beams and lath, and replaced the slate.

"And last night?" said Renard, trying not to sound impatient. Solesme smiled at Renard but ignored his question.

Louis had stopped by her house and introduced himself shortly after he arrived. A retired gentleman from the United States, he had spoken halting French. His French had gotten quite excellent over the years, didn't Renard think so? She liked his accent, found it charming, cultivated. She smiled at Renard again.

"Louis Morgon has become a trusted neighbor and a friend." He helped her with little things, like repairing a shutter. Of course, he liked to speak about painting. He was passionate about painting. She knew nothing about painting, but she admired his paintings.

Renard shifted impatiently from foot to foot. *So far I haven't learned a thing about the murder,* he thought. *Meanwhile, I have heard all about their friendship.* Solesme's loquaciousness masked her care and discretion. Though Saint Leon was a small village, and everyone knew everyone else, no one, not even Louis's friend, the gendarme Jean Renard, knew that she and Louis were lovers.

Solesme began to talk about the events of Monday night. She had fallen asleep at the window as she did most every night. She had fallen asleep with the window still open. She awoke as a car passed by slowly. It drove without lights, which made her take special note. And it stopped near the bottom of Louis's driveway, out of sight of his house but not entirely out of sight of hers. It was partly obscured by a small stand of trees. The car stopped in the road, not on the gravel. The engine was shut off.

Two people got out of the car. Or maybe more. Solesme could not be certain how many there were. They did something together, but she could not see what it was. She thought that they might be lovers, but they did not stay long. They may have been there for five minutes. They may have opened the trunk. She couldn't be sure. She thought one might have stepped down the road a few meters, then back up to the car.

"What did he do down the road?" asked Renard.

"Nothing. I don't know. He may have dropped something. I don't know." She sounded apologetic that so much could have happened that she was unsure of.

"The others were already in the car. He got in the driver's side, I think, or in the backseat behind the driver, and they drove off." She had not been able to read the license of the car, but she thought it was a BMW. Renard was surprised that she would recognize a BMW in the dark, but she seemed fairly certain.

"A big one. Black or some dark color."

"Did you see any of their faces?" asked Renard.

"The inside light did not come on when they opened the door."

"Could you tell if they were white men or black?" asked Renard. He did not know what Louis might have told her. He might have been giving away more than he wanted to.

"Black?" said Madame Lefourier. She seemed surprised at the question. She thought for a moment. She decided she had been unable to tell.

"What about the brake lights?" asked Renard.

"The brake lights came on briefly. But I couldn't read the number. The light was too dim."

"Did you notice anything else about the car?"

She thought for a long moment. "There was a small white oval," she said finally. "A decal of some kind. I couldn't read it."

"Which way did they leave? Up the road or back down?"

"Up the road. I thought they would turn around and come back down. But they must have known the road, or they would have turned around. What do you think this is all about?" she asked.

Renard sighed. He wanted to be somewhere else. He preferred mediating disputes between neighbors to investigating murders. Then you did not have to lie and conceal things from people. You did not have to fear the arrival of the big officials with their smooth hair and their suits and uniforms.

"Madame," he said, adopting his official tone, "you have been very helpful. If you think of something else about what you saw, please let me know. And now, one last question about the other night: Do you know what time it was when you saw the car?"

"It was just before three," she said without hesitation. "The clock rang three right after they left."

"Thank you again, madame," said Renard and stood to leave.

"One moment," she said. She stood slowly, pressing herself upward off the chair with strong arms and hands. She led the way out to her cave. Though she walked with difficulty, she moved with surprising grace and even agility. Solesme Lefourier, Renard could not help noticing, was a beautiful woman.

She picked two jars of honey from a sagging wooden shelf and handed them to Renard. "For Isabelle," she said, handing him the one then the other. "And for your mother."

V

RENARD DREW A LARGE CIRCLE ON THE MAP WITH HIS FINGER, retracing the circle he had drawn earlier with a red pencil. It took in a quarter of France. "The African was killed," he said, "within three hours' drive of your house. He was still alive at midnight. And he was drunk." Louis sat looking at the map Renard had spread on his table.

"How do you know he was driven the entire way?" asked Louis. "Orly, Charles DeGaulle, and other smaller airports are well within your circle."

Renard chose not to respond. "He was brought here by at least two men in a dark BMW just before three o'clock in the morning. They carried him up from the street and left immediately. We do not know the license number. The car had a white decal, an oval, perhaps from the *corps diplomatique*."

"Solesme Lefourier," said Louis with a smile. He met Renard's eyes. "She misses very little." Renard looked at Louis sharply. Renard had the distinct feeling that he was missing a great deal.

"They drove without lights," said the gendarme finally.

After having made lists of what he did and did not know, after staring for hours at the map spread out on the desk in his office, he had decided to share what he knew with Louis. He had folded the map and walked past the police car to his own car. He did not like to use the police car unless he had to. People might think he was putting on airs.

He had wound along the road that followed the Dême. The shadows of poplars splashed across the car as he drove, causing the sunlight to flicker pleasantly in his eyes. He had turned up the lane, passed Madame Lefourier who stopped tying up her tomatoes and looked after him. Now here he sat. He could think of nothing more to say. He shrugged and drank the last of his coffee. He lit a cigarette.

The more Renard told Louis, he reasoned, the more likely Louis would be to move into action himself. And his snooping around would stir things up. That, Renard reasoned further, would inevitably turn up more information.

"Why are you telling me this?" Louis asked.

Renard shrugged again. "Maybe you will tell me what you know."

Instead of telling Renard anything, Louis got up and took down a dusty bottle from the mantel. He poured a centimeter of clear liquor in the still-warm coffee cups. Each man dropped in a sugar cube and cradled the cup under his nose to take in the heady aroma of plums. The two men sipped at the sweet brandy in their cups until it was gone. "I only know what you have told me," said Louis.

"What did you have to do with Africa?" asked Renard helplessly.

Much to his surprise, he got a question in response, and a very interesting question at that.

"Why did the people that brought him here go to such trouble to identify him as an African?" said Louis.

Renard waited.

"When your men carried the body to the ambulance yesterday, the cap would not stay on his head." Renard remembered his own experience at the morgue. "And yet, there he lay, after being drunk, having his throat slit, having his shirt changed, bouncing around in a car, being carried up the driveway in the dark, there he lay with his cap on. Why?"

"Unless he is not an African," said Renard.

"Unless he is not an African," said Louis.

"Why are you telling me this? This in particular," said Renard.

"It is something I noticed," said Louis. "It puzzled me. Whenever people want me to look in a particular direction, I find it useful to look in the opposite direction."

"And now you want *me* to look in a particular direction," said Renard.

"It is something I noticed," said Louis. Then, after a long pause: "I need something from you."

"Aha," said Renard.

"It will be of use to you too. I need to find out about this car. It is a BMW." He pushed a slip of paper with the license number toward Renard. It was a Paris number.

"Where did you see the car?" asked Renard.

"It may have been following me, and it may not. I don't know."

"Why should I help you when you have been entirely uncooperative?" asked Renard. He did not try to conceal his frustration.

"What else do you have?" asked Louis and smiled.

In his car, Renard thought about the ruse of the dead man's cap. Had it been meant for the police? He had, of course, been taken in completely. He cursed his own stupidity. Or had it been meant for Louis, who had not been taken in at all? Or had the murderers known who would and who would not be taken in? Were they trying to lure the police in one direction and Louis in another?

And what about the car that had followed Louis? Of course, it might be the same car that Solesme Lefourier had seen. But, for the moment, Renard was more interested in *where* Louis might have been followed. Solesme had seen him leave for his daily shopping trip and then leave again later that evening.

Renard went home. Isabelle was in the kitchen. She was not happy to learn that Renard intended to sit outside Louis's house and then to follow him when and if he left. Jean Marie, their only son, was home for a visit. Until recently, his job with the customs service had had him stationed in Tours. Then they had seen him frequently. But now he had been promoted and transferred to Paris. He was stationed at Charles DeGaulle Airport where he was undergoing training as a telecommunications specialist. He did not come back to Saint Leon that often.

"A murder has happened," said Renard helplessly. "And I have to investigate."

Isabelle gave him a thermos of hot coffee. He drove back to the office and changed cars. If he was leaving Saint Leon, he would rather be in the police car. There would be less explaining to do if he needed help. He drove back out toward Louis's house. When he got within sight of the driveway, he pulled off the road behind a tall hedge beside the Dême. This was a spot where he liked to fish for the trout that swam in the swift little stream. He turned off the engine and waited. He worked a crossword puzzle. He read the newspaper. He sipped a cup of coffee and wished he were home with Isabelle and Jean Marie. Soon they would be eating her roasted chicken.

Then Louis's car came down his driveway and down the lane. He turned onto the road going south. When the old Peugeot was out of sight, Renard pulled out from behind the hedge and followed.

VI

*L*OUIS DID NOT LIKE PLAYING CAT AND MOUSE WITH RENARD. IT DIS-
tracted him from the larger enterprise. Still, Renard was smart and
could take care of himself, and, for the moment, it was something of
a comfort to think that Renard might be following him. Louis did
not see him, but he hoped he was back there. Louis drove slowly and
kept to the main roads.

Once in Villandry, he took his suitcase from the car and went
into the hotel. It was six o'clock. The chateau and gardens had just
closed, and people were streaming out through the gates. The tour
buses had started their engines, filling the air with clouds of
exhaust. The tour leaders pumped their bright umbrellas up and
down to call their stray charges back to the buses. The street was
filled with families walking back to their cars. The girl from the
day before signed Louis into the hotel. She gave him the key to
room twelve. Upstairs, first floor, the bath was down the hall, she

explained, the w.c. next to the bath. Louis had asked for a room without a bath so that he could prowl the halls if necessary. And he had asked for a room overlooking the street.

The room was clean and modern, with flowered wallpaper, a sink, a bidet, a bed, a dresser, and a television. The bed was comfortable. Louis slept for an hour. He slept on his back. He slept without dreaming. He got up and put on his shoes. On his way to the bathroom, he listened at the doors of the rooms next to his. He heard nothing. He went downstairs to eat. "Do you prefer to eat inside or on the terrace, monsieur?" asked the young woman. She showed him to a table on the terrace. It was barely seven o'clock, so the only other guests were an English couple. They were puzzling over the menu. "What the devil is *'lotte'*?" said the Englishman loudly, as though presenting him with a French menu had been a personal affront. "It's fish," said his wife in a loud, urgent whisper, looking pleadingly in Louis's direction. Louis kept his eyes on his own menu. He ordered an omelette, a *salade composé*, and a half bottle of red Chinon, an '89 Domaine Alain, a wine he regarded as an old friend.

Renard left the police car in a nearby *allée* under a row of plane trees, and walked to the hotel. He showed the young woman who greeted him his identification, and looked at the hotel registry. Louis had reserved room twelve for one night. He had paid in advance with cash. At this moment, Monsieur Morgon was having dinner on the terrace. Did the gentleman wish to speak with Monsieur Morgon?

Renard could see Louis on the terrace, through the dining room door. He sat with his back to them. He held a glass of wine in his hand and seemed to be studying its color. No, he did not wish to speak with Monsieur Morgon, said Renard. His voice was angrier than he had meant it to be. He was thinking of Isabelle and Jean

Marie and the roasted chicken. "Thank you for your help, madame," he said. He hurried back to the car. Maybe they would not have finished with dinner at home. He was glad to be driving the police car. He could speed with impunity.

Louis's omelette was slightly overdone, the vinaigrette on the salad was a bit too tart, but the Domaine Alain was just as good as he knew it would be. He had a piece of goat cheese and then a cup of coffee. He left the restaurant and strolled up and down the street as the last daylight faded. The sounds of television and laughter from the campground, the church bell ringing ten thirty reassured him somehow. So did the cool air from the river. He went to his room to wait, though he did not quite know what he was waiting for. But he had made his presence apparent, and if anyone was interested, then they knew by now that he was there.

Louis did not have a gun with him. He had never owned one, though he had known since serving in the army how to use one. He had been trained in the use of various weapons. In his work at the Central Intelligence Agency, he had been required to carry a pistol on occasion, though, even then, he had strapped the holster under his arm with great reluctance. He had felt that carrying a gun into a tight spot offered but one more way things could go wrong. And yet, now, lying alone on the bed waiting for a visit from assassins, it seemed to him as though he might find considerable comfort in feeling the hard steel of a pistol under his pillow. But there was none.

Louis regarded his body in the mirror as he undressed for bed. He was trim and muscular for a man in his sixties. Still, the hair on his chest was white, his waist was thick, his hips and legs were starting to get thin. He was acquiring the body of an old man. "A gun won't change that," he said aloud and started at the sound of his own voice in the small room.

He had intended to lie under the covers fully clothed. Perhaps it was simply the force of habit that had caused him to remove all his clothes before getting into bed. Whatever the reason, he decided to wait in bed without clothes. *Like the proverbial sacrificial lamb.* He smiled to himself.

Before turning on the light, he stepped to the window and looked out onto the street. A black BMW like the one he had seen the other night was parked just opposite the hotel. He could not see the license plate or if it had a decal, but he thought it must be the same car. "Let's see what they do," he said. This time he did not notice that he had spoken aloud.

The little lamp with the frilly shade gave off a faint light, so that he had to lean toward the lamp and hold the book almost under it in order to read. He was just beginning *Anna Karenina*. When Louis had come to France to live, he had decided at the same moment to read only time-proven masterpieces of world literature, as though to make his departure from "the sordid world" absolute and complete. He gave up all contemporary writing, all newspapers and magazines, and began to work his way through Shakespeare, then through Balzac, then Goethe, Schiller, Plato, Aristophanes, through Thomas and Heinrich Mann, Zola, Faulkner, Graham Greene, Musil, Hugo, one by one, chosen at random, as the spirit moved him. Nothing but great writing held his attention. Now all of Tolstoy, all of Dostoevsky, Ibsen, Strindberg lay ahead of him, then Hamsun, Tagore, Kafka, perhaps Kraus, Hemingway, Dante, Molière, and on, and on. The prospect made him happy, as if he were facing a magnificent and endless feast.

He had never read *Anna Karenina* before, or any of Tolstoy. He opened the book and began: "All happy families resemble one another, each unhappy family is unhappy in its own way." He let the book sink to his chest slowly and gazed past it into the darkness. Louis had not pictured Sarah for a long time. And now, suddenly, there she sat before his mind's eye, her pretty face furrowed with anger and unhappiness. He had not seen her for more than twenty years, so she appeared to him now the way she had looked the day he had left. He had been unable to bear her looking at him there at the front door, so he had simply turned without a word and gone. Now he could not turn away. Nor did he want to. He closed his eyes in order to continue seeing her face, but it disappeared.

Louis and Sarah had married before graduate school. He had just finished two years in the army, serving as the signal officer for an antiaircraft missile battalion in Germany. Sarah had just graduated from Ohio University. Somewhere deep in their minds, they must have both known that getting married was the wrong thing to do. But, to the young, marriage often seems like the solution to the loneliness which youthful friendships and parties cannot make go away. And to Louis's generation, marriage was simply the next step after college. It did not require preparation or thought.

He could not recall now, lying in the darkness so many years later, whether he had even loved Sarah, much less whether she had loved him. He had certainly felt attached to her. He had liked her company, felt close to her. They had shared opinions and ideas. They were outraged and amused by the same things. That must have seemed like love at the time.

They set up housekeeping. They bought towels and dishes at Sears. They rented a small furnished apartment in the top floor of a house lived in by Manny Ricosi, a grocer, his wife Florence, and their three children. Louis and Sarah had to walk through the Ricosi's living room to get to their apartment, so that, on their way in or out, they saw with trepidation what a long marriage could become. The Ricosis screamed at one another with shocking abandon. Florence ate cake and donuts and got fatter and fatter. Manny hit Florence when things boiled over for him. The two youngest children watched television or fought with each other. Ronnie, the oldest of the three, shut himself into his room and listened to rock and roll records he played at full volume. He sang along in an atonal wail. The sound found its way through the ceiling into the Morgon's small apartment.

Some nights, *many* nights, in the first years of their marriage, after Louis had turned out the lights, Sarah lay in bed weeping. She wept silently so that he would not know, but he felt her trembling beside him as her sadness filled the room. Louis would stare into the darkness, feeling helpless and alone. "What's the matter?" he would ask finally. "Tell me what's the matter."

"It's nothing. Sometimes I just have to cry," she said. They went to sleep finally, neither one knowing anything more about the other, neither one feeling any less lost. They were so young and inexperienced, they did not even know how to ask each other questions. Had he loved her? Had he felt the generosity of spirit, the sense of joint purpose, had he been interested in their differences, curious about her particularities? Did he possess even the remotest knowledge of any one of that entire complex of good impulses which he now regarded as love?

He had been twenty-five years old. Louis tried to remember what that was like. He remembered that he had been entirely absorbed in being a graduate student of international politics. He was excited by his studies, by the intellectual challenges of graduate school, by his own emerging expertise in international relations. He had come up with the idea that, if by applying cybernetics to the study of politics, you could make the study of politics more scientific, then you would eventually be able to organize men and events to achieve a desired outcome with a high degree of predictability. He began to develop new structural frameworks, new methodologies to make this new approach to politics a reality.

"My God." Louis heard himself, now, these many years later, sighing in the dark: the arrogance, the hubris, the sheer craziness of the idea! What had he known then? What could he possibly have been thinking?

Louis's mentor had been Professor Kascht, a man whom he had not even thought of for decades. "Professor Johann Kascht." He pronounced the name slowly; it felt unfamiliar in his mouth. Tolstoy's first sentence had released a torrent of memories, and Louis could not have stopped their washing over him if he had wanted to. He pressed ahead, struggling through the memories surging and rising like dark floodwater around him, as though recalling these things might be of the greatest urgency. And in some sense it was of the greatest urgency. For Louis believed this was where the dead man's journey to his doorstep had begun, that this crime had its beginnings in his past.

When Louis had begun studying with Kascht, the professor's own studies of Middle Eastern politics had, for some time, been helping to shape American foreign policy. Louis worked diligently to learn what Kascht had to teach him. And Kascht, in turn, introduced Louis to important people at the State Department. So it happened that even before Louis had begun writing his dissertation, he was awarded a contract to apply his cybernetic models to relations between Egypt and Israel, Syria and Israel, Jordan and Israel.

In a series of papers, Louis laid out a systematic plan which, he argued, would guarantee Israeli strength, security, and autonomy, while, at the same time, keeping the three Arab states out of the

Soviet orbit and dependent on the United States for their eventual security and prosperity. Meanwhile, at night, Sarah, his wife, lay weeping beside him. Science and cybernetics failed him at night. *That should have told me something.*

Louis and Sarah did what many couples do when they see their marriage failing. They had a child. Then they had a second. Their love for their children was limited by their failure to comprehend who they were, just as their love for one another was limited. They did not consider, could not even remotely understand, what Jennifer and Michael might learn by watching their parents manufacture their own unhappiness. Now their children were grown and estranged from them both and from one another, and only now, these many years later, did Louis understand how that had happened.

At first, upon making this discovery, he had blamed himself. Then he had simply tried to put it out of his mind, thinking that his insights had come much too late to help anyone. Louis did not fear life. He accepted things as they came. But he did fear life's shadows and reflections—the memories, the recollections, the reconsidering, the thinking things over. And so he had determined, unconsciously perhaps, to count his family—Sarah and the children—as but one more aspect of "the sordid world," which he had come to France to escape. But now he realized, in fact, just in the last two days since the dead man had been deposited on his doorstep, that in leaving behind what he could leave behind, he had also tried to leave behind what he couldn't.

The papers he had written for the State Department were received with great interest, so that he found himself sitting one day with Johann Kascht and an undersecretary for Middle Eastern Affairs in the large reception room of the office of the secretary of state of the United States. They were ushered into the secretary's office. It was even larger than the outer office and was paneled entirely in walnut. The floor was covered with plush, royal blue carpet with the seal of the United States in the middle. There were bookcases built into the walls. These were filled with leather-bound books and mementoes, mainly photographs of the current secretary with every imaginable dignitary, including several with the president. A large semicircle of overstuffed couches, chairs, and small tables bearing vases filled with cut flowers faced the desk where the secretary sat. Behind him stood a wooden standard holding an American flag. A portrait of the president hung above and behind the secretary in an elaborate gold frame.

The secretary rose from behind his great mahogany desk and, shaking hands with Kascht and Louis, gestured toward the chairs that had been set right in front of his desk. His assistant brought coffee in a silver pot on a silver tray for the three visitors.

The secretary had Louis's papers in front of him. "I am told that you have done some important work here," said the secretary. He folded his hands on the small stack of papers. His thin fingers laced together smoothly and perfectly, and Louis recalled thinking that the secretary might have actually practiced this gesture. "You come highly recommended by Professor Kascht and Undersecretary Bowes. I don't have to tell you how explosive things are in the Middle East. The Soviets are making great gains in Syria and Egypt right now. We need to bring some new thinking to the problem. I would like for you to come aboard as part of our team at State. Yours would be primarily a research position, to begin with, but you would report to the undersecretary and would be expected to make policy recommendations. I think you can make an important contribution." He gazed at Louis with cold blue eyes and waited for him to say yes.

VII

*A*NNA KARENINA LAY HEAVILY ON LOUIS'S CHEST. THE LIGHT BREEZE moved the curtains in the window. The dim, little light left the corners of the hotel room in darkness. *It is in the corners,* Louis thought, *that I need to see.* He gazed ahead of himself, into the darkest corner, but saw nothing.

When his appointment to the State Department had finally been confirmed, Louis and Sarah had bought a house in Arlington in Virginia, across the river from Washington. Sarah finished her dissertation and was hired as an assistant professor of French at George Mason University in nearby Fairfax. Louis left for his office each morning before seven and some evenings did not return until after the children were asleep. He accompanied the undersecretary on trips to the Middle East with increasing frequency.

"You're on a fast track, Louis," said Hugh Bowes, laying his arm across Louis's shoulder. Hugh Bowes knew about fast tracks. His career trajectory was legendary. He was barely thirty and already an undersecretary of state. Bowes had come to the Department of State from Princeton University where he had been a protege of H. William Kendall, the dean of foreign policy analysts and founder of the Institute for Middle Eastern Studies. Within a year, Kendall had retired from the institute and Bowes was in charge.

For Bowes, it was only a short step from Institute director to undersecretary of state. He understood many things, but above all he understood how to make himself indispensable to those above him. He was soon invited to policy meetings, whether they concerned the Middle East or not. He often traveled with the president and advised him on the domestic ramifications of his foreign policy decisions. He stood in the background at press conferences, in case his expertise was required. He appeared as an administration spokesman on television news shows. When he spoke publicly, he articulated the administration's views with clarity and wit. His manner was both competent and self-effacing. In person, he was charming and engaging.

Bowes invited Louis to attend a policy briefing at the White House. Bowes put his arm around Louis's shoulder. "The president and the secretary will be there and could use the benefit of your thinking on . . ." Louis could no longer remember what the specific issue had been. But he could remember the excitement he had felt at being invited to attend this meeting. He remembered the sense of his own importance which easily overwhelmed any wariness he ought to have felt. Now, though, as he remembered the weight of Bowes's arm across his shoulder, a little shiver ran through his body, and he pulled the blanket higher.

Louis and Sarah had shopped together for a new suit for the occasion. They drove to Lord and Taylor. They picked out several blue and gray models; then they weighed the cut of each suit, the width of the stripe. They laid neckties across each suit. This suit had the correct air of importance, but its cut gave Louis a narrow, pinched look. That tie was too bright. It might upstage the president or the secretary. As they talked over which suit, which tie, this detail and that, their voices were hushed, their brows knit in concentration. The salesman waited dutifully through the long silences while Louis and Sarah thought about what the other had said. They might have been discussing their future together, or their children. But they were talking about buying a suit.

"Mr. President, Mr. Secretary, I think you will all be interested to hear Mr. Morgon's thoughts in this area," said Hugh Bowes. He brushed his thinning hair back with his hand and turned to peer at Louis through his thick glasses. What Louis said was not new to Bowes. In fact, what he offered was a synthesis of his own views and points that Bowes had made when they had spoken earlier that morning. Though Louis's ideas were controversial, Bowes assured him they coincided with his own ideas on the subject.

After some discussion, Louis's ideas met with general approval. "Watch out for this young man, Hugh. He could be after your job," said the president to general laughter.

"I will, Mr. President," said Hugh.

The policies which were designed and implemented out of Louis's suggestions met with success. In the peculiarly bloodless language of the State Department, the desired outcomes were achieved. As Sarah later pointed out to Louis, Hugh Bowes's prestige and influence had been enhanced without any risk to himself. After all, Louis was his man, and he was Louis's sponsor. With success, all power accrued to Bowes; when things went wrong, all blame would accrue to Louis.

In fact, as Louis eventually came to realize, Sarah, who had certainly been less naive than he in such matters as the thirst for power and the venality it engendered in high government circles, had still grossly underestimated the resourcefulness and cunning of those who desired power, as well as the intensity of their desire and the ends to which they would go to fulfill it.

They desired power above everything else, but were, at the same time, only dimly aware of their desire. When they thought of power at all, they saw it as a neutral force that could be used for good or for evil. They did not recognize how it could make virtue seem like weakness. Power required what the powerful called toughness, but what often enough turned out to be murderous brutality.

Louis thought with alarm of other bodies which had turned up during his time at the State Department. He recalled the case of Wilson Pemberough. A graduate of Harvard University and a Rhodes scholar, Pemberough started his career as an officer on the Soviet desk. He then received diplomatic postings in Cairo, Beirut, and Vienna, where he performed his duties with efficient enthusiasm, rendering the United States "exemplary service," as one citation he received when he left the government put it. Pemberough was the embassy's political officer in his last two postings, which meant that he concerned himself with political events in the country and compiled daily reports about them which he sent back to Washington.

This work, which was fairly routine and easily dispensed with, was a cover. For, as was often the case with embassy political officers, Pemberough was also responsible for running the United States' secret agents in the country where he was posted. This work consisted mainly of receiving the agents' reports and passing on assignments to them. This was done mainly by dropping messages at agreed-upon sites, but sometimes by means of secret rendezvous.

Pemberough was the only person at the embassy who knew who these agents were.

Pemberough had also recruited, and was running, a few agents that no one else knew about at all. He had done this on his own initiative. Such freelance work was frowned upon, but was often tolerated because of the intelligence it afforded. One of Pemberough's agents was a young secretary at the Soviet Russian embassy in Vienna named Ines Palyatskaya. Pemberough was handsome and sensitive. He showed concern for Ines's well being. She gave him information about her work. She smuggled photocopies of diplomatic papers to him. In return, Pemberough gave her love and affection.

That is not to say that Pemberough felt either love or affection for her, though it is true that he enjoyed their passionate hours together. But he pretended that he loved her in order to get the information he desired. His caresses, his tender words were part of his job.

Pemberough had a young wife. When Pemberough put off going back to Moscow with Ines, as he had promised he would, she threatened to tell his wife. Ines's body turned up in the Danube canal. Since his superiors knew nothing about Ines, Pemberough did not feel obligated to tell them of her death. But an enterprising Viennese police detective was able to establish her connection to Pemberough. Pemberough insisted that she had been done in by the Soviets, but he was recalled to Washington. He was forced to leave the foreign service. Still, so as not to ruin his possibilities outside government service, he left with citations from his superiors and a nice pension.

Louis realized now that Pemberough, or Hugh Bowes, for that matter, might not even understand that they wanted power, let alone how badly they wanted it. They thought of themselves as men of principle. Very often they were. Take Wilson Pemberough and his superiors, for instance. They all were certain that Ines Palyatskaya's death had been an unfortunate necessity, that she was a sacrifice to the higher good.

Hugh Bowes believed in democracy, the right to life, liberty, the pursuit of happiness, and the extension and dissemination of those rights to the rest of the world. Whatever power Hugh acquired was only acquired in the service of his principles. But Hugh was also a pragmatist. His study of politics and political philosophy, and then his own experience, had shown him the impossibly intricate interconnectedness of all things, and he had eventually come to understand that the world's problems would be solved by those who could develop and master the most detailed understanding and control of this impossible complexity, including the seamy and clandestine complexity represented by the Wilson Pemberoughs.

For some reason, the sight of Hugh Bowes eating now came back to Louis with astonishing clarity. Hugh always had his supper delivered to his desk, carried in on a silver tray. It was always a steak, well done, a baked potato, and a salad. He washed everything down with great gulps of Coca-Cola or coffee. He continued to read, dictate, and take down notes in his small, cramped hand. He never spilled or dropped anything. Yet he did not even seem to notice that he was eating. Louis was reminded of pictures he had seen of great bombers refueling in midair. Five minutes after the food had been delivered, nothing remained but the tray, the dinnerware, and the crumpled foil from the potato.

Anna Karenina slid to the floor, and Louis awoke with a start. It was nearly midnight. The curtain hung still in the window. The corners of the room remained in impenetrable blackness. The only sound was the rhythmic chirping of crickets outside. The world was at peace, and yet Louis's heart raced with terror. By making inquiries the night before, and now by waiting in this hotel room, he had made himself the bait in a dangerous trap.

Louis took the phone off the hook and turned out the light. A dim glow from the street lamp below shone through the window and cast pale squares on the ceiling. The dial tone sounded very loud in the dark. After a minute, the phone went silent. Louis waited naked in bed. He fought to remain alert. But the stream of his memory which had swept him along this far, and his dawning understanding of the murder, of his life, of everything seemed irresistible.

A State Department official, even one so new as Louis had been, was sought out by reporters, by diplomats lobbying for their own interests, by other policymakers in other departments. He was sought out for recommendations and advice, for influence that he might be able to exert, for pressure he could bring to bear. Louis was an amiable colleague, eager to learn how the government worked, curious about his colleagues and the work they did. He was bright, friendly, and attractive, with an intelligent and attractive wife. He and Sarah were invited to parties at embassies, at the homes of undersecretaries and assistant secretaries, and he found that, just by virtue of these contacts, which, as far as he could tell, he neither sought nor encouraged, he began to have some small measure of power and influence, which is to say, he began to be perceived as having power and influence. His opinions were listened to as though they were more than opinions. He listened to himself as he spoke in order to be certain that he conveyed the proper balance of helpful instruction and restraint. He watched his own face in the gilt-edged mirror behind the person opposite him, watched his own lips move, saw his hair, his clothes, saw himself smile, as though he were watching someone else, or rather, as though he were watching a part of himself he had never seen before. "Of course, the president cannot be certain that this particular new policy vis-a-vis Jordan will succeed. It is a risk, as any untried policy is, but it is a calculated risk, and I believe he knows that, and, having carefully weighed all the alternatives realistically available to him, the president thinks a possible favorable outcome far outweighs the risk." The others around the table would listen and nod as though he had just told them something not only new but useful. While he had said nothing that was untrue, he often had the uncomfortable feeling that he had nonetheless been dishonest, that the face he had watched in the mirror was the face of an imposter.

He was quoted as an "unnamed administration source" in a *Washington Post* account of policy meetings and a decision taken. Those who toiled daily in the State Department labyrinth and in the press knew from reading the particular points being made who this unnamed source was and immediately adjusted their view of him to take this new information into account. Or, if they didn't know, they set about finding out, since in their minds, from the absence of knowledge of this sort it was only a short fall to the absence of influence.

Louis had been invited to appear on a national television news show to explain what King Hussein of Jordan might be hoping for from his forthcoming meeting with the president, and what he could more reasonably expect. Louis was on the air, answering the anchorman's questions and explaining why His Majesty's expectations might be unrealistic, for a full thirty seconds, which one of the show's producers assured him, as she was removing the microphone from his jacket, was "a lot of air time, a lot of exposure. Ten million people watch this show."

Johann Kascht, his old professor, invited him back to the university to address the political science faculty and graduate students.

Louis spoke to them with wit and assurance about how policy was actually formulated in Washington and what misconceptions about policy formulation he had brought with him to Washington. He did not speak to them about his unease. He did not mention the dark undercurrents, the intrigue, and duplicity his work had laid open before his eyes. The more he studied the Palestinian question, for instance, the more he found assassination, organized violence, and betrayal not only condoned, but encouraged in order to promote what were known as "American interests," but which were often something not quite so virtuous, or so easily defined.

Even then, Louis had found his smooth ascent not only heady, but also disconcerting. Disconcerting, but to his astonishment now, nothing worse. The intrigue, the danger, none of the dark business had touched him in any way. At least not until now. Louis was certain now that the murdered man's footprints led back through his recollections to his State Department past. But try as he might now, he could not find the nugget that would illuminate the course things had taken.

It was true that Louis had been enticed, even seduced, by the attention he got, by the weight and the feel of power. But it was also true that with each small success his unease had grown. Undressing after a dinner party, looking at his children in their little beds, looking at Sarah studying herself in the mirror, the feeling of loss and confusion and loneliness would not be driven away.

Certain changes in United States policy during the Six Day War in the Middle East, taken at Louis's recommendation, had not had the desired outcome. Several members of the National Security Council had issued a report in which the loss of Israeli and Egyptian lives was attributed to this mistaken direction, although that was probably an overstatement of the case which they made for their own reasons. Nevertheless Hugh Bowes, instead of distancing himself from Louis, as Sarah had predicted he would in such a moment, spoke up in a cabinet meeting and assumed responsibility for the failure himself. Everyone there knew that Louis was the author of the failed policy.

"We expected that things would develop otherwise," said Bowes. "We did not expect such a quick and decisive victory by Israel. We made a serious miscalculation. I take full and complete responsibility." In the corridor at the State Department Louis thanked Hugh Bowes. Hugh laid his arm across Louis's shoulders. "We're a team, aren't we, Louis? It's already been taken care of."

In fact, when the opportunity arose for Louis to be promoted in grade and to be attached to the Central Intelligence Agency as the representative of the secretary of state, Hugh Bowes supported him enthusiastically. They met with the secretary in his great paneled office to formalize the appointment. "Langley is a world all its own, Louis," said Hugh afterward. "Let me know how things develop for you out there."

Jesus, thought Louis. He sat up in bed. His eyes were wide open now. His body was tense: that, he realized for the first time, was the moment of betrayal. How could he have missed it? He had been promoted out of the mainstream, away from influence, and into a secretive world where his destruction could be accomplished without leaving a trace.

Louis now gauged the depth of his obliviousness, his staggering naivete, by the fact that he had preferred working at CIA headquarters in Langley to working at the State Department in Foggy Bottom. It was a great sprawling campus with modern, low buildings and tree-lined walkways. In fact, it had felt to him like a modern university, but for the high wire fences, the cameras mounted everywhere, the guards. And despite the secret and duplicitous nature of their business, he had found the people at CIA headquarters possessed of a peculiar and eccentric innocence—he could think of no better word for it—which he found appealing. They all had arcane specialties at which they worked earnestly and single-mindedly without any apparent ambition beyond the desire to do their job as thoroughly as it could possibly be done. And they all seemed to believe that they could make deceit and intrigue their livelihood and still lead normal lives. Louis had joined them in this belief.

The director of central intelligence, whom Louis realized only now had been the appointed instrument of his undoing, was an amiable man who had, prior to his nomination to the directorship, been a federal judge in Texas. He had made large contributions to the president's election campaign and had subsequently expressed interest in serving the president as his head of the CIA, which entirely explained why he had been nominated. There were no obscure reasons for his nomination or secret plots afoot, though everyone expected that the president and the director were up to something. People always thought that way when the CIA was involved. The one thing of enduring value that Louis's failed career had taught him about government was that people—including those in government—almost always had the wrong idea about how government worked.

The director had served in the justice and defense departments in a previous administration. He had had no experience in any intelligence service, and the senators who voted overwhelmingly to confirm his nomination were all convinced that he was being led like a lamb to the slaughter. But, in fact, the Judge, as everyone from the president on down still called him, thrived at the CIA. His amiability and, above all, his earnest resolve to change nothing, to leave things as they were, a resolve which he expressed repeatedly and as often as he could to everyone he encountered at Langley, assured his success as the director. "If it ain't broke, don't fix it," he said with a determination and firmness that made it sound almost as though he were actually calling for something to be done.

Louis had been attached directly to the director's office. His job was to see that evolving State Department policies were represented in policy meetings at the CIA and, to the extent that he could, to make certain that changes in CIA policy were in accordance with State Department objectives. Louis reported to the secretary of state. Still, when he filed reports and recommendations, he found that it was Hugh Bowes who called. When he was summoned to the State Department, it was Hugh Bowes he met with.

Louis had believed he understood the various tensions and conflicts, not only between Israel and its neighboring states, but also the internal political conflicts within Israel and each of the Arab states, the rivalries and power struggles among their leaders, the ambitions and jealousies that drove the engines of politics. He had thought he knew who was vying for power and how they were using the extant political conflicts and forces to do so. He had thought he knew about the incipient revolutionary movements in Jordan, Syria, Egypt, and even within Israel. His unease about the true nature of world politics, as he saw it, diminished to a faint hum in the background of his life, like the noise of distant traffic. Just as with Sarah's silent sobbing in the early years of their marriage, since he could not think of anything to do about his unease now, he had chosen to ignore it. His reports to the secretary of state were met with apparent satisfaction.

Hugh Bowes announced one day that he was getting married. That is, the State Department made the announcement in the daily press briefing. Louis had been as surprised as anyone to learn this news. Bowes was frequently described as one of Washington's most eligible bachelors. He was, after all, a young man of great intelligence and charm, with an extraordinary number of accomplishments already under his belt and a boundless future. He appeared at the best parties and found himself celebrated on the pages of the *Washington Post*'s style section more often than he liked. However, the picture Louis had of him, even at the time, was of someone whose life was completely filled with himself, for whom love and companionship must certainly have been, if not alien concepts, then at least peripheral ones.

Of course, Louis had himself all but crowded love out of his own life. How Sarah's work was going, how she spent her day, life in her department at the university, these things were all pretty much a mystery to him. He never asked, fearing that if he did ask, and she answered, he would be forced to acknowledge how little he knew. She had also stopped asking him about his work. "I can't talk about it," he said, whether he could or not.

From time to time, when Jennifer and Michael had jumped into his arms, or snuggled on his lap, or when he had made their supper while Sarah was away at a conference, he wondered to himself, *Who are these little people? Do they really have anything to do with me?* Their expectant, open faces, their sheer self-centered neediness aroused in him something that must have been paternal feeling. That his children had seemed strangers beneath whatever familial feeling he had been able to muster may have been due to his own incapacity, his own unwillingness to know them. As with Sarah, he had always been too eager to stop their tears without learning where they came from.

Yes, he was certainly defective, but so was the world. It was unreliable, dangerous, and filled with false hope. Whatever love there was in the world was often so limited and so damaging to others that it sometimes seemed worse to him than no love at all. He was tempted now to miss his children. But he knew that what he really felt was regret and sorrow which, despite the shape it took, had very little to do with them.

VIII

*T*HE PALE SQUARES OF LIGHT ON THE CEILING FLUTTERED. SHIFTING only his eyes, Louis looked to the window where the curtains moved lightly. There was not a sound except for the almost imperceptible rustle of the curtains on the windowsill. The door from the hallway was in complete darkness, but Louis knew it had opened. Someone was in the room with him. When the curtains stopped moving, he reached over and turned on the light.

The man squinted, though the light was feeble. He backed against the door, fumbling to find the latch. Then he moved toward Louis. "Don't come any closer. I've been expecting you," said Louis in French, as if his expectation alone might somehow save him. Louis's voice was calm and was made to seem even calmer by his American accent. "Don't try to leave. Don't try to harm me." He motioned toward the phone. "The gendarme from Saint Leon, Monsieur Renard, is listening nearby. If you try to leave or to harm me, you will be apprehended." He paused. The man was dark skinned with dark curly hair. He wore a blue double-breasted suit over a gray knit shirt. He held his hands in front of him in a gesture that was meant to be submissive. He smiled nervously. He had a gold tooth that glinted in the pale light. "I only want to talk," said Louis. "Do you understand?"

"Yes," said the man and he smiled nervously again. He turned his head slightly as though he were listening, considering the possibilities.

"Do not put your hands in your pockets," said Louis as the man shifted. "Who are you? What are you doing here? Why did you break into my room?" asked Louis. He sat up in bed so that the covers slid from his shoulders. The sight of Louis's pale, naked chest seemed to frighten the man.

"Why are you following me? Why are you asking questions about me?" said the man in rapid, heavily accented French. *He is North African,* thought Louis.

"I have been inquiring about you because I think you are involved in a murder. You know why I have been inquiring about you. Tell me what you know about the dead man who was dumped on my doorstep."

"Murder? I do not know anything about a murder. I do not know about your doorstep." The man changed his tack. "I was on my way to the bathroom, and I came into your room by mistake." He smiled again. His nervousness had disappeared. He suddenly seemed unconcerned about Louis's questions or his threat to summon Renard. "Call your gendarme. I came in here by mistake, and you accuse me of murder." But he did not leave.

"Which embassy do you work for?" asked Louis, trying to keep his voice calm and flat.

"First I am a murderer, now I am an ambassador," said the man as he laughed. "If I want to kill you, I can kill you, and your gendarme cannot help you."

"It's all right, Renard. Not yet," said Louis in the direction of the phone. Then to the man, "I just want to talk. I do not want you to be arrested. I just want information. The answer to some questions."

"Ask your questions," said the man. "I will answer if I like."

"Which embassy are you with?" said Louis.

"I cannot tell you," said the man. "I am not allowed."

"Not allowed by whom?" said Louis.

"The dead man was one of our agents," said the man. "We just learned from the French that he had been killed. Through our intelligence service. We learned through our intelligence service. I do not know who did it, or why he was deposited at your doorstep. Or even if that is what actually happened. I do not know, perhaps even you might have killed him. In any case, we are conducting our own investigation. It could become an international incident. We are trying to avoid that. Now, suppose you tell me why you are following me." The man put his hands in his pockets.

"Take your hands out of your pockets," said Louis. The man took his hands out of his pockets. The right one held a small silver pistol.

"Is this what you are afraid of?" said the man, holding the pistol up for Louis to see. He stepped to the bed. He pushed the barrel hard into Louis's right ear. With his other hand he hung up the phone. "Renard is not in Villandry. He's home snoring in Saint Leon. Do you think I am stupid? I am going to kill you for playing stupid games with me. I have already told you too much. Now I have to kill you."

Louis smelled the sweat from the man's suit. He smelled the

wine the man had drunk while he was waiting in the bar down-stairs. The curtains hung lifeless in front of the windows. The night outside was black and silent.

"If anyone finds out what you know, about Hakim's murder, about the embassy. We cannot afford to let you live."

"You cannot afford to kill me. There is Renard now." And, in fact, at that moment a car could be heard racing through the night.

"I am not a fool," said the man. But he took a step backward toward the door. Louis's ear throbbed where the barrel had pressed into his flesh. "Renard is not here." He pointed the gun at Louis.

"Then go ahead and kill me," said Louis. He said it in English. At the same time, he threw the covers off his body. "Shoot me," he said, again in English. There he lay, pale and old. The white sheets only emphasized the pallor of his skin. The thin hair on his head stood in tufts like an unruly halo. His hands, twisted slightly by arthritis, lay palms up at his sides. His chest rose and fell slowly with each breath. The muscles in his arms hung slack. The cloud of white hair on his chest gave way to his wrinkled stomach, his narrow hips, the folds and wrinkles of his penis and testicles, his thinning legs, his ankles, his feet splayed outward. His sad watery eyes were fixed on the visitor.

"You crazy bastard," said the man in French. He put the pistol in his pocket as he ran from the room.

Louis lay motionless for a few long seconds. Then he turned out the light, got out of bed, locked the door with the key, and went to the window. He watched as the man walked quickly across the street and, without looking back, got in the passenger side of the BMW. The speeding car had already passed, and the sound of its racing engine disappeared into the night. The BMW started its engine and slowly pulled away from the curb. Louis did not watch to see whether it carried the insignia of the *corps diplomatique*. He knew that it did, but he was also certain that it meant absolutely nothing. He dressed in the dark, packed his few things into his suitcase, and left the hotel. An hour later, Solesme heard him drive by. She opened her eyes and watched as he turned up the driveway.

IX

$\mathcal{H}$E HAD NO INTENTION OF KILLING ME," SAID LOUIS AND TOOK A SIP of his coffee. Renard peered at him through the smoke curling from his cigarette. "Besides, I told him you were just outside."

"You crazy bastard," said Renard.

"That's what he called me," said Louis and smiled.

"He's right," said Renard, needing the last word.

The two men sipped their coffee in silence. "A little taste?" said Louis, and Renard shrugged his assent. He scowled into his cup. Louis poured brandy from the slim bottle. He patted the other man's hand, but Renard's anger would not be assuaged. He was angry with himself for not remaining in Villandry. And he objected to Louis's putting himself in such danger without even informing him. For what?

"For knowledge," said Louis. Each man cradled a warm cup in

his hands, each closed his eyes and inhaled the plum fragrance of the *eau de vie*.

"The car was rented," said Renard. "It is not a diplomatic plate. The name and address of the renter are false. He paid cash. It was rented in Paris. When they are finished with the car it will turn up abandoned."

"It will turn up abandoned in Paris," said Louis. "I would guess at the airport." Renard waited, but Louis didn't say any more.

"What knowledge?" said Renard. Probably, because he did not expect an answer, he got one. It was always that way with Louis.

"The answer. Who did it. Who the murderer is."

Renard lit his cigarette again. "You know who the murderer is." It was not a question so much as a request for confirmation of what he thought he had just heard.

"I have a good idea of who the murderer might be. I don't know why the murder was committed just now or who the murdered man was. But, before I tell you about my suspicions, answer one question for me."

"What question?"

"When are the national police arriving?"

"The national police? They're not coming." Renard pushed back in his chair and stared at Louis for a moment. "I was notified this morning that they're not coming. The case is to be handled locally. That is very unusual for a case of this sort. After all, my jurisdiction ends at the edge of town. It means nothing will be solved. Although I have to admit, I'm relieved not to have to deal with the bigwigs. But you knew that, didn't you, that they're not arriving? How did you know?"

"Then I am right in my suspicions," said Louis. It was his turn to push back in his chair. He smiled, but it was a chilly smile that made Renard want to button his sweater. "It is Hugh Bowes. The murderer—though he probably did not actually kill the man—is Hugh Bowes. I will tell you everything." Louis examined the backs of his hands as though they had just revealed some mystery to him.

Renard looked at him in amazement. "Hugh Bowes?" he said finally. He knew the name. "The American secretary of state?"

"When I knew him, he was not yet the secretary of state, although we were all certain that one day he would be. It was nearly thirty years ago. He was about to marry Ruth Chasen. She was a famous television reporter.

"Ruth Chasen was a rising star at the television network, CBS. She was one of the first generation of female television reporters: smart, pretty, and ambitious." These were all qualities that appealed to Bowes, if not viscerally, then at least theoretically. Hugh Bowes had seemed indifferent to sex, and Louis surmised that he regarded love of any kind with a mixture of fear and contempt. However, one strong component of Bowes's enormous ambition had to be his desire for normalcy. Ambition always has that desire as a part of itself.

"Hugh Bowes must have known Ruth Chasen from press briefings he had held, maybe from an interview he had given her. Beyond that, how their courtship unfolded was a mystery to everyone. So, when they announced their marriage, everyone was taken by surprise. The wedding was to take place in New York where Ruth Chasen's parents lived.

"Her father was Anhold Chasen, the famous tenor." Renard had never heard of Anhold Chasen.

"The wedding was to happen at the Pierre Hotel only a few

weeks after the engagement was announced. It would be a lavish affair with dinner for five hundred guests.

"I was securely ensconced as the State Department liaison at the CIA. What that means is not important. What is important is that I owed my job, if not my career, to Hugh Bowes. It did not surprise my wife, Sarah, that I wanted to give a dinner party for Hugh and Ruth to celebrate their engagement." Renard listened in continued astonishment. After so many years, the floodgates had opened, and Louis was finally giving shape and detail to what he had always simply referred to as "the sordid world."

"It is necessary that you know," said Louis simply. "I need for you to know," he added. After a pause he continued. "She, Sarah, made the arrangements for a catered dinner. For fifteen couples. Sarah looked lovely in a green satin dress." Louis's voice was flat and unemotional, as though he were simply laying out the facts of the case. But the story was a sad one, and Louis dwelt on the details. Renard did not mind.

"The long dining table was filled with great cascades of flowers. The room was lit by the light of many candles. They were on the table, on the sideboard, on the buffet. Everyone's face glowed in the golden light. We drank good wine and ate filet mignon with new potatoes and roasted vegetables. We spoke about the rapidly escalating situation in Vietnam. We spoke about the theater, about movies and books. The conversation was lively and interesting."

"I did not think you w-w-would get m-m-married," said Johann Kascht, who had come to Washington for this party. A long suppressed stutter had reemerged in recent years. And he had gotten fat. His face was flushed from the wine, and he was puffing on a cigar.

"Really? Why not, Jack?" said Hugh. He smiled at Kascht and folded his hands in front of him.

"Marriage suits some p-p-people, like Louis and Sarah, here, and others it s-s-seems to l-l-leave alone." Everyone laughed. Kascht's eyes twinkled. Sarah and Louis looked down at their hands in a gesture everyone took to be modesty.

"I choose not to be left alone," said Hugh, and smiled at Kascht again. Ruth watched Hugh from across the table. She smiled when he looked her way.

"Who proposed?" someone asked. It was meant to be a joke.

"The secretary of state," said someone else. The laughter was thin, and nervous.

"I made a toast," said Louis. "All I could think to say was: 'To the happy couple.' The men all stood while everyone raised their glasses to the happy couple."

After leaving the table people stood around talking. Hugh Bowes found himself by the piano. "Who plays?" he asked. "The children take lessons," said Sarah. Hugh opened the keyboard, sat down, and, after staring at the keyboard for a few seconds, began to play a Mozart piano sonata in D major.

"It is a light, playful piece of music," Louis explained to Renard. "One that everyone has heard," and he hummed the melody by way of identification, waving one hand gently as he sang. "It is not an especially difficult piece. And it possesses many of Mozart's most familiar melodic figures. So it has come to be favored by piano students for use in recitals. But, as Hugh Bowes played it, it became something other than Mozart. His fingering was perfect. But he played the piece with a brittleness that made the notes sound like shattering glass. He had divided the melody into awkward and peculiar phrases. He had all the requisite technical skill. And yet, he not only had no conception of what Mozart had in mind for his music, Hugh Bowes seemed to have only the remotest conception of what music was at all. It was as if the pianist's principal preoccupation must be to produce a particular sequence of sonic disturbances according to a prescribed set of dynamics, now loud, now soft, but without the slightest sense that they fit together as a whole, that they were evocative, or expressive, or meaningful, or, for that matter, beautiful.

"No one had even known that Hugh Bowes could play the piano, and, being a particularly unmusical group, everyone applauded with delight and surprise. Only Johann Kascht, himself an amateur cellist, stood aghast in the back of the crowd. His eyes were open wide, his cigar was dangling, forgotten, in his hand, spilling ashes on the rug. And Ruth Chasen, the daughter of Anhold Chasen, the famous tenor, stepped from the room, with a look on her face that can only be described as horror. It was as though she had just had a terrible premonition." A dark shadow clouded Louis's face, as though he himself had just had a premonition of his own.

"What is it?" asked Renard, but Louis did not answer. Instead he continued with his story.

"The wedding at the Pierre came off without a hitch. It was a glamorous event. The room was filled with luminaries from across American society. We all get married too young. I remember, I said those words to the director of central intelligence as we stood in the Pierre ballroom watching the newly married couple have their first dance. Of course, I was thinking of myself and Sarah as I spoke."

Louis and the Judge had gotten to know one another fairly well in the months since Louis had gone to work at the agency. They enjoyed a cordial, if slightly wary, relationship. The Judge seemed to regard Louis as Bowes's inside man at the agency, which, in some sense, Louis probably was. The Judge had been married to the same woman for more than forty years, which he had accomplished by means of what he described as extracurricular diversions. His wife had discovered diversions of her own, and so each found his own happiness without imposing his lusts on the other. When, after several glasses of champagne and more conversation in the same vein about marriage and family, Louis mused aloud whether he and Sarah would stay married, despite their unhappiness, the Judge raised an eyebrow and leveled a baleful stare at Louis. "If it ain't broke," he said, "don't fix it."

Now Louis paused for a long time. To Renard he seemed to be thinking about how, or even whether, to continue. Renard sat as quietly as he could, fearing that he might somehow break the fragile spell, and Louis would retreat back into his silence.

Renard was wrong about this. Louis was thinking about what he had already said, and what came next. He was thinking about the Judge, thinking about Ruth Chasen. He was wondering, for instance, what her fearful premonition might have been.

In fact, he was on a sort of archaeological expedition begun the night before, excavating the layers of his past to unexamined depths. The story he was telling was revealing its secret truths to him even as he told it. His abrupt starts and stops came about as he was piecing together his new, darker understanding. "Murder does that to you," he would explain to Renard much later. "Murder is unimaginably radical. It changes everything, casts everything in a different light. It makes death something other than it was before, and, therefore, it changes life too."

"Back in Washington," he said now, "I was unexpectedly summoned to a meeting with the secretary of state. I had no idea what the meeting was about. I arrived at the office of the secretary of state at the appointed hour to find the director of central intelligence, the secretary, two deputy secretaries, and a Marine Corps colonel attached to the national security council waiting for me. Hugh Bowes was away in Hawaii on his honeymoon." This was a fact to which Louis now seemed to attach some significance.

"As I was shown into the room, the other men stopped talking and quickly took seats at the conference table. They did not greet me. They did not look at me. They did not smile. The secretary formally opened the meeting and quickly turned it over to one of the deputy secretaries, a man I knew only vaguely. The marine colonel took notes."

Louis had then listened in shock while a long catalogue of charges of his ineptitude and incompetence were enumerated. The deputy secretary peered through his half glasses at the portfolio from which he was reading, as though it were some great distasteful insect. Louis's malfeasance had begun during the Six Day War. Since then, his misperceptions and political missteps had caused severe damage to the United States' efforts in the region. He could not have done more harm if he had been trying to, which had led some to believe that he had, indeed, been trying to somehow impede American foreign policy goals.

Every effort had been made to salvage things, but, thanks to Louis's ineptitude—again, some in the department wondered whether it wasn't outright treason—Israel had turned into a recalcitrant and reluctant ally, while the Arab states had drifted closer to the orbit of the Soviet Union. No one in this room wanted to believe that Louis was a traitor, though secrets to which he had access had found their way into Israeli hands. Still, he was at least a dangerous liability. His security clearance was being revoked immediately, his appointment with the State Department was being terminated immediately. He could pick up his personal effects at Gate B at CIA headquarters in Langley.

His pay was being frozen, and his personal bank accounts would be frozen until the charges that he had committed, or allowed, serious violations of national security had been thoroughly investigated. No, he could not know who had made the charges, but he could be assured that they had come from more than one knowledgeable and unimpeachable source. If and when he was cleared of all charges, his bank accounts would again be available to him, and he would receive whatever pay was owed him. "Though," added the deputy secretary, closing the file and looking at Louis with continuing distaste, "incompetence is a kind of treachery all its own, isn't it?"

Louis had tried to speak, but the secretary had raised his hand to stop him. "You may leave any questions you might have with my secretary outside. She will see that you are given any notice you might be entitled to. You may go now." He knit his hands together in that perfect gesture. Louis turned to look at the Judge. The Judge met his eyes with a look that showed neither recognition nor concern. Louis left the room. A security guard escorted him to the garage where his car was parked. Then the guard took away Louis's identification card.

"I drove home in a sort of stunned trance. I was relieved that no one was there. Sarah or the children. I sat and looked out a window. My years of study of international politics, of American politics, of political philosophy, of cybernetics, of everything else that I had read and studied, had led me to an understanding of life as something that proceeded in an orderly and predictable fashion. Not that you knew what was going to happen next, but you could be certain that what did happen next would inevitably grow out of already existing circumstances. What happened, inevitably happened because of what had happened before. There was a logic to it, wasn't there? But this was like an accident, a truck careening suddenly onto the sidewalk and killing a pedestrian.

"Not that I regarded the end of my political career as a catastrophe. In fact, in those days, just after I was fired, when I tried to discover how I felt about what had happened, I could find anger and humiliation among the feelings that shot around in my head, but I could not find sorrow, or even anything like regret, at losing my job. Even in these very first confused and turbulent hours, I mainly felt something resembling relief. Still, there was something catastrophic about what had just happened. Not that it was important. But it was catastrophic in the sense that it had been sudden, unforeseen, and unforeseeable.

"It should not have been such a surprise. But I did not recognize that the treachery and deceit which permeate the political world had now entered my own life. Someone had set out to ruin me."

Sitting in his chair and gazing into his own backyard, it had seemed to Louis as though he were somewhere he had never been before. He sat and watched, perhaps for the first time, as the leaves of the dogwood and the hosta moved about slowly, first here, then there. The pyracantha—firethorn: it sounded like the name for a jet bomber—rustled where a brown bird pulled at red berries. Maybe it was a thrush. A different kind of bird landed on the lawn. It carried a wriggling insect in its mouth.

The week before, he had been mowing the lawn, going back and forth across the yard thinking of something else, when he saw the mower pass over a fallen bird's nest with three babies in it. They were under the mower before he could stop. He pushed the mower along, terrified by what he would certainly find. But after the mower had passed over them, there they were: pink, featherless, blind, and alive, their outsized beaks wide open. When he stopped the engine, he could hear their feeble sounds. Were they being fed? It was doubtful. It might have been better had the mower chopped them swiftly to pieces. But who could know such things? Louis had put the nest in the crotch of a dogwood.

After sitting a long time, he stepped through the French doors into the garden. The air was full of the sounds of an airplane passing far overhead, of dogs up the street, of birds singing, of distant traffic. Louis smelled something fragrant, then something acrid. He was still wearing his suit, but he lay down on his back in the grass. He unbuttoned his jacket and spread his arms wide, palms up. He felt the grass prickling his skin through the thin suiting. He felt something crawling on his hand. It was a tiny yellow spider, and it moved across his thumb as if it had to cross the entire world. He looked straight up through the leaves of the tree into the pale sky. A sense of freedom and terror came over him, and he watched as his eyes filled with tears.

X

*N*OT KNOWING WHO ELSE TO TURN TO, I WENT TO VISIT JOHANN Kascht," said Louis. Renard now had the sense that Louis could have been entirely alone and he would have kept talking. He seemed to Renard to be entirely lost in his own thoughts. But just at that moment, he leaned toward Renard and said, "Be patient. This all leads somewhere."

Kascht had stood as Louis entered his office. The clutter of bookshelves stuffed with books and papers, of stacks of papers on his two tables and on nearly every available chair, was reassuring to Louis. But Kascht was not friendly. "I d-d-don't think we have a great deal to talk about," said the professor, sitting down again and resting his arms on his great swollen belly. He drew on a cigar until the end glowed, then blew clouds of gray smoke at Louis. "You have, by your combined ambition and incompetence, not only b-b-betrayed your country, the United States"—he named it as though

reminding Louis of his country's name would further his shame—
"but you have also betrayed the university, and me, and the confidence I so m-m-mistakenly placed in you."

"I didn't protest my innocence. There was no point in protesting. How could I prove that I was innocent, since I still had only the vaguest idea what I was supposed to be guilty of?" Why protest, if his own professor, who knew his work and had recommended him to the State Department, could believe that he was incompetent, or worse?

Johann Kascht had always been an unswerving disciple of the scientific method. He scrupulously gathered and organized endless data when researching his books. But now he had decided on Louis's guilt in an instant. And the *entire* evidence on which this meticulous scientist had based his judgment, that Louis had committed some terrible wrong, was that someone had told him so. Kascht had been astounded to learn of Louis's failures. But he had also immediately believed what he had been told.

"What d-d-do you want of me? Why have you c-c-come? I hope you do not think, for a moment, that I will r-r-recommend you to anyone. You have betrayed your country, me, and the p-p-principles of social science. I cannot, no, I *will* not p-p-possibly do anything to help you.

"However," he said, after a thoughtful pause, "I will not d-d-do anything to stand in your w-w-way. I w-w-will not withdraw my previous letter of recommend-d-dation from your f-f-file. I w-w-will not say anything n-n-negative about you. For S-S-Sarah and the children." Louis was grateful for Kascht's lapse of principle. As he left, he heard Kascht stammering through the closing door, "Y-y-you are a d-d-disgrace and a f-f-failure."

"To my surprise at the time," said Louis, "Hugh Bowes took my call. In fact, he offered to meet me for dinner. He greeted me warmly and, before saying anything else, expressed regret at what had happened. He was, he said, completely baffled—'profoundly puzzled' were his words—as to who could have filed the charges, and why. He sat shaking his head. What is most astounding, in retrospect, is that I believed him. He flattered me. He told me my work was first rate. If he could do anything to help, please let him know. He put his arm across my shoulders."

Hugh Bowes had written a letter for Louis's file. It was filled with generous and extravagant praise. It recounted Louis's successes and achievements in glowing detail. It made no mention of his appointment at the State Department having been terminated or of the reasons for the termination. The Judge, likewise, agreed to write a letter of recommendation for Louis's file. It was brief and perfunctory and had been backdated six months.

"I found an academic position without too much difficulty, just as I had expected I would. I was hired as an associate professor of political science at George Mason University, where Sarah was teaching. The chairman of the department was a tall, gloomy man named D. William Stone. He had once been an administrator for the Marshall Plan, and then had been the American ambassador to Iran.

"Ambassador Stone, as he liked to be called, was happy to have me in the department. He saw me as the only other member with 'hands-on' experience. He talked to me in confidential tones about life as a diplomat, about the Department of State during the Eisenhower years and other such matters, about which I had neither knowledge nor interest.

"I taught graduate courses in policy studies and Middle Eastern politics. My students aspired to join the foreign service or the State

Department, to become 'public servants.' Once a week they gathered around the seminar table and discussed their papers about arcane moments in the ongoing drama in the Middle East.

"Their papers were overly long. They were laced with references to this study or that other study and written in a style that could best be described as being without style. They believed, as I must have once believed, that, by means of this bland and soulless prose, they could somehow accomplish what no one else had been able to accomplish before them, that they could drain all passion, all murderous feeling, all despair, all desire from the world, and with simple strokes of logic—a, b, c—could solve whatever problem needed solving.

"I sometimes remembered Sarah's unhappiness as I listened while my students read their papers aloud. What were their lives like? Some were married to hopeful spouses, some already had young children. I wondered whether any one of them had applied their intellectual skills to their own nascent unhappiness.

"After about two years, our confiscated bank accounts were unfrozen. The salary and leave payments that were due me arrived in the mail. They arrived without explanation. And I sought none.

"I stayed at the university for only five years. I had, after all, lost my faith in science. Not just in science. I had lost my faith in knowledge. Not in the value of knowledge, but in knowledge itself." Louis suddenly stopped speaking. He did not move. He remained silent for a long moment. It happened now, from time to time, that the disorder of things appeared suddenly before him with blinding clarity. Life's unruly and turbulent nature became simply inescapable. Then, in such moments, the utter chaos of human being, no, of all being simply overwhelmed him and swept his entire understanding of life on earth into shambles, as a great tidal wave might have done.

Then he fell into silence, wherever he was, whatever he was doing. What else was there for him to do?

Louis did not regard either this glimpse of chaos, or the ensuing silence, as a bad thing. On the contrary. He found it exhilarating to face a world empty of meaning and significance. After all, with meaning and significance gone, he reasoned, treachery, dissembling, and deception lost much of their force, could not ultimately change anything, could not do harm. Things were as they seemed. No, things were as they were. The great wave swept aside all seeming too.

"But we are searching for knowledge now," said Renard. He immediately regretted having spoken.

"You may be, my friend," said Louis with a faint smile. "But I am trying to put a stop to something, to bring something to conclusion. To make something terrible which has happened, as though it did not happen. That is all."

Louis continued with his story. "Dealing mainly with opinion, as it did, treating knowledge a little more lightly, a life in journalism seemed to me a less grandiose, and more honest, way to earn a living, though it did not interest me any more than teaching did. So, I began writing reports on the Middle East for specialty publications like *Petroleum Monthly* and *The Middle East Review*. Occasionally, I worked as a consultant for companies doing business in the Middle East. It seemed like fairly honest work. When I finished the work, I was paid for the work I had done. The money was irregular but sufficient.

"The Vietnam War came and went, the race riots, that flared up across the United States in the late 1960s, occurred far in the background of my life. Though I had once worked at the heart of the political world, I hardly noticed these events. I was convinced the war was stupid and unnecessary, but I didn't join the protests to stop it. I watched the racial animosity, the struggle by black Americans for civil rights, all the social upheaval of the next years, without participating in it in any way. In fact, I only watched because it all occurred within my field of vision. I did not watch with interest or curiosity.

"I saw Hugh Bowes only once more. It was a few years after I had quit teaching, the week after I had left Sarah and the children. I came back to the house to pick up some clothes. I rang the bell, but no one answered, so I let myself in. I heard sounds coming from the bedroom. There I found Sarah sitting astride Hugh Bowes, facing him, her back to me, bouncing up and down and moaning. I had always found her moaning during sex to be disconcerting. It was a high-pitched, drawn-out sound which could as easily have been an expression of pain as one of pleasure. But, as I listened now, it seemed familiar and almost soothing. Hugh lay with his head pressed back in the pillow. His glasses lay on the night table. I had never seen him without his glasses. Seeing the glasses there on the table embarrassed me almost more than the sight of them having sex.

"Hugh's full lips were pulled back, his small teeth were bared in a kind of ecstatic snarl. They both saw me at the same time. Sarah screamed and jumped up. She grabbed her robe and held it in front of herself. Hugh Bowes quickly pulled the covers above his chin. Only his eyes were visible."

Renard shifted uneasily in his chair. "Please, don't tell me this. Please. It has nothing—"

Louis raised his hand to stop him. "Just wait. You will see that it has *everything* to do with what has happened.

"'You son-of-a-bitch, you're supposed to ring the bell,' Sarah shouted, as she wrapped the robe around herself. I paid no attention to her. I looked at Hugh Bowes who was watching me. Was Hugh Bowes actually smiling? I couldn't believe it. I stepped to the bed. I moved slowly, without thinking. The most important thing to me, at that moment, was to answer that question: Was Hugh Bowes smiling? I took the corner of the sheet in both hands and tore it back. Hugh tried to hold onto the top of the sheet, but he couldn't and his hands landed at his side." Hugh had not been smiling. He lay there naked, pale, misshapen. His erection wobbled from side to side. Otherwise, he lay silently. His arms were fat and white, his breasts sagged to the side, the red nipples still aroused. His body hair was wet and matted against his chest, across his stomach, around his groin. His hips were wide, his legs heavy, his feet pink and wrinkled, like the feet of a baby. "Nobody moved," said Louis. "Nobody said anything.

"Finally, I turned to leave, to get the clothes I had come for, and leave. And Sarah showered me with curses. She followed me to the bedroom door screaming at me to just get the hell out. But I stopped to look at Hugh Bowes once more. He had not moved. He looked back at me with dead eyes."

Renard breathed a deep sigh and sat back in his chair. His back hurt from sitting so long. The evening sun was poised just above the horizon, too low for Louis's umbrella to do any good. Renard shielded his eyes with one hand. "And this makes you think it is Hugh Bowes." He was astonished. "How do you know it is Bowes? How could it possibly be Bowes? That is madness. The whole idea is insane. Why would he? The whole business with pulling off the sheet. It's crazy."

"Because everything points away from him," said Louis. He was unmoved by Renard's incredulity. "It points away from him, just as it did then. That is how he operates. When I was fired, he was my mentor. He was in Hawaii. He wrote me a letter of recommendation. That is why I am sure it was him." Louis did not sound bitter or angry. And he did not sound crazy. He sounded as though he were simply stating an absolute fact.

"But that is not proof," cried Renard in mounting exasperation. "That is not proof. Everything points away from everyone. Everything points away from . . . Madame Lefourier," he waved his arm in the direction of the neighbor's house. "Everything points away from . . . from your wife, Sarah?" It was the first time Renard had known her name.

"Sarah."

"From Sarah. Everything points away from Sarah. That is no proof."

"You are wrong. Everything *does not point toward* Sarah. That is different from pointing *away* from her." It was a subtle but important distinction.

Renard looked at Louis for a long moment. "That is still not proof," was all Renard could think to say. This was what you got when you dealt with a man who did not believe in knowledge.

"If it is Hugh Bowes," said Louis, looking into the evening sky, "if Hugh Bowes is the murderer, then he will deliver the proof himself."

"How do you mean?"

"He may have already begun to, though not intentionally, of course." Louis sat up a little straighter. "Tell me: Why did the national police not come to investigate the case? Why do you think they did not come?"

"You think they did not come because the American secretary of state is involved and was able to stop them from coming."

"That seems like one very good possibility."

"It is only a possibility," said Renard, lighting a cigarette. "It is a possibility. But that is all. There are other possibilities. All we have are suppositions."

"All we ever have are suppositions," said Louis. "If it is Bowes, then he knows by now that I know it is him." Louis smiled. "I sent him a message."

"A message?"

"My body. My naked body in bed."

Now it was the policeman's turn to sit up straight. He peered intently across the table into Louis's face. "You're not serious," said Renard. Louis did not smile. "Do you really believe he remembers that moment from thirty years ago? Do you honestly think, if he even hears about what you did, throwing the covers aside, that he will make the connection?"

Louis looked across the fields as though he had been asked to assess the coming weather. "If the dead body was a message from him, then he will be waiting for a response from me, and he will certainly remember that moment. In that moment in my wife's bedroom, Hugh Bowes was humiliated by me. I believe it is possible that not a day passes when he doesn't think of it." Louis paused. The policeman shifted in his chair, rubbing his hands together, while the smoke from his cigarette curled about his face.

"I know. You cannot imagine," Louis said, "that such a small thing as this humiliation could stay with anyone, with Hugh Bowes, all these years, much less that it could elicit such strange and extreme measures." Renard did not answer. "That is because you are unfamiliar with the psychology of the powerful. It does not seem possible to you that Hugh Bowes, a man of power, a man occupied with important affairs of state, a man who spends his days negotiating with other world leaders, would even remember a moment like that.

"But Hugh Bowes regards his life in the same way as a painter regards a painting." Renard let out an exasperated groan. He certainly did not want to hear another dissertation on painting, especially now. He drew deeply on his cigarette and angrily exhaled a cloud of smoke into the darkening sky. "Bowes's life," said Louis, ignoring his friend's reaction, "is to Bowes's way of thinking his own creation, his masterpiece. One could say he sees it as a work of art which, whatever its contradictions, has to have its own internal consistency if it is to be great. And it *must* be great. He wants his life to be a public monument to power and to achievement.

"I am certain Hugh regards his own frailty as a mortal sin against the life he is constructing. It is a terrible violation of who he wishes he were. And I am just as certain that he loathes me for having been witness to it, worse, for having called it to his attention."

"And why just now, after all these years?" Renard demanded.

"I don't know the answer to that," Louis answered quickly. He had wondered the same thing. Perhaps it was because the murder, whoever it might have been and for whatever reason entirely unrelated to Louis, finally offered him a convenient opportunity to even the score. "To kill two birds with one stone. But your question is a proper one. And I don't know."

"And what did he hope to achieve by doing this thing, by leaving a dead body on your doorstep?" Renard asked.

"I don't know that either," said Louis with a sigh.

"And you?" asked Renard. "Have you thought of him all these years?" Louis turned to look at the policeman, then looked away. The evening star had appeared. The two men sat silently as night fell. The sky darkened gradually, imperceptibly. The evening star brightened, and other stars appeared. On the next farm, the Ducloses' dog barked. Both men turned to watch as an owl swept through the yard above them. Its heavy head and thick body made its flight improbable, and yet it flew slowly, silently, gracefully, and without apparent effort.

Louis finally broke the silence, his voice a whisper. "All these years," was all he said.

It was dark by the time Renard spoke again. He spoke calmly now. "If he is the murderer, and he receives and comprehends your message, all of which seems extremely unlikely, but if it is as you say it is, then he might now try to have you killed."

Louis corrected him. "If he wants to, he will have me killed. There is very little you or I, or anyone else, can do to stop him. Perhaps that has been his purpose: to set up a little duel with me, to play with me, in order to restore his superiority, before he kills me. That doesn't seem like his style to me. But I don't know."

"That is unacceptable," said Renard. "It cannot be allowed to happen." Louis could imagine the scowl on Renard's face. He breathed deeply to smell the smoke from his cigarette. The smell of the smoke was reassuring. He liked the policeman. He was glad to have him there.

"I have a plan," said Louis. Renard waited, but Louis did not say anything more.

XI

$\mathscr{R}$ENARD AND ISABELLE SAT OVER THE REMAINS OF THEIR SUPPER. IT was nearly midnight. They had eaten a rabbit Isabelle had bought from Madeleine Picard. Isabelle had stewed the rabbit in a red wine sauce made with garlic and shallots. The sauce was almost black. They ate the rabbit along with roasted new potatoes, red peppers, and onions from the garden.

Renard had mopped up the last of the sauce with a piece of baguette. Now he used his knife to press the last few crumbs of a goat cheese onto the bread. Isabelle had begun to clear the table. Renard had told Isabelle what he had learned about Louis Morgon and the trouble he was in. "I am worried," he confessed. "My job is to protect the old man, but I cannot protect him from this."

"You cannot protect him at all," she said. "You do not need to protect him." She said this in such a way that it caused Renard to stop, a morsel of baguette and cheese halfway to his parted lips, and look at her. "He looks like an old man, but he is not." She was right. "Besides, he is operating in a world we know nothing about. I would let him take the lead. I would go to him tomorrow and tell him that you trust him to take the lead, that you will follow his lead."

"This is a deadly business, Isabelle." He thought a long moment before he corrected himself. He hated exaggeration, so he avoided extreme words when he could. "A dangerous business."

"You could stay out of it," said Isabelle, knowing that he couldn't stay out of it.

"I will go see him first thing in the morning," said Renard.

When he arrived at Louis's house the next morning, the chain hung across the driveway. He stepped across the chain and walked up the driveway, but he knew what he would find. The house and barn were locked. The shutters were closed and bolted. The old Peugeot was gone. "He left before dawn," said Solesme Lefourier. "I will water his geraniums. I can't take care of the garden. Dominique will have to do that, although somehow she never gets all the weeds. Quite likely things will be in a terrible state by the time Louis Morgon gets back." She spoke his whole name in this peculiar, elegiac way, which caused Renard to look at her more closely and wonder what she knew that she wasn't telling him.

Louis had driven to Le Mans and caught an early TGV, the fast train, to Paris. Though he considered the trip urgent and necessary, he still had left early enough so that he could drive slowly. He would have driven slowly even if his car had been newer and faster. He did not like leaving. He wanted to drive in such a way that he could watch the countryside emerging from the night. There were no other cars on the road. The farms he passed were dark and shuttered. The ponds were capped with shallow clouds of fog. In the fields, the cows were lying down, some sleeping, some already chewing, clouds of steam coming from their nostrils.

In the little towns he came to, one after another, the houses were shuttered. There were no lights. In Courdemanche, a woman emerged from a barn as he passed. She wore a patterned smock over her black dress and woolen stockings. She held a silver milk pail in each hand. She leaned against the great wooden doors in order to close them.

The little road passed over a series of bridges where the narrow Dême snaked its way back and forth, its grassy banks sheltering trout, rows of newly planted poplars casting pale reflections on the water. The first rose color shone in the sky. An ancient willow hugging the bank had, for the hundredth time, sent out new branches from its scarred and knobby trunk where those from the year before had been cut back. A thin column of smoke rose straight up from the chimney of a cottage. Eventually, the country gave way to the city.

As the train sped toward Paris, he watched the countryside go by in the dawn. It passed too quickly for him to feel any further connection to it. He saw his own face reflected in the glass, superimposed over the undulating fields, the villages, manor houses, and woods. He looked at his face looking back at him. He looked like someone other than the person he thought himself to be.

In less than an hour, he stepped from the train into the noise and tumult of Montparnasse station and Paris. Solesme Lefourier had been to Paris a few times. But, as she had assured him, she had no desire to go back. "There is nothing there I want. Would I be able to sleep in Paris? That is really all I want: to be able to sleep."

As strange as it might have seemed, Louis had never enjoyed

travel either. One summer long ago, he had gone to Cape Cod with Sarah and the children. He and Sarah had sat beneath a fluttering yellow umbrella on a glorious beach. Little white clouds drifted far overhead, while the children laughed and played in the gentle surf. Another time, they had driven to the Smoky Mountains where they had camped in the misty silence and hiked up and down steep trails. But to his mind, these vacations and the other brief excursions they had made out of Washington were for Sarah and the children. His part had been as the driver, organizer, and tour guide. And like everything else he did, his participation had been somewhat perfunctory and of less interest to him than it should have been.

Louis had not traveled widely in Europe either. He had been stationed in Germany for eighteen months in the army, but he had used up most of his leave returning to the United States to be with his dying parents, and he had never gone back. However, some years after his divorce from Sarah, after Jennifer had left Washington for the first time and Michael had left college, Louis decided to visit France. Someone had suggested it. He or she—who had it been?—had said, "There is a reason that the rich—people who could live anywhere in the world—choose to live in France. And the misanthropic." Whoever it was had presumably included the misanthropic for Louis's benefit.

The suggestion that he see France had somehow stuck in his mind. Who knew how or why? It was perhaps for no other reason than that it had been made at just such a moment as Louis was feeling caught in his unhappiness over how things had turned out, no, how *he* had turned out, how he had misread life, how things had all gone wrong, and how he, though further along down the road, was still as far as he had ever been from understanding anything. He was feeling sorry for himself. Running away to some other part of the world, leaving the world he eventually came to call "the sordid world" for a while, seemed the perfect thing to do.

After doing some research, Louis decided that he would walk across France, across the entire country. He would follow one of the ancient Christian pilgrim routes that crossed the country and eventually led over the Pyrenees and along the northern coast of Spain to Santiago de Compostela. During the Middle Ages and later, pilgrims had come from every corner of Europe, converging along trails, finding their way from sanctuary to sanctuary, from church to church, wearing the scalloped shell which came to be the universal symbol for this journey.

In his mind Louis saw himself among them. He pictured the friars in their rough robes, saw Eleanor of Aquitaine on her horse, wearing silk and gold, surrounded by guards and servants, saw the merchants and tradesmen who had left their families and the wealth they had acquired from their tanneries, stables, and vineyards to walk across France and Spain, and there to prostrate themselves on the spot where Saint James, the Apostle, had landed in Europe. To prostate themselves and to be redeemed. After all, Louis was a pilgrim if ever there had been one.

Louis did not think he was exactly in search of redemption. Yet this long walk, day after day, alone with himself and his thoughts, felt like something he had no choice but to do. He equipped himself with a backpack, sturdy shoes, and a thick packet of maps and books, and flew one day in late May from Washington to New York, and from New York to Charles DeGaulle Airport in Paris. The plane arrived in the morning twilight. The day was overcast. The runway was wet; the grass beside it seemed exceptionally green.

He retrieved his backpack from the baggage carrousel, showed the customs agents his passport, and started walking. His first steps were around the great donut-shaped airport terminal. He was tired from the overnight flight and restless at the same time, so that it only slowly dawned on him what a new place this was he was walking through. The faces around him were different in subtle and inexplicable ways. Was it how they held a cigarette, was it their animation, their shrugs and gestures when they spoke? The language was different, of course, but so was their use of it. A woman's voice announced the incoming flights softly, it almost seemed so as not to disturb anyone who didn't need the information. Chimes rang out before each announcement on the public address system. Outside, policemen in blue uniforms stood by a small car and watched the goings on. Little trucks and cars whizzed around and around the terminal building.

It was chilly. There was a drizzle. It took him half an hour to walk out of the airport by a service road which took him through a little-used gate. When he was approached by airport police, he explained in his halting French that he had just arrived and was beginning a walking tour of France. They understood his French and, to his surprise, seemed to accept without question his explanation for being on foot in the middle of the airport. They looked at his passport and then wished him a good journey, *"bonne route,"* touching their hats as they watched him go.

This back gate from the airport opened directly into the town of le Mesnil-Amelot. Because other airport exits led to all the main highways, there was no traffic in the town, despite the airport's proximity. The street was broad and cobbled and lined with ancient plane trees. Their mottled tan-and-white bark shone brightly against the backdrop of dull stone houses. Despite the damp chilly air, windows were open, and here and there mounds of white bedding hung over the sill. Someone had hung a canary cage in the window. The little yellow bird hopped from the perch to the side of the cage and back again. It sang as Louis passed below.

From le Mesnil-Amelot, Louis headed northeast along a narrow farm road lined with poplars. The new leaves on the poplars shimmered in the silvery light. He walked the three kilometers to Moussy le Vieux. From there, he turned northwest along the Biberonne which was overflowing its narrow banks. He reached Moussy le Neuf and went on to Saint Ladre, which, although it was on his map, was little more than an ancient, rambling farmstead. The high gray walls that enclosed the farm did not allow even a glimpse of what went on inside.

Louis studied the map carefully. The route he meant to follow— it was indicated by a small wooden sign stuck on the wall, painted with a bright red GR-1—was a double-rutted farm track that disappeared between tall hedge roses on one side and an ancient stone wall on the other. He peered down the way and then back at his map. His hesitation came neither from fear nor uncertainty, but rather from something that most closely resembled exhilaration.

Louis moved his finger slowly on the map along the route he had taken to Saint Ladre where he stood, hesitated a moment as if his finger were himself, then moved it along the route he intended to follow from there. It was as though he hoped that, seeing the roads and towns reduced and summarized on the map, reading their names to himself like some lovely poem might even further intensify his joy.

The airport, with its great jets, lay less than three hours' walk behind him. If he had listened for them, he might have heard the airplanes taking off and landing. But now he was walking where pilgrims had walked many centuries before. The little wooden sign indicated by means of its GR-1 that this was the Grande Randonnee number 1, the first of many ways and paths that led through towns and fields and forests. These old walkways, farm roads, and tracks had gradually been consolidated into a system of walking trails which now covered the whole of France. Another even smaller sign indicated that Beaumarchais lay two kilometers through the fields to the north. He set off again.

The bell in the tiny church at Beaumarchais chimed noon as Louis reached the town. He found a small store and bought a baguette, some Gruyere cheese, and a bottle of grape juice. He stopped beside the small stone obelisk in the middle of the town square where the names of the children of Beaumarchais—*"les enfants de Beaumarchais"*—who had died in the two great wars were listed on bronze plaques around its base.

Louis read through the two dozen names—an unthinkably large number of war dead, an unspeakable loss for this hamlet with its few dozen houses. Halfway down the list of dead from the First World War, he came to the Morgons. There were nine of them: Charles Morgon, Felix Morgon, Gaspard Morgon, Gerard Morgon, Guy Morgon, Jean Marie Morgon, Jean Pierre Morgon, Louis Morgon, Onesime Morgon. Were they cousins? Were they fathers and sons? Were they all brothers? There was no way to tell since it only gave the year they had died. That fact, their violent and futile deaths, had obliterated everything else about their lives. The shorter list of dead from the Second World War included no Morgons. Perhaps all the Morgon men had been killed in the first war. He read through the nine names once more, and after that could recite them from memory for the rest of his life.

Louis knew he was not related to the Morgons of Beaumarchais. His grandfather's grandfather had come to the United States from Odessa, and before that, from a stetl in the Ukraine. He had arrived in America in the 1850s. The exact date was uncertain. He had held onto his first name—Avraham. But his last name had disappeared into oblivion. He was renamed by an immigration agent on the docks of New York. You were given one opportunity to state your name. The agent wrote down what he heard, handed you a paper, and you moved on.

Avraham did not mind the loss of his old last name. To him that name had represented persecution and poverty. His new name—Morgon—signified a brand new beginning. In Avraham Morgon's case, as in countless other cases, the great American melting pot had not only worked, it had done so instantaneously. A few years later, still carrying around a thick Russian accent, Avraham, or Abe, as he now proudly called himself, joined the Irish Brigade being put together by William Meagher, an Irish nationalist, himself newly arrived from British imprisonment in Tasmania. Avraham swore he was Irish when he was asked and proudly wore the distinctive orange and green epaulets at the battle of Manassas, where he distinguished himself and was made a sergeant.

Louis knew Avraham Morgon's story, so there was no reason he should feel that he was kin to the dead Morgons of Beaumarchais. Maybe it was just the fact that nine from one family in that tiny village had died. Maybe it was seeing his name nine times on that stone on his first day in France. Whatever the reason, when he moved to France and considered changing his name to make it more difficult for others to find him, he could not bring himself to do it. Before now, he had felt no loyalty to the name that was his by accident. But giving it up now, even in a provisional way in order to take on an alias, would have seemed a betrayal of the Morgons of Beaumarchais, toward whom he felt a strong and inexplicable allegiance.

In some mysterious way, Louis's arrival in France had echoed

Avraham's arrival in New York. His name, which had been a fiction founded in an almost comic mistake, now had suddenly taken on the weight of tragic history, again by accident, this time the accident of his walking through a village and reading the list of its war dead. Just as suddenly as Avraham had lost his name five generations ago, Louis had found his.

Louis ate the lunch he had just bought, sitting on a bench in the square in Beaumarchais, not far from the monument. The town presented a somber, gray face across the square. The sky was overcast. A wet, chilly wind blew in from the west.

XII

$\mathcal{L}$OUIS FOUND LODGING FOR THE NIGHT, HIS FIRST NIGHT IN FRANCE, eight kilometers further on, in a small hotel over a bar in the village of Ermenonville at the edge of the great forests of Ermenonville and Chantilly. He slept deeply that night. He dreamt of dead horses floating down a great river, then of bees swarming together into great balls of bees, trying to fly together, lifting off briefly, buzzing frantically, then falling, stirring up clouds of dust, and lifting off again.

The next day, Louis walked through the forests of Ermenonville and Chantilly. Great masses of rain clouds rushed in from the English Channel where the late spring storms were still following one behind the other. The storms brought cold, windy showers. These were interrupted, as suddenly as they had come, by blue sky and sun that shimmered in the water dripping from the leaves and lying in puddles along the forest roads.

Yellow birds flashed across in front of him, sounding their alarm. Once, two wild boars, small low creatures that seemed to be half head, crashed out of the brush ahead of him. They galloped along the muddy road for a short distance, and then bolted across and into the brush on the other side. The forester passed in his small truck, moving swiftly along the parallel tracks as Louis stood aside. Even the familiar sound of the truck did not diminish the sensation Louis had that he was walking in a new world, inhabited by different creatures, where different laws prevailed, where life was ordered along different axes, to different ends.

Louis turned south, once he was past Paris, then west, then south again. He walked through fields, along small roads, along canals, over tiny rivers. He stayed in small village hotels, when he found them, where the room often cost less than supper, where there was no bath and the toilet was down the hall. When there were no hotels, he found rooms by asking where a room might be found. To his astonishment, he was often welcomed into people's homes and given a meal and a bed for the night. When they learned he was American, they wanted to talk about the liberation. It seemed, when they spoke of it, as though it had just happened. They described how the American tanks had come through town, how there had been a battle in the next town where the Germans had had a fuel dump. Emboldened by the approaching Americans, the local partisans had blown the dump sky high. They drank a toast to the Americans, to the liberation.

He crossed the Seine at La Roche Guyon, at the great bow the river makes just above Giverny. He did not visit Giverny, where Monet had had his house and splendid gardens, but instead continued southwest. East of Dreux he joined the Eure River—that was how he thought of himself now, as having a relentless motion of his own, which allowed him to join rivers. The Eure led south into the great flat plains of the Beauce.

The storms ended. The dry summer season took hold. The days, which had seemed endlessly long already, got even longer, and he began to sleep under the stars. He set out each morning with the sun already high in the sky, and he walked until it dropped beneath the brim of the straw hat he had acquired. He enjoyed seeing the farmers, the shopkeepers, the housewives working their gardens as he passed.

He studied the map or read until it got dark. Then he lay down under his blanket, savoring the chilly air on his bare arms and face, watching the sky fill with stars as it slowly darkened, watching the Milky Way emerge from the blackness, until the entire sky seemed to be made of stars, a skein of stars, a quilt of stars, an ocean of stars. He could not find the words. Then, every night as he lay there, the same thing happened. And that was, that the great arching bowl of sky turned into space. That is, the sky suddenly took on something resembling its true nature—vast empty space—and assumed, to the extent that Louis's mind could apprehend it, its own true immensity. Louis was overcome by a terrifying and simultaneously delicious dizziness, and he spread his arms into the tall, cool grass, grabbing bunches of it in each hand, so that he would not go hurtling off into space.

"I am coming undone," he thought to himself. The thought made him happy. It was undoubtedly a kind of madness, this new state of mind into which he was finding his way. But he found the idea that he might be going mad, may indeed have already gone mad, to be far less of a worry than it was a relief that he had left his old madness behind.

One night, Louis slept in a pasture beside a broad pond. It was a clear moonless night. He awoke suddenly, and had the short-lived recollection that he had heard an animal cry in his dreams. He saw the dark shape of an owl move between him and the stars above him. He stood up. He had taken to sleeping naked. He walked through the tall grass to the edge of the pond and, after a moment's hesitation, walked into the pond. The muddy bottom oozed around his feet. He walked in until the black water was up to his chest, then he stopped and stood unmoving. The surface of the pond became still again. And as it did, it filled with the reflection of stars. Now it was as if he were completely surrounded by stars, above and below, surrounded by the universe of stars, as if there were no earth that could fling him from its surface, as if he were the center of the universe, the planet of Louis Morgon, providing his own gravity, his own reason for being. "Reason for being." He spoke the words aloud to himself, then repeated them, so that the planet of Louis Morgon would have its own sound.

The vast fields of wheat were turning yellow, as Louis approached the great cathedral town of Chartres. He saw the cathedral much as the early pilgrims had seen it, in the twelfth century, when it was first built, rising bright and enormous out of the vast treeless plain of the Beauce. It lay before him for hours. Louis slowed his pace to hold it there longer. The site had been chosen so that the cathedral seemed to actually emerge from the wheat as one approached, with the town, below and around it, only becoming visible as you reached its outskirts.

From Chartres he walked south and joined the tiny Loir—not la Loire, with an "e", but *le* Loir, a tributary of the larger river. The landscape gradually became rolling again. It began to be laced with small river valleys, with villages in the valleys, and farms an orchards on the plateaus above the valleys. The fields were smaller than in the vast Beauce and produced a greater variety of crops—wheat, soybeans, but also sunflowers, corn, and apples, pears, asparagus, tobacco, and hazelnuts. He followed the course of the river. It led through Chateaudun, with its feudal chateau and fortifications, to Vendome, where the Loir, by now a full-fledged river, split into branches dividing the medieval town into islands, then reunited and flowed on to Lavardin, with its ruined castle fought over during the Hundred Years War, and its ancient church of Saint Genest.

Louis had started visiting churches when he was still near Paris. His true purpose was unclear. The explanation he offered himself was ironic: he was a pilgrim, and pilgrims stopped at churches. At first, he was relieved when the church doors were locked, as they often were, and he could walk on without losing time. But at Chars, in the pretty Viosne valley, the church's heavy oak door had been unlocked. He had pushed it open and stepped across the raised threshold. The church had massive columns supporting the gray ceiling with its clumsy and rudimentary vaults revealing the first beginnings of the gothic age. The church's windows were pointed and narrow and unexpectedly graceful. Their glass was plain, letting in the gray daylight.

There had been no one in the church at Chars. A few votive candles flickered in front of a small side altar. He smelled the paraffin from the cheap candles. Louis heard cooing and the flapping of wings from pigeons that had found their way in through a broken pane or through the bell tower. They had made their nest somewhere in the shadows above.

He took off his pack and sat down. On the worn bench beside him lay a black lace glove. It was small and exquisitely made, a glove to be worn at a funeral, perhaps at a wedding, certainly at some solemn ceremony, not the kind of glove to be taken off. He picked it up with great care, as though it might have lain there for centuries and might disintegrate at his touch. The glove was so light and insubstantial, that he could only tell he was holding it by seeing it lying in his hand. The initials AMM were embroidered on the back. Without thinking, he raised the glove to his nose. To his surprise, he detected a faint perfume. He had a strong sense of the woman's presence. He turned around to see whether the glove's owner, perhaps having removed the glove to light a candle for someone recently dead, might still be in the church.

He might have found the owner, AMM, if he had chosen to inquire at the market that was going on in the town square. He might also have stopped at the cemetery as he left Chars, to see whether there were any new graves. He did not seek the glove's owner, but from then on, he stopped at churches, and regretted it when the doors were locked.

The church of Saint Genest in Lavardin was decorated with frescoes from the Middle Ages, which had only recently been discovered, and were just now being restored. They were of mythical beasts and saints, all in red and ochre, crowding shoulder to shoulder, along the ceiling, and up and down the columns. Since that first visit on foot, Louis had come back many times to look into the oval eyes of the saints, the lions, the lambs, and to revel in the glorious solitude of his life in Saint Leon, which lay just half a day's walk further on.

XIII

*A*s IT HAPPENED, THE DAY LOUIS HAD ARRIVED IN SAINT LEON SUR Dême for the first time was June 21, the summer solstice, the longest day of the year. The town sat astride the Dême. It did not strike him as an exceptionally pretty town. Just in the last few days he had come through half a dozen which were more beautiful. In fact, this was a corner of France where the villages were said to be particularly charming, owing, at least in part, to their being typically sited on a stream in a protective valley, and owing also to the creamy stone and the bluish slate roof tile from which their houses were constructed.

Saint Leon was a plainer version of the typical town. It was a farm town mainly, with an unremarkable medieval church and a small, rather plain chateau from the fifteenth century. The chateau was privately owned and mostly hidden from sight behind high stone walls in a forested park. The town consisted of several streets of houses, which had seen better days, and a few small shops—a bakery, a butcher, a grocer, a small bar—which managed to provide their proprietors with a comfortable, if modest, living.

The Hotel de France had eight rooms which now remained mostly empty. Nonetheless, its windows were flung open expectantly each morning, on the chance that guests might suddenly arrive. Great masses of trumpet vine and Virginia creeper climbed up the sides of the building, and cascades of red geraniums spilled from the flower boxes hanging everywhere.

The Hotel de France was run by Monsieur and Madame Chalfont, even then. The Chalfonts were very friendly, and Madame had a way with flowers. Louis was astonished—and disappointed—to learn that the Chalfonts had once actually visited Washington and even knew where Arlington was. Louis decided to eat lunch at the hotel. He could then walk on to Bueil en Touraine, where several pilgrim trails came together, and where there were, according to his guidebook, two interesting adjoining churches. They contained some old tombs with carved lids, and the remains of old frescoes. He would, he had already decided, sleep near Bueil.

"But, monsieur," said Monsieur Chalfont in alarm, his eyebrows arching skyward as he gestured with upturned palms around the square. He indicated the loudspeakers, which had been installed on strategic lampposts, and which were being tested at this very moment. He pointed here and there at the red, white, and blue bunting, at the small tricolor flags that fluttered everywhere, at the small stage, which had been set up opposite the hotel in front of the Gendarmerie. "It is the Festival of Music, monsieur. It will be a night to tell your friends about when you return to Arlington."

Louis remembered having seen similar preparations being made in other towns he had passed through. Since Bastille Day was still more than three weeks off, he had assumed they were preparations for local festivals. But, as Monsieur Chalfont explained with great animation—and with incredulity that Louis could have walked this far through France without knowing anything about the Festival of Music, all over France in every city and village from Paris to . . . to Saint Leon sur Dême!—tonight was the Festival of Music. Tonight, an entire country, all of France, welcomed the summer by singing and dancing through the night.

Yes, the festival would certainly be celebrated in Bueil en Touraine, if Monsieur chose to go there. But—and here Monsieur Chalfont's voice dropped to a whisper, Bueil was smaller than Saint Leon, and its celebration would be a *much* more modest one. In fact, Saint Leon was well known for its elaborate Festival of Music celebration, and people came from the surrounding villages, including Bueil, to take part in it. The celebration began after sundown— probably at around ten thirty, and different musicians would play through the night. The square would be transformed into one large dance floor. Of course, this one night the Hotel de France was completely full, but the Chalfonts had opened a small annex for the occasion, and a small room was available for Monsieur. He would be their guest. Louis could see no way out. He accepted their invitation.

Monsieur Chalfont brought Louis the room key and described how he could find the annex just across the Dême and through a narrow alley. Louis had a trout for lunch, accompanied by small, boiled potatoes, and a bibb lettuce salad with vinaigrette. He sat under an umbrella in front of the hotel and watched the preparations for the night's festivities. He watched people come and go— some English tourists stopping to buy ice cream from the freezer stationed just outside the hotel entrance, the people of Saint Leon buying their provisions for this evening's supper and visiting with their neighbors. He saw some fishermen heading toward the river.

Louis found the annex without difficulty. His room was cool, dark, and quiet. Lace curtains billowed into the room. The mattress sagged on its old iron frame. The dark paint on the wood floor had been worn away by a thousand scrubbings. Louis was unaccustomed to stopping this early in the day. In his journey thus far, he had rarely spent more than a few daylight hours in one place. He lay down on the bed to take a nap but was too restless to sleep. He tried to read but couldn't.

He walked through the streets of Saint Leon where he unexpectedly encountered Monsieur Chalfont who, to Louis's considerable discomfort, greeted him like an old friend and introduced him to the two men with whom he had been speaking. Monsieur Chalfont inquired whether the room was to his liking and enthusiastically repeated to his friends that Louis was on a "pilgrimage."

As quickly as he was able, Louis excused himself and walked out of town. Up a small hill, just past the walled cemetery, he found a shady patch of grass under some poplars. He could see part of the town below him—the roof of the chateau through the trees, the church tower with its peculiar slate dome. In the fields around him, the wheat had already been taken, the wheat straw had been baled. A tractor pulled a flatbed cart slowly through one of the fields, while a farmer and his wife swung bales onto the cart. Their young son drove the tractor. The wheat stubble was almost crimson in the shimmering summer light. The shadows were purple. Because the breeze came from the south, Louis could not hear the tractor. Louis had never painted before and had never, until that moment, felt any inclination to paint. But the way everything was spread out before him, it seemed like an exquisite painting waiting to be made.

Louis lay back in the grass and gazed up through the branches, watching the leaves twist and turn on their stems, the golden clouds moving past above them. An occasional bird swept through his field of vision, but he did not follow it with his eyes. The first thing he was aware of when he awoke was the sound of children playing. He opened his eyes and saw three women looking down at him. All three were dark skinned, with black hair, and striking blue eyes. The youngest, a girl in her late teens, smiled broadly, shamelessly it seemed to Louis, revealing very white, but uneven, teeth. She was pretty. The other two were fat, their skin was leathery, and their teeth were turning black.

Louis sat up quickly. He was embarrassed to have been found sleeping. The women wore plain cotton shirts, partly unbuttoned in front, and not tucked in. Their brightly patterned, full skirts hung nearly to their feet, which were bare and dusty and flat. Behind them, several children were racing around a tall, wooden wagon, chasing, and in turn being chased by, a mongrel dog. The smallest of the children was naked. A man in a broad felt hat led a horse off, then tethered him to a long rope and left him to graze. The man went about his business, apparently paying no attention to Louis or the women.

"Did you have a good sleep?" asked one of the women in heavily accented French. She rolled the r's like a Spaniard. Her tone was mocking, as if she were teasing Louis for allowing himself to be taken unawares by three gypsy women.

"Yes, thank you," said Louis, wanting to tease them back, but possessing neither the immediate wit nor the facility in French to do so. Still, the women laughed uproariously as if he had said something enormously clever.

"Hey!" shouted the man holding up a half-made basket and shaking it in their direction. He shouted something in another language. One of the women shouted back at him, shaking two fingers in the air, then all three of them giggled behind their hands, as if they were all—Louis included—in on some delicious conspiracy.

"Why were you sleeping here?" asked the same woman who had begun the conversation and had shouted the curse at the man. Her arms were crossed. She looked into Louis's eyes.

"I was taking a walk and I fell asleep," said Louis.

"You fell asleep while you were walking?" The three again laughed uproariously. The man moved in their direction, followed by a boy of perhaps sixteen. The man had removed his jacket, but he still had on the broad-brimmed hat. His shoes were dusty, his clothes wrinkled and stained. As he approached the group, he suddenly ran at the women, kicking out with his feet, but he missed them, and they laughed and scattered as they ran from him.

He turned toward Louis, and as he did, the scowl dropped from his face, as though it had been a mask. He was dark like the women, with the same blue eyes. He had thick lips framed on top by a black pencil line of a mustache. He was shorter than Louis, with narrow shoulders, thin arms and legs, and a pot belly that pushed at the buttons of his shirt. But despite his almost comic appearance, there was something authoritative and imposing about him. When he kicked out at the women, it was almost as though he were doing an extravagant series of dance steps. He came to rest in front of Louis, his hands resting lightly on his hips. Louis half expected him to remove his hat and sweep into a bow. As it was, he smiled broadly, showing off a mouthful of gold teeth, leaned his head slightly to the side and said, "My sincerest apologies, monsieur." He exaggerated the honorific in what might have been construed to be a sarcastic manner, and the way he stood there could hardly have been less apologetic. In any case, Louis did not know whether the man's apology was for his own behavior, or for some impropriety he might have perceived on the part of the women. So Louis simply greeted the man in return.

"I am Phillipe," said the gypsy, offering Louis his hand. He did not introduce the young man who stood just behind him. "Welcome to Saint Leon sur Dême," he said grandly, gesturing to the town just beyond the cemetery below them. "You are here for the night of music."

"I am passing through," said Louis. He was not eager to get involved in a conversation with Phillipe, but he was uncertain as to how to avoid it.

"As are we," said Phillipe, with another broad smile and a wink that seemed meant to suggest that they might be accomplices in some plot. "Where are you going, monsieur?"

"South," said Louis, looking for the shortest possible answer that might also allow him an easy exit from the conversation.

"Ah, Provence. You are English, aren't you? The English all love Provence. We have come from there. Marseille. By way of Orleans. Or is your trip business? Yes? And what business might that be? We are business travelers ourselves, in a manner of speaking." He seemed to find this very amusing, and turned with a laugh to the young man behind him, acknowledging his presence for the first time. The young man laughed dutifully, a high, whinnying laugh.

"Why don't you join me for a drink?" said Phillipe, at which point the young man darted off to the wagon, and returned carrying a small table, two folding chairs, an unlabelled green bottle, and two glasses. Louis protested and tried to excuse himself. "I must be getting back," he said. But back to what, wondered Phillipe. Just have a drink. There were hours to go before the music began. He was in town for the music too, said Phillipe, and he and the boy laughed again. He put a chair behind Louis and gently pressed him down onto it. When he was quite satisfied that Louis was not going anywhere, he sat down on the other one. The chairs wobbled unsteadily on the uneven ground, so the two men balanced more than they sat, their legs spread wide to steady themselves. Phillipe put a glass in front of Louis. He took Louis's hand in his own and wrapped it around the glass. Phillipe's hand was long and fine, almost delicate. "Hold the glass while I pour," said Phillipe. "Don't let it spill." He poured a half inch of clear liquid into Louis's glass, then into his own.

"Do you know what this is?" asked Phillipe.

"No," said Louis, wishing he had known.

Phillipe stared at him for a long moment. "Brandy. Plum brandy. *Eau de vie*. The water of life." He said it again: "The water of life." Then: "Sip it slowly." He took a careful sip, keeping his eyes on Louis over the rim of the glass. Louis raised the glass to his lips, and the odor of ripe plums and alcohol filled his nose. It almost made him sneeze. The brandy was cool on his tongue and burned his throat. He took another sip.

"The best *eau de vie* is made from the Reine Claude plum that grows only here in the Touraine, a little plum with yellow-green fruit, and a skin so delicate that, by the time it is ready to eat, it is invariably covered with bruises. It ripens in August. It is the sweetest fruit on the earth. What is your name?"

"Charles," said Louis.

Phillipe tilted his head to the side for a long moment and smiled. He looked into Louis's eyes. "What do you know about the Rom, Charles?" Louis did not answer. "We are the Rom, Charles, the Tsiganes, gypsies. What do you know about our people? Who we are? Where we come from?"

"Very little," said Louis and took another sip, thinking, if he drank a little more, he could leave.

"The Rom came from India originally," said Phillipe.

"It is time for me to go," said Louis putting his glass down and starting to rise.

"Stay," said Phillipe and put his hand on Louis's. "Stay while I tell you about the Rom. Then you can go." He kept his hand on Louis's. "Please, monsieur," he said and smiled so that his gold teeth flashed. Louis sat back down. Phillipe took his hand away. He looked at Louis. He took a thoughtful sip of the plum brandy.

"The Rom, which is what we now call ourselves, came from India originally. We were called the Dom there, where we were one of the lower castes. We were not exactly driven out, but we were persecuted, so that leaving became our only alternative." Phillipe spoke as though he had personally lived through the entire Rom history. "We first landed in Europe in the Middle Ages, and then went in all directions. Every country tried to break our backs, to regulate our trade, to stop our wandering, but we survive to this day as wanderers. The Rom are a people whose life is movement, who wither in houses, who die when they stay in one place. We are despised everywhere.

"You are a Jew, aren't you, Charles?" He did not wait for an answer. "And you are a man who travels on business. You have seen the world. And you know about persecution. Your people, the Jews, have been persecuted for all time. So have we. My father and all his sisters and brothers died in Poland. They were rounded up in France and Italy and sent to Auschwitz where the Nazis used them in medical experiments. The Rom were disposable, not even people, *Zigeuner*, viewed as thieves and confidence artists, someone to be despised and gotten rid of. Did you lose people in Auschwitz, Charles?" Phillipe took a sip and studied the glass. He took the bottle and poured more into both their glasses. "Go on and drink, Charles," he said. "It is the water of life.

"I have a question for you, Charles."

Louis waited.

"Why did you say your name was Charles, when it is not?" Again he did not wait for an answer. "We are fellow travelers—the Jew and the Rom—strangers to each other, who share a history, and meet in our travels. We stop for a moment in the same place. I see you asleep in the grass. I see that you are alone. I am courteous, I am hospitable. My women are friendly and courteous to you. My son treats you as an honored guest. And still you are afraid of us. You hardly answer my friendly questions. You say that your name is Charles. You are fearful that, what? I will rob you, cheat you, do all the things you have heard and read that gypsies do?

"When I was little, my father taught me to read. But after a while, I stopped reading. It is too easy to write lies without even knowing you are doing it. You are a traveler. You travel for business. You have found in your travels that the world is a dangerous place. Perhaps your clients are not to be trusted. Maybe they have tried to cheat you. Or worse. True, the world is a dangerous place. Nobody knows that better than I do. Jews know that too. How could they not? But it is important not to allow a possibility to dictate your behavior, not to become a prisoner of your suspicions and fears. You are a young man, Charles." Phillipe was no older than Louis, but he spoke now as though he might have been speaking to someone much younger. "You shouldn't believe things, even if they are written, until you know them to be true.

"You are an educated man, Charles, I can tell." He continued to call Louis Charles, and each time he did so he flashed his golden smile. "You know, education is often poisonous, I have found. People who are educated often seem to believe that education has given them knowledge, no, not exactly knowledge. What is the word . . . ?"

"Certainty," said Louis. "People who are educated believe they have acquired certainty."

Phillipe looked into his eyes. Then he nodded his head emphatically. "Certainty. Yes. Certainty. That is it. But to pay for their certainty, they surrender their understanding, their compassion, their humanity. That is a high price to pay for certainty, especially when it is a false certainty, a mirage, the certainty of Auschwitz.

"Now, you may leave."

Louis took a last sip of the *eau de vie*. "I thank you for your hospitality." He gave Phillipe his hand.

"Maybe we will see each other tonight at the Festival of Music," said Phillipe. "Or along the road. In any case, I wish you a good journey south."

XIV

$\mathcal{M}$ONSIEUR AND MADAME CHALFONT HAD TAKEN IT UPON THEM-
selves to reserve a table for Louis in front of the hotel on the sidewalk facing the square. People arrived and mingled as they had
earlier in the day. American pop music came from the loudspeakers,
its sound made even more raucous by the loudspeakers' poor quality.
Paper lanterns had been hung over strung lights. They glowed in the
early twilight. Louis sat at his table enjoying Monsieur Chalfont's
excellent coquille Saint Jacques. Eyelets of golden butterfat floated
in the cream sauce. The scallops were tender, the potatoes perfectly
roasted. He soaked up the last sauce with pieces of baguette. He
drank a local wine he had never heard of before.

A few people danced. Some teenagers lit firecrackers, and
laughed and chattered when they went off. Beer, wine, and soft
drinks were being sold by the glass at a bar that had been set up
beside the stage. The square had filled with people. The other tables

were all occupied. Monsieur Chalfont joined Louis at his table, still wearing his wilted white jacket and dirty apron, and a handkerchief knotted around his short neck. Beads of sweat stood on his red face. He spoke rapidly and excitedly to Louis about the Festival of Music, and then, yet again, about his stay in Washington. He wondered if Louis knew the hotel where they had stayed, whether Louis had lived in Washington when they had been there. He pointed out everyone he knew. When anyone passed close enough, he introduced them to Louis.

Suddenly, the recorded music was turned off in midsong. After a brief pause while the microphone was adjusted, the live music began. *Musette* is dance music usually played on an accordion, which for many foreigners, rightly or wrongly, has come to characterize France. Its rhythms are light and energetic, but there is an underlying sadness, a feeling of loss, about it too, a sense of the lilting, skipping, unstoppable passage of time.

Musette came into being in the dance halls of Paris at the end of the nineteenth century, when the accordions of Italian immigrants took up the folk songs of migrants from the rural Auvergne. Perhaps it was the music's contradictions—the joyful melancholy it expressed—that made it irresistible. The musicians who played in the dance halls, at the *bals musettes* were soon incorporating gypsy music, tangos, swing music, and jazz into their songs. The *musette* flourished and spread all over France.

Paris dropped the *musette* in the 1950s to embrace rock and roll, the new music from America. There is, after all, something hopelessly naive about the *musette*. And the accordion is an unrefined musical instrument. Its sound is mechanical and without nuance. It is inescapably reedy. It is too clumsy to be delicate, and yet too soft to be forceful. Both the instrument and the music it plays feel dated.

But in the smaller towns of France, in the countryside, where people heard in the *musette* the sad, and happy, and slightly outdated rhythms of their own lives, and where the accordion, for all its awkwardness, sang in a voice they knew, they did not let the *musette* disappear, or the *bal* where they could dance to it. It is true, that even in the countryside people now listened to rock and roll or to jazz on their radios. But when it came time to dance, even the young, who scoffed at the *musette* and groaned when it began to play, could not resist its enticing rhythms.

Now the crowd on the square at Saint Leon—old, young, children, everyone—began to dance. They paired up, and moved, and twirled to the quick step as though it were their normal means of locomotion. The dance moved them at different speeds, but all in a counterclockwise direction around the square. It appeared to Louis as though this moment must have been rehearsed. The accordionist played with what sounded to Louis's unschooled ears like extraordinary skill and dexterity, elaborating and embellishing notes, weaving new intricate melodies around the implied melody, while the great bobbing crowd swirled past, just in front of the table where Louis sat.

Louis had never enjoyed dancing, although whenever Sarah had forced him onto the dance floor, he had acquitted himself with a natural grace that surprised even him. Dancing was the kind of public display he found embarrassing and, if he was completely honest with himself, slightly dangerous. It embarrassed him to move in a way that was both so sensual and so public. Moreover, it felt calculated and dishonest to him, alien somehow to his person, the same way using slang had always felt alien. So, when Madame Chalfont invited him to dance, and Monsieur Chalfont chimed in, insisting he could not possibly appreciate the pleasures of the Festival of

Music without dancing, Louis insisted just as adamantly that he could not and would not dance. The two ignored his protestations. They simply would not accept his refusal. Their insistence and determination that Louis should, no, *must* dance grew stronger, the stronger his resistance became.

He was suddenly struck by the absurd intensity of his refusal. It reminded him of his earlier wariness toward the gypsies. Or maybe it was simply the reflected light of the lanterns playing in the glass of wine that stood in front of him. Whatever the reason, Louis soon found himself in the crowd, circling around the square, holding Madame Chalfont in his arms. She smiled and spoke encouragements to him as, to his surprise, he quickly found his way into the music. Madame Chalfont was a stocky woman, with a red face, crooked teeth, and eyes—one blue and one gray—that looked in slightly different directions. She danced lightly, high on her toes, and unabashedly pressed her body against his.

This was what felt dangerous about dancing. After all, dancing was barely sublimated sex, a fact which everyone else seemed to have no trouble putting out of their minds, but which Louis never forgot when he was dancing. What they were doing seemed illicit to him. He danced with Monsieur Chalfont's wife while Monsieur Chalfont waved approvingly from the table. He felt her bare arms on his, smelled her hair, felt her breasts, her belly, felt her thighs moving against his, as intimately and as sensually as if they had been in bed together. Madame Chalfont threw her head back and laughed as though she knew exactly what he was thinking.

They danced among the other couples—young lovers, children in their fathers' arms, couples married for decades, pairs of young girls—circling around and through each other, moving like traffic at different speeds, but all moving, whirling around the square, carried by the accordion's spinning melodies, adrift in space on the *musette*, as if the music were yet another small planet, and the dance were life itself. To dance was to live. To dance with Madame Chalfont, to be in orbit with all these other people, reminded him of standing in the pond that night amid the stars. It seemed in that moment as though life and death, happiness and unhappiness, all the contradictions of being were reconciled and given coherent meaning that could never be spoken. It could only be danced.

The music stopped, but within seconds the accordionist struck up another tune. Madame Chalfont was willing, and it was as if they had started life anew, were newborn, were children, were lovers, were dying, all at the same time. The accordionist began to sing as they passed the stage. He sang in a high tenor, and had that rapid vibrato that is exactly right for the *musette*. It was a clear, startling voice. Louis looked to see the musician as they passed by. It was Phillipe, the gypsy. He wore a bright green suit that was too tight around the middle, a yellow plaid shirt, and a flowered tie. He swayed and sweated as he played and sang. His broad hat kept his face mostly in shadow. Louis could not tell whether Phillipe had seen him or not. But the words that he sang made it seem certain that he had.

> *Charles the great has come at last,*
> *Come at last to stay.*
> *He knows not where he's going, though*
> *He thinks he knows the way.*
>
> *He thinks he knows the way to love,*
> *Through flowered fields and highways.*
> *He does not know what love is or*
> *That I will love him always.*

A pretty girl there waits for Charles,
To ease his pain and kiss his eyes,
To circle him with chains of love,
To show him love and make him wise.

Charles the great might disappear
While thinking you can see him.
But life is short and art is long,
And she can live without him.

When the song was finished, Phillipe began another. The Chalfonts introduced Louis to their neighbor, Madame Bernard, a tall woman with a shy closed-mouthed smile. Louis immediately invited her to dance with an urgency in his voice that made everyone laugh. Madame Bernard's body was lithe and quick, her back was muscular and arched. She did not press herself against him as Madame Chalfont had. But as they followed the music, their bodies brushed against each other in ways Louis found thrilling. They danced many dances together until they were both tired, and sat down.

Madame Bernard was soon invited to dance by another man, and so Louis found himself asking a woman sitting alone at the next table to dance. She said nothing, but she tilted her head slightly, and smiled at him with raised eyebrows. She appeared to be about his age. She had a pretty face with a long, straight nose, a high forehead, and a cloud of loose brown hair she had pinned up here and there, but to no avail. It tumbled in every direction.

This was Solesme Lefourier, his future neighbor and lover. As she took his hand and stood, he saw that her back was twisted unnaturally. Louis began to apologize, but Madame Lefourier smiled and nodded toward the dancing throng. "I love to dance," she said.

She danced more carefully than the other women had, taking small, gliding steps while the crowd eddied around them. With each step, she turned her shoulders slightly, and he felt her breasts moving like a soft wave across his chest. She leaned into his right shoulder, pushed her face against his neck, and he found himself looking through the great cloud of her hair.

The square had emptied somewhat when they stopped dancing. Most of the older people had gone. So had the children. Madame Lefourier said she was tired, and Louis apologized for having kept her so long. She thanked him and said how much she had enjoyed dancing. He took her back to the table where her husband now sat. Pierre Lefourier was even then a ponderous man, shaped like a pyramid, and apparently as old. He greeted Louis with a broad, but indifferent, smile.

Later that evening, after the Lefouriers had gone home and the square had emptied, Louis sat with the Chalfonts and gazed at the colored lanterns. "I met the accordionist today," he said. "Phillipe."

"Who? Phillipe?" asked Monsieur Chalfont, mopping his red face with the handkerchief he had removed from around his neck. He was still out of breath from the last dance. "Who is Phillipe?"

"The accordionist," said Louis. "The gypsy. I met him on my walk."

"But his name is Henri," said Monsieur Chalfont. "Henri Kadusco. He comes every year to play for the Festival of Music. He is quite well known all over France for his *musette*. But he comes to Saint Leon every year, for many years. Phillipe? No, no. It's Henri."

"Ah, well, the gypsies," said Madame Chalfont. "They lie about everything."

"But what a musician," said Monsieur Chalfont.

In his room, Louis lay on the bed, his hands behind his head. He looked at the dark ceiling. The tall, lace curtains billowed gently into the room, moved, it seemed, by the music that still came from the square.

> *A pretty girl there waits for Charles,*
> *To ease his pain and kiss his eyes,*
> *To circle him with chains of love,*
> *To show him love and make him wise.*

> *Charles the great might disappear*
> *While thinking you can see him.*
> *But life is short and art is long,*
> *And she can live without him.*

He woke up once in the early dawn to hear music still playing. The next time he woke up, the sun was high in the sky and he heard only birds.

At about ten o'clock, Louis thanked the Chalfonts for their extraordinary hospitality and set out for Bueil. From there, he walked on to Saint Paterne-Racan where he slept in a field across from the Chateau la Roche-Racan by the little Ecosais river. He walked on south—Sonzay, Parnay. After two more nights, he crossed the broad Loire at Langeais. He walked through the great Foret de Chinon, where he slept one night, and awoke early to find himself surrounded by a herd of grazing deer. He crossed the Vienne at Sazilly and entered the broad vineyards by Ligre south of Chinon. He walked through the town of Richelieu with its twenty-eight mansions lining the Grande-Rue.

July found him entering the Charente. In his mind, time and space had merged. He walked across the changing face of France, as if his walking were the motion of time, as if time would stop if he were to stop. He was spinning out a silken cord as he walked further and further from equipoise. In his mind, this point of balance, this his own personal version of magnetic north, slowly consolidated and came to be located exactly on the square in the village of Saint Leon sur Dême on the night of the Festival of Music.

One day toward the end of July, he was leaving a small stone church just south of Angouleme. The church stood alone surrounded by fields of lavender. It was an ancient building—from the ninth or tenth century he guessed. Its builders had barely known how to construct an arch. They had stacked up stone on stone to make walls three feet thick with one narrow window, oddly placed high and off-center above the door. It was cool and dark inside the church, and completely empty of any furnishings except for a wooden cross in front and a bell rope hanging down to the hard dirt floor. He had pulled down on the rope until he felt the weight of the bell. But he let it go carefully, not wanting the bell to ring after all. The rope swung briefly against the floor as he released it. Then everything was silent.

It was bright and hot outside. He saw something moving toward him along the track through the lavender. As it drew nearer, he saw it was a horse-drawn cart, and when it came nearer still, he was startled to see that it was the gypsy musician. It was like unexpectedly meeting an old friend. But as the cart approached and Louis stepped off the track and said "Bonjour, Phillipe"—it somehow did not seem proper to call him anything else—the gypsy raised his hat and said, "monsieur," as if they had never met. The youngest of the women sat beside him, and she smiled at Louis broadly as she had done weeks before. The gypsy spoke angrily to the horse as the cart rolled past. Louis turned to watch. Phillipe's son sat on the back of the wagon, dangling his legs. Louis waved. The boy waved back. The wagon rolled past the little church and into the distance.

Over the weeks, Louis had sung what he had come to call the Charles song to himself over and over again, sometimes aloud, sometimes silently. He sang it again now in a whisper as though he had suddenly discovered its incantatory powers.

> *Charles the great might disappear*
> *While thinking you can see him.*
> *But life is short and art is long,*
> *And she can live without him.*

Had he disappeared? He had. Walking had transported him further from his life than he had wanted it to, than he had imagined it could. He did not decide to stop then and there. He walked on into Spain, and all the way to Santiago. But now he walked looking backward, wondering whether the delicate cord that spun out behind him would have the strength to pull him back.

His trip had ended, and he had been back in Washington for months, visiting his children, doing research and writing articles about the Middle East and the politics of oil, even consulting with the State Department again, before he had decided to move to France. No, not just to France, but to Saint Leon sur Dême. For he gradually discovered that, despite what he had imagined—that once he was back in Washington his pilgrimage would be gathered into his life and assimilated, would become a part of the whole of who he was, and that his center of gravity would remain, at least for the foreseeable future in Washington, near Jennifer and Michael, and, yes, near Sarah—in fact his center, his point of equilibrium, remained where he had first found it, in Saint Leon sur Dême.

To the utter bafflement of his friends, and the dismay of his children, Louis sold the apartment he had bought after the divorce, put his belongings in storage, and went to Saint Leon to buy a house. When he returned, he told his clients that he would no longer be writing articles for them. Like his friends, they stared at him, uncomprehending. "What will you do there?" they wanted to know. He did not know what he would do there.

"What are you thinking of?" Sarah demanded. "Your children are here. They need their father." Louis did not have an answer that would even begin to assuage her anger. He acknowledged both the abruptness and the enormity of his decision. "It seems foolish to me too, when I think about it, foolish and . . . to suddenly leave my home for a strange place? I can't begin to understand or explain it."

The truth was that Louis was a stranger in Washington. He had always been a stranger in Washington and, for that matter, wherever he had lived. He was a stranger in his own life. He lived on the edge of his life, unconnected to anyone or anything except in a tentative way, by their expectations of him, by his sense of his obligations and his duties, but not by his heart. These tentative connections seemed the truest thing about him. And now, somehow—as preposterous as it seemed, it must have been the dance—he had plunged into the life of Saint Leon with such intensity and force that his absence from there felt violent and insupportable, making his obligations insignificant in his own mind. He could never have said so to Sarah or anyone else. He could barely allow the thought to enter his mind. But the fact was that the only home he knew was a place where he had stopped for a night.

XV

WHEN LOUIS HAD ARRIVED BACK IN WASHINGTON AFTER WALKING TO
Santiago, it had seemed as though he were arriving from another
planet. Now, arriving at Dulles Airport after having been away for
these many years, Louis felt as though he had only just left. The
friendly green hills of Virginia rose up to greet the plane full of
travelers. The moist heat enveloped them as they left the plane. The
passengers sighed or laughed as they felt it. They were relieved to be
off the plane. Louis squinted into the brightness of the day. But time
and memory play tricks on us. Except for the white light, the heat,
and the verdant landscape, almost nothing was the same.

A great hall had been built to receive international passengers. It
was chilly inside. The immigration officials in their open-collared
shirts, festooned with silver badges and bright patches, typed each
passport number into a computer, then greeted each passenger as
they handed back his passport. "Enjoy your stay, Mister Morgon."

Louis's suitcase came down the chute amidst assorted cases and parcels, and wobbled along the conveyor belt to where he waited. At the exit, officials took the declaration form he had filled out on the plane and waved him past.

He made his way through the crowds of travelers, and found a taxi which sped him along the airport road into the city. The Dulles Airport access road had been built to the distant airport through open country with funds specially allocated by Congress, so that its members would not have to wait in traffic on their way in and out of the city. Now this road was lined with office buildings of steel and glass, surrounded by expensively landscaped grounds and discreet signs tastefully announcing their occupants—THE AIRLINE PILOTS ASSOCIATION, GENSYS, UUSA, ALLIED ELECTRONICS, THE ASSOCIATION OF ENGINEERS—to businessmen and political operatives speeding in and out of the city.

The trip to the George Washington Colonial Court Motor Hotel in Falls Church took twenty minutes and cost thirty-five dollars. Louis had remembered the hotel as a reasonable and convenient place to put out-of-town guests. He had dialed information from Saint Leon. Was the hotel still listed? "Hold for the number," said the operator. An automated voice recited the number. He called and reserved a quiet room away from the street. "Are you a senior citizen, sir?" the clerk asked. A senior citizen. "We have a special weekly rate for seniors," said the clerk brightly.

The motel looked much the same as Louis remembered it, with its sign depicting George Washington in silhouette, its broad lawn scattered with turquoise colored plastic chairs, its grandiose colonnaded porch, the vivid blue swimming pool, the two brick wings with their rows of white doors. He walked past the humming ice machine to his room. The air conditioner was set on high; the heavy, double vinyl curtains were closed against the light and the heat. He turned down the air conditioner but left the curtains closed.

Louis had been back to Washington only twice since he had left, both times when Jennifer had had medical emergencies. On those earlier visits, he had anticipated his arrival with an exaggerated sense of delicacy, with the expectation that he would need time to adjust to things. He had the same expectation now: that he would have to sit in his room or walk slowly around outside, touching things, naming them, as though he had just been born or released from prison, as though he were starting from scratch. Instead, he found himself wanting to get moving, to allow whatever changes had occurred in the place to catch up with him.

The Metro was filled with people going home from work. Despite the heat, the men wore suits; many of the women did too. Everyone read or looked into the space just in front of them. They seemed familiar to him, like the rattling, humming ice machine at the hotel. As he got off at Foggy Bottom, crowds of students and government workers squeezed past him through the doors into the cars. He rode the escalator up out of the Metro station and stopped to look around. He walked against the tide of people surging toward the station.

Inside the main entrance of the familiar granite building that housed the State Department, a security guard sat beside a metal detector through which everyone entering the building had to pass. Two other guards stood against the wall behind him, leaning toward one another as they talked in confidential tones. The seated guard looked at Louis expectantly but did not speak. Louis stepped to the side to look past the metal detector and the barrier that blocked the way. "May I help you, sir?" said the guard, intending perhaps by means of his impatient tone to remind Louis where he was and what he had to do. Louis continued to look at the great lobby with its tall windows and wooden paneled walls, its corridors leading off to the left and right, the three central marble stairs that led to staircases left and right, the tall flag standard in the center. "May I help you!" said the guard. The other two guards had stopped talking.

"Yes," said Louis. "My name is Louis Morgon. I would like to see Secretary of State Bowes."

The guard looked at him for a moment. The other two guards looked at one another and stood up straighter, in case Louis turned out to be one of those people who showed up wanting to give the secretary a piece of their mind.

"My name is Louis Morgon," said Louis again in a voice that did not sound irate or, for that matter, even troublesome. "I know of course I cannot simply stop in and see the secretary. But if you could tell me how one goes about seeking an appointment, I would greatly appreciate it." The guard could not remember that anyone had ever asked how to make an appointment with the secretary of state. Either you had an appointment, in which case your name was on the printed daily schedule distributed to all security guards each morning, and you arrived by limousine, usually through the underground garage entrance, or you didn't have an appointment, and, as far as he knew, you couldn't get one. The secretary's days were planned weeks, even months, in advance. In fact, he was rarely in the building, spending most of his time, when he was in town at all, in his suite of offices at the Old Executive Office Building next to the White House. The guard studied the clipboard in front of him and said, without looking at Louis, "You have to call his office for an appointment." He knew this answer was unsatisfactory, but he busied himself writing something and hoped Louis would just leave.

"Could you please give me his office number so that I can call for an appointment?" said Louis. One of the guards who had been watching stepped up to the table. He was older than the other two and wore the stripes of a sergeant on his blue uniform sleeve. "What did you say your name was, sir?" he said peering at Louis through his steel-rimmed glasses.

"Louis Morgon," said Louis, and added, "I used to work here."

"I thought you looked familiar, Mister Morgon. It was a long time ago, wasn't it?"

Louis looked back at the man but could not remember him. The man wrote a telephone number on a slip of paper and handed it to Louis. The number ended in three zeroes, so it was probably the State Department switchboard number. "Call this number, Mister Morgon, and they'll be able to help you. It was nice to see you again after all this time."

Louis left the building. He walked the several blocks to the Old Executive Office Building. The streets were filled with traffic. The broad sidewalks were full of people—government workers going home, as well as tourists. The tourists wore baggy shorts and bright T-shirts with the names of sports teams on them. They watched carefully as the government workers passed, searching for a recognizable face, someone they might have seen on the news.

The Old Executive Office Building is a gray Victorian mansion, a forest of pillars and gables and windows, chimneys and mansard roofs. "My name is Louis Morgon," said Louis to the guard on duty in the small guardhouse just outside the building, "and I would like to see the secretary of state." The effect here was the same as it had been at the State Department. That is, the guard not knowing what else to do, gave Louis the number of the State Department switchboard. He watched as Louis walked away and then wrote down the time—17:15—and his name—he spelled it Morgan—in the daily log: "Man says name Louis Morgan wants to see secy. of state."

There had been several recent breaches of security at the White House, including a tourist who had somehow entered the grounds with a crowd of visiting dignitaries and had been found wandering the corridors of the West Wing. He was caught far from the president's quarters and seemed to have no other purpose than to see the inside of the building. Still, the apparent ease of this "penetration," as it was called, was particularly worrisome to the Secret Service and the FBI, and as a result, security guards at all government office buildings had been reminded to note any and all unusual activity in their daily logs, along with details.

At the end of the day, the shift commanders reviewed the logs and entered any incidents of note into the computer. So it happened that on this particular day Louis's name found its way into the computer twice, once misspelled, and after a few moments was matched with the extensive FBI file that already existed under his name. The guard at the State Department, the one who had remembered Louis—Leroy Burwell was his name—was the shift commander there, and so he was the one to enter Louis's name, correctly spelled, into the computer there. An abbreviated version of the FBI file came up on Burwell's screen. Then he remembered exactly who Louis was. There were those officials who spoke to the guards when they entered the building and those who didn't. Louis Morgon had been one who did. Leroy had watched that day as Louis was escorted from the building. The guards had all talked about it. Louis seemed all right to them. They wondered to each other what he had done. But nobody ever told them anything.

The complete file, which was available only to the highest officials, gave Louis's date and place of birth, his social security number, army identification number, blood type, and other vital statistics. It also included information about his former wife, his children, and their whereabouts. It included fingerprints and an old photograph from when he had first joined the government. And it included a summary history of his dismissal from government service and the lifting of his security clearance, along with references to the correspondence between the officials involved. Any official able to access this correspondence found that it was complete, except for any record of who had initially filed the charges leading to Louis's dismissal. Recent updates to the file included Louis's address and telephone number in Saint Leon sur Deeme—spelled wrong—a recent photograph, and the number of the French passport under which he currently traveled.

The file had been flagged by a secret account within the State Department so that any amendments to it were automatically forwarded to that account holder's electronic mailbox. An amendment had already been forwarded to that mailbox earlier in the day as a result of an entry made by the Office of Immigration and Naturalization: "Entered U.S. using French Passport number 154656, Dulles International Airport, August 6, 14:40."

After Louis had first settled in Saint Leon, he had exchanged occasional letters with some of his old friends in Washington. He had written them about buying the house in Saint Leon. He had written about taking up painting, how it had then come rushing into his life, and how it seemed to fill some part of himself that he hadn't even known was there. They wrote back about their work, about their children growing up, getting braces, going off to boarding school, wrecking Dad's car. But because of the distance between Louis and his friends, and because of their divergent lives, their connection to one another had grown tenuous over the years. And after a while neither Louis nor his friends had any real sense any longer of whom they were writing.

In his first years in Saint Leon, the Steinbergs and then the Mullers had visited him, the Steinbergs after a barge tour in Burgundy, and the Mullers while they were traveling through Europe. They wrote: "When are you coming back to D.C.? Whenever it is, you know you are welcome to stay with us. It would be a pleasure for us to have the time together." But they knew he was not coming back.

Now Louis sat on the edge of the motel bed with the heavy Virginia telephone directory on his lap. He found the Mullers, Arnold J. The Steinbergs were unlisted. He still had their old number. He found Milton Hamsher's number. He searched for and found the names of people he had no intention of calling: former neighbors he barely knew, an editor he had once worked with, friends who had stopped calling when he got divorced, a woman he had been involved with for a while, the lawyer who had helped him settle things when he moved to France. He found Sarah Morgon. He found Michael Morgon. He found J. Morgon. Jennifer. He touched the pages of the telephone book as one might touch the names engraved on gravestones in a cemetery.

Louis had not told anyone he was coming. He dialed the Steinbergs' old number. Arlene answered. She was out of breath. "Hello?"

"Arlene?" he said.

"Louis," she answered. Then again: "Louis."

"How did you know it was me?" he said, immediately feeling foolish for asking. "After all this time?"

"I recognize your voice," she laughed. "How else? Even with

your French accent. Where are you? Are you in Washington? When did you get in?"

"Yes. I just got in."

"For how long? Where are you staying?"

He mentioned the hotel. He told her he was staying for several days, that he was there on business, that he would love to see them.

"Come for dinner tomorrow. No, come tonight. Or are you too tired from the flight? Wally will pick you up at seven. I'll call him at the office. God, Louis, it's fine to hear your voice." The "fine" sounded wrong. It didn't matter. She had taken a chance by saying something friendly so early in their conversation. They all would have to find their way back across the great distance which had grown between them.

When Wallace Steinberg turned into the drive of the George Washington Colonial Court, Louis was sitting under an umbrella on one of the turquoise chairs. Louis allowed him to get out of the car and enter the motel office. He saw the clerk rise and point in his direction, saw Wally turn and toss his head back in recognition and then stride his way. Wally was tall with a squarish body that had only gotten a bit thicker. He still had a boyish face, but his hair now consisted mainly of a white fringe above his ears.

"Louis!" he said, and again, "Louis! . . . Louis!" marking the closing space between them with periodic exclamations of "Louis!" until they met, and Wally took Louis's hand in his own huge hand and pumped it happily, clapping his shoulder with his other hand and saying "Louis!" yet again.

The Steinbergs lived in a large house across the river in Potomac, Maryland. When Louis and Wally arrived, Arlene came out to greet them, followed closely by Arnold and Joanne Muller, whom Arlene had called and invited to come see their old friend Louis Morgon.

"He's here?" said Arnie on the phone to Arlene. "Unbelievable." Louis shook hands and embraced everyone, and they all exclaimed how none of them had changed in . . . how many years had it been?

"Too long," said Wally, and again, "too long." He spread his long arms and herded everyone into the house.

Wally and Arlene were attorneys. He had always been in private practice, doing deals that rarely had anything to do with the government. Arlene had been at the State Department years ago, but she had left about the time of Louis's departure, to enter a private firm devoted to public relations and government access. The Steinbergs had two grown children who were both out of medical school and doing their residencies in New York. In fact, the Steinbergs had two new grandchildren.

Wally and Arlene had both recently retired. "We're thinking of getting a place in New York to be near the kids," said Wally. "Of course we'd keep this place. This is home."

"Here are the grandchildren," said Arlene, producing photos. "Samantha is Joe's . . ."

"Joe and Susan's," said Wally. "Joe *and* Susan's."

". . . and Noah is Jennifer's, Jennifer and Tom's."

The Mullers had seen the pictures before. And they had grandchildren of their own, so they watched magnanimously as the Steinbergs passed photo after photo to Louis. He looked at them helplessly, stacking them precariously on his knee. People who had been young when Louis had last seen them now had grandchildren. He did not have grandchildren. He did not want grandchildren. He wished sometimes that the Morgon family line had ended with him.

Louis asked about Milton Hamsher who had once been his best friend. Milton had gotten divorced from Susan, had married again, a much younger woman—was her name Tierney?—and had gotten divorced again. Milton's career had derailed. He no longer answered his phone or returned calls. They thought he was a freelance journalist now, but no one knew whom he worked for. No one had seen him in years.

Arlene announced that she had made a bouillabaisse. She invited everyone to the table. "Since you left, Washington has finally grown up. It's a big city now, with good restaurants, bakeries that offer good bread, good seafood shops."

"French wine!" said Arnie brandishing the bottles of Saint Emilion he had brought. "In your honor, Louis," he said.

"Tell us what your life is like in that lovely French village," said Joanne Muller. She and Arnie remembered their visit fondly. They had spent three nights at the Hotel de France, and Louis had shown them the local sights—the Chateau at Amboise, the one at Azay, the gardens at Villandry, Vendome, the village of Lavardin. "How is that sweet man that runs the hotel? Monsieur . . . ?"

"Monsieur Chalfont. He is not very well, I'm afraid," said Louis.

"My life there is really quite simple and quite wonderful," said Louis. "I spend a lot of time painting." He spoke a little about his recent painting experiments.

"You said you're here on business," said Arlene.

"It's personal business, Arlene," said Louis. "Nothing that would interest anyone. Something from long ago that I have to wrap up. Some loose ends I have to tie up." He liked finding his way back into the American idiom, the sense of speaking without effort, of not being heard immediately to be a stranger, someone from somewhere else. But of course he sounded just like a stranger. He was not entirely at home in any language any more.

"If there's anything we can do," Arlene said, "any way we can help?"

"Thank you. But I don't think so," said Louis. "What I really need to do is talk to Hugh Bowes." He tried to make it sound less serious: "Have a word with Hugh Bowes."

Arlene's eyes narrowed momentarily, and then she spoke softly. "That's probably not going to be easy."

"Nobody sees Hugh very much anymore," said Wally. "Since he became the secretary, of course."

"He travels in different circles now." This was Joanne. "Has for the last few years, actually."

Finally, after a long pause, she added, "I take it you don't know that Ruth died." Louis felt his heart stop. He clasped his hands together under the table and stared at Joanne.

"Yes," said Joanne. "She just died. I'm sorry, did you know Ruth? You look shocked. I'm sorry, Louis. Well, we all were shocked. Did you know her well? She just died, very suddenly.

"And even before that, well, Hugh had pretty much cut himself off from everybody he used to know. They had only the one child. He had to be institutionalized. You knew about him. Ruth had a stroke. It was completely unexpected. Shocking and very sad. Terrible." Joanne finally fell silent.

"We've reached that age, Louis, where our friends start dying," said Wally, smiling gamely, trying to keep the dreadful silence from settling in. "We've reached that age."

During the long silence, Louis saw Ruth Chasen before his mind's eye. "When exactly did she die?" he asked finally.

"It's only been a week or ten days at the most, hasn't it?" said Joanne.

"A week, maybe," said Walter. "Maybe ten days. Let's see: the memorial service was last Sunday."

"Hadn't she just come back from Paris, Walter? I think she had been in Paris."

"She died of a stroke?" Louis kept his hands clasped beneath the table. The bouillabaisse sat forgotten in front of him.

"She had been to school in Paris as a girl, I think," said Arlene. "I think she went there often." Louis did not ask further. He did not want to betray too much interest. He felt his heart beating.

"How is Sarah?" Louis asked finally. His voice was steady, betraying nothing. It was an innocent question, a question he could ask, one that led nowhere. "Is anyone in touch with her?"

"We're not in touch with her. But I saw her recently. She looked terrific. We talked briefly. It was in Georgetown. She's lost some weight. She looks really good." This was Joanne Muller, relieved to be speaking about the living. "She was going to get married again; a professor, I think; maybe you knew him. What was his name? I don't think it worked out though. You probably knew that?"

"No, I didn't know that. I'm sorry it didn't work out," said Louis. He did not ask about Michael and Jennifer, whether anyone saw them. He was afraid he might learn something any decent father would have known about his own children, like: "Jennifer is married again and has three children. Didn't you know?" The occasional letters back and forth between his children and him were cool and impersonal. Michael seemed angry and pinched. He reminded Louis of himself as a young man. Louis wondered how it could be that, despite the vast distance between them for most of Michael's life, the son could have come to seem so much like the father.

Jennifer too was bitter. She was back in Washington after a brief failed marriage to someone Louis had never met. And though she wrote to Louis regularly, just below the surface of her letters he heard recrimination and sanctimony. "Your life in France sounds idyllic—no family, no responsibility. What more could one ask for?" He had not seen Sarah or his children for ten years. He imagined Jennifer being slightly plump, wearing ill-fitting skirts, with her hair pulled back and no makeup, a version of the Sarah of long ago. His letters to them contained sober good wishes and sad, empty sentences about this and that.

XVI

$\mathcal{S}$ARAH ANSWERED THE PHONE. THAT LOUIS KNEW HER VOICE IMMEDI-
ately from her hello startled him. He had expected that she would
sound different than he remembered, or that her voice would have
changed. But it was as if he had never stopped hearing it, as if hardly
any time had elapsed since their last conversation.

"Hello, Sarah. It's Louis. Morgon," he added.

"Louis," she said after a moment's pause. "My God."

"I am in Washington. I don't get here often." She did not
speak. "I'm sorry to surprise you with this call. I should have written first."

She laughed uneasily. "You have a French accent. You actually
have a French accent."

"Not, unfortunately, when I speak French. How are you,
Sarah?" He wished he hadn't said her name.

"I'm doing well," she said, her voice already sounding warier, cooler. "I moved to a new townhouse. I have an endowed chair at George Mason. I'm a full professor now."

"I know," he said, feeling the conversation already beginning to go sour. "I heard from the children, about your townhouse, about the promotion. Congratulations on all of it."

"Collective congratulations." Was her laugh angry? He couldn't tell.

"Sarah, . . . I wonder how you would feel about meeting somewhere for a cup of coffee."

"I don't know how I would feel about it," she answered. "Why?"

"I need to discuss something with you."

"We can't do it over the phone? All right. It's so sudden and unexpected."

"I should have written, Sarah. I'm sorry."

They met at a coffee shop near his motel, which was also, as it turned out, not very far from her new townhouse. He stood to greet her as she came in the door. That way she would not have to search the room for him and then look startled when she found him. They shook hands. Sarah had become more beautiful. Her skin had wrinkles now, but the shape of her face had sharpened. Lines lay around her eyes and mouth and across her cheeks in such a way that her eyes appeared larger and more liquid, her nose finer, and her mouth and chin more delicate than they had been when her skin was smoother and fuller.

They talked uneasily about the children. Sarah didn't see much of them, although all three of them lived around the city not far from one another. "They do not approve of me either," she said with a tight laugh. "And, to be honest, I do not like being with them very much. Either of them. They seem old before their time. Do you intend to see them?"

"I don't know," said Louis.

"They support themselves and live their own lives. Jennifer talks about going back to school, but I doubt that she will do it. Michael's illustration work is enough to keep him going. But, frankly, I don't think he's very good at it. His drawings seem overworked, tight, I think. But what do I know? He told me that you are a painter. He doesn't approve. He seems to think you should be doing something more serious. Isn't that sad? What must he think of his own work? They're both old way before their time. Maybe they'll grow younger as they get older." She did not laugh. She looked at her watch. "What did you want to talk about?"

"I wanted to talk to you about Hugh Bowes," said Louis. He cradled the hot coffee cup between his hands and watched her face.

Sarah's eyes narrowed, her neck stiffened. "I haven't seen Hugh Bowes for twenty years. And I can't think of anything we might have to say about him."

"You could be a great help to me," said Louis. "I want your opinion about Hugh Bowes, about his personality, about his character, about something he may have done." Louis told her the whole story beginning with the dead man on his doorstep. She listened in astonished silence.

When he had finished she looked at him for a long time before she spoke. "You actually think Hugh Bowes would kill someone and dump them on your doorstep in faraway France to avenge some perceived humiliation?"

"How did he act that morning after I left the house? What did he say? What did he do?" asked Louis.

Sarah cocked her head to the side and studied him for another long moment. "You've got some nerve, Louis, dredging up that crap after all these years, whatever fantastic scenarios you may have concocted. I haven't thought about it for a long time, and I don't intend to think about it now, just because you, the silent man, the reappearing man, suddenly treat me to a cup of coffee." The other people in the coffee shop lowered their heads and pulled their newspapers closer. "You really are a son of a bitch, Louis," she said as she remembered her own humiliation. Sarah got up and left the coffee shop.

At the public library, a librarian explained that the card catalogues and reader's guides to newspapers and periodicals had all been replaced by computers. By typing in a word or series of words, you could instruct the computer to do a search of books or newspapers. Within seconds it would offer up a chronological list of works about the subject you had named. In the case of certain newspapers, like the *Washington Post* and the *New York Times*, you could get a list of all the articles in which the subject-word even appeared, whether it was the main topic of the article or not. The librarian beamed triumphantly at Louis, as if this remarkable technological advance were of her own devising.

At the blinking cursor Louis typed: Hugh Bowes. The screen went dark for a moment and then indicated that there were 749 entries from the most recent two years alone. "Change to database 1990–1994 for additional entries." Louis started the search again and typed: Ruth Chasen. The computer offered 27 entries. He scrolled through the list and quickly found an account of her untimely death and, in the same issue of the *New York Times,* her obituary.

Ruth Chasen Dead
Secretary of State's Wife Dies of Sudden Stroke.

CHEVY CHASE, MD; July 25—Ruth Chasen, the wife of Secretary of State Hugh Bowes, died suddenly this evening at their home in Chevy Chase. She was 59. Secretary Bowes found his wife lying on the floor of their bedroom. Emergency rescue workers called to the scene were unable to revive Ms. Chasen. She was taken to Walter Reed Hospital where she was pronounced dead of a massive cerebral hemorrhage. A memorial service will be held Sunday, July 30, at the Washington National Cathedral.

An obituary on the last page was accompanied by a photograph that must have been fairly recent. She was blond and pretty and smiling.

RUTH CHASEN

Ruth Chasen died suddenly at her home last night of a massive stroke. She was 59. Ruth Chasen was the daughter of Mathild Chasen, née Pendergrass, and Anhold Chasen, the renowned tenor. She was born in Manhattan and grew up there and at Quogue on Long Island where her parents also had a home.

Both their East Side apartment and their sprawling Hamptons cottage were often filled with visiting musicians, artists, and writers, so that Ruth "was privileged to frolic as a child in a sea of art and intellect," as she once said in an interview in *Vanity Fair* magazine. During her teenage years, she often traveled with her father when he was on tour, visiting every part of the United States and many cities around the world.

She attended the Millbrook School in Millbrook, New York, and then graduated *magna cum laude* with a bachelor of arts degree with majors in French and philosophy from

Mount Holyoke College. Having spent her junior year in Paris, she returned for a year of post-graduate study at the Sorbonne.

Upon returning to New York, she joined CBS as a news researcher but soon began doing news spots during the nightly newscast. "I was there when things opened up for women," she said, "and the camera loved me. It was as simple as that. It was luck." But to her colleagues at CBS News, Ruth was a brilliant and talented on-air reporter who was able to project both competence and glamour.

In 1964, she left New York and moved to Washington to marry Hugh Bowes, who was then an undersecretary of state. She continued to work in broadcasting, but no longer in the news. She was the host of a 1969 special "Women of the Peace Movement" and of a 1976 special "Three First Ladies," both of which were broadcast on CBS. She was also a co-host of the weekly news show "Washington Speaks" which ran on public television stations around the country from 1976 until 1980.

Ruth Chasen gradually left broadcasting, as her husband rose in prominence. She devoted herself to charity work, helping to organize charitable fund-raising events. Her special interest was in charities that helped children. "Of course her arts, media, and political contacts were important," said Thomas Jackson, one of her colleagues at the World of Children Foundation, "but her enthusiasm and energy are what inspired us all. She could not have children, so she regarded all the world's children as hers."

Ruth Chasen is survived by her husband, Secretary of State Hugh Bowes, by her mother of Quogue, and by her

half-brother Robert Pendergrass of Paris, France. Her
father Anhold Chasen sang with the New York Metropoli-
tan Opera until 1958. He died in 1980.

Ruth Chasen had died on the same day as the man on Louis's
doorstep. Louis typed the name Robert Pendergrass into the computer. After a moment's hesitation, the computer showed two
entries: one was the obituary which Louis had just read, the other
the *Washington Post* obituary which said, after mentioning Bowes
and her mother, "She is also survived by Robert Pendergrass her
half-brother of Paris, France."

Louis read the other articles the library had about Ruth Chasen.
He read the *Vanity Fair* interview. The interviewer had asked her
about her life in Paris. She still went to Paris frequently, she said.
She loved the city, for its culture, for its beauty, for the friends she
had there. Louis searched the earlier databases, but learned little
that was new and nothing that seemed important.

The announcement and then the description of the Bowes-
Chasen wedding in New York did not mention Robert Pendergrass.
Louis did not remember that Ruth Chasen had ever mentioned a
brother, or that he had seen him at the wedding in New York. The
computer offered no references when Louis combined the keywords
Ruth Chasen and child, other than references to Ruth's charity
work. Maybe Joanne had been mistaken about the institutionalized
child.

Back at the George Washington Colonial Court, there was a
message asking that Louis call Sarah at her home. "Hugh Bowes lay
there for a long time, I don't know, maybe several minutes after you
left. I remember, that though his eyes were squeezed shut, tears were
seeping out and running down his cheeks the whole time. I stood

and looked at him because he looked so strange. His body was completely rigid, like someone having a seizure of some sort. He was fat, but you could tell his muscles were all tensed. Then all of a sudden he let out a scream. But it was more than a scream. It was a howl, like an animal, and he howled long, while tears rolled from his eyes which were now wide open and looking everywhere but at me."

"Did it frighten you?" asked Louis.

"It scared the hell out of me," said Sarah. "I got out of there as fast as I could. When I came back, he was gone.

"You know," she added, "I saw him not too many years ago at a party at one of the embassies. I had forgotten about this." She paused. "Our eyes met. But in the instant they did, his hardened, and it was as if he looked right through me. He didn't greet me, didn't speak at all."

"Thank you for calling me back, Sarah. It was very generous of you to do it. And please don't tell anyone about our conversation. Don't even tell anyone you saw me. For your own safety. Just in case I'm right."

XVII

$\mathcal{R}$ENARD AND ISABELLE WERE FINISHING THEIR LUNCH WHEN THE telephone rang. "I need a favor," said Louis when Renard picked up the phone.

"I am not surprised," said Renard angrily. "Where are you?" he demanded. But he knew Louis was in Washington. "What time is it there?"

"It is seven o'clock in the morning. Listen: find out what you can about somebody named Robert Pendergrass who lives, or lived, in Paris. He is Hugh Bowes's brother-in-law. And see if there is a phone or address listed for Ruth Chasen, Hugh Bowes's wife. If you don't find it under Chasen, it may be under the name Ruth Bowes, or try Ruth Pendergrass."

"Why should I?" said Renard. He was, after all, the police officer in charge. Isabelle gave him a look that caused him to turn his back to her and look out at the garden. "Tell me what you've learned," he said into the phone, trying to sound more cooperative. He listened for a while and said, "I will call you." He paused. "Yes, I wrote them down. All right: you call. Tomorrow at the same time." He paused again. "She is fine." Then: "A pork roast with rice and lentils in a tomato sauce." Then: "It was. Be careful."

"I have to go to Paris," he said to Isabelle as he hung up the phone. "I have to find out about some people there. I'll stay the night and be back tomorrow morning."

"Is he all right?" she said.

"Hugh Bowes's wife died on the same day as the man whose body turned up here. Louis sounded frightened."

At his office Renard checked the national telephone directory and found a listing for R. Chasen on the rue Jacob in Paris. He found a listing for Robert Pendergrass on the boulevard Raspail. In his ancient and tattered *Guide General de Paris*, he found that both streets were near the Montparnasse train station, and they were close together, for which he was grateful.

He called Jean Marie. Jean Marie's machine answered. His son had an answering machine. Renard knew the boy would never live in Saint Leon again. He told the machine that he was arriving in Paris on business, and that he hoped they could have supper together. He would call at the end of the day. "All right, Jean Marie . . . see you soon." How did you say good-bye to a machine?

He looked through his phone directory and dialed the number for Julien Petitot in Paris.

"Police, Petitot."

"Julien, it's Renard in Saint Leon."

"Jean Renard! Can it be?"

"It can be, and it is, Julien. How are you?"

"I had a heart attack, Jean."

"That was two years ago, Julien. I know about the heart attack. You told me when we talked at Christmas."

"We talked this past Christmas? It can't be this past Christmas. What's up, Jean?" Julien Petitot and Renard had known each other since they had started their police careers together at the national police academy. They had liked each other immediately. No one besides Petitot called Renard Jean, except for his mother.

"I need you to look into something for me," said Renard. "It's about a murder."

"In Saint Leon?! Impossible! In that nest?" Petitot laughed. In fact, he had grown up in the village of Villedieu, which was less than twenty kilometers from Saint Leon and even smaller. But he had stayed in Paris after the academy, had married a Parisienne, and now they even took their country vacations in the Cevennes, where her parents had lived, and where she had inherited an ancient farmhouse. Renard and Isabelle had visited them there the summer of the famous heart attack.

"It didn't happen here, but the body ended up here. I'll explain later. Right now I need you to see what information you might have on a Ruth Chasen, an American, who died recently in the U.S., listed at 66 rue Jacob. And anything on Robert Pendergrass, her half-brother at 131 boulevard Raspail."

"Why not call their precinct, Jean?"

"Julien, I need this all on the quiet, and I need it right away. This murder is not being investigated. When you start looking, you'll see why. Be *very* discreet. Be *very* careful. Don't tell anybody that you're looking. Nobody."

"The captain—"

"Especially not the captain."

"All right, Jean. Give me a few hours. I'll call you back."

"I'm coming to Paris. I'll call *you* when I get there."

Renard did not go to Paris often, even though it was so close by train. He did not like the ordeal of going: driving to the station, then paying to park, waiting in line to buy a ticket, then sitting in the train, even if it was just for an hour. It was always too hot or too cold. And his knees were jammed against the seat in front of him. He didn't like sitting next to some stranger, seeing the landscape fly by. He was always hungry in the train, but whenever he ate, he invariably spilled something down his front or on his pants.

Once he was in Paris, well, he liked Paris. He even envied Julien Petitot a little for his life in Paris, his apartment in the Marais, his modern office with all the latest computer technology, the interesting crimes that came his way. He liked seeing the shops, hearing the noise, seeing all the people.

There were usually musicians playing for change on the Metro. Once, he had heard a gypsy boy singing a song to his own guitar accompaniment. The boy's voice had been so startlingly beautiful that nearly everyone in the car had given him money. He liked watching the people strolling through the Jardin du Luxembourg gazing at the intricately planted beds of flowers. And the Tuilleries. And the Palais Royal. And the de Parc Monceau. And on and on. All of them.

When Renard reached the rue Jacob, it suddenly started to rain very hard. He stood in the doorway across from 66 and brushed the rain from his hair and arms. Two young women jumped into the doorway, laughing to each other about the rain. They glanced at him and went on with their conversation. There were such women in Paris, thin and tall and beautiful. You saw women like that nowhere else on earth, he was certain of that. They had impossibly long, narrow legs and tiny waists. They were a species all their own.

The doorway where they stood led into a bookstore that special-
ized in art and travel books, and, on the other side, into an art
gallery that was closed for the August vacation. Renard peered
through the glass door, but he couldn't see anything. An elderly
American couple stepped into the doorway too, along with a French
woman.

The man was speaking. "Of course, I'm retired," he said. "When
Alice and I retired, we sold everything—the house, the car, gave
some of the furniture to the kids, got rid of the rest. We've been
traveling ever since." His wife glanced around at the others, and
then busied herself with her plastic rain hat. "Last year we were in
Israel, then Turkey, then Singapore. Of course we go home to see
the kids. Like that. But we travel. And you know what? People are
nice every place we go. Just nice. This is our anniversary trip. We've
been married fifty years." He looked around and smiled at the girls,
at Renard, a broad, encompassing smile that was meant for everyone. "How ya doin'?" he said, embarrassed that he hadn't included
everyone in his conversation. They, of course, had not understood a
word he had said.

The rain let up. The American couple left with the French
woman. The girls dashed off. Renard watched them go. He walked
across the street to number 66. There were no names outside, only a
small electronic number board for residents to punch in a code, and
below it, a bell for the concierge. He pressed the bell and waited.

The concierge opened the door a crack, saw that it was still raining, quickly looked Renard up and down, and opened the door so
Renard could step into the corridor. Renard thanked her. The hallway was nondescript and modern. The elevator was to the right,
beside a frosted glass door that led to a courtyard. Opposite the ele-

vator, the door to the concierge's apartment stood open. The sound of a television came from inside.

"Well?" She was short, sixty years old perhaps, had short gray hair, a plain face, and wore the most extraordinary eyeglasses Renard had ever seen. The turquoise-colored fronts were teardrop shaped with the rhinestone-studded corners sweeping up a good two centimeters. The temples of the glasses were undulating black and gold plastic stalks, also dotted at regular intervals with rhinestones.

"Excuse me, madame, but I have to say how I admire your glasses."

She smiled, revealing several gold teeth, and thanked him. But she was not one to be distracted. "What do you want?"

"I am sorry to bother you, madame, but I am from the police." He showed her his identification which she peered at, actually leaning forward holding her glasses on with one hand. He closed his wallet before she could read his name. "I am here about Ruth Chasen who owned an apartment in this building."

The concierge corrected Renard. "The apartment is still in her name."

"I don't know if you are aware, madame, but Ruth Chasen died not too long—"

"Of course I am aware. People have been appearing on this doorstep since the day she died to tell me that. Police and more police."

"They came to tell you that Madame Chasen had died?"

"I'm certain that is not why they came. But in the course of their business they told me that she was dead. Of a stroke. A massive stroke. Her husband found her in their bedroom. Not here. He was never here. Or hardly ever. In their home in Washington."

"You know her husband?"

"I saw him once. Before he was . . . whatever he has become."

"Secretary of state."

"Yes, that. He came here once and asked to be let in. I refused. It is not my right to let strangers into my apartments. I told Madame Chasen later, and she said I was correct, and that I was never to let him in."

"These people who came after she died, who were they?"

"You know," she said, looking at Renard curiously, "you are the first one to actually ask questions. I told you, they were police, like you. But they didn't ask anything."

"What did they want?"

"They wanted to be let into the apartment."

"Did you let them in?"

"They were the police. They are not the secretary of state, they are the police. Of course, I let them in."

"Did they take anything from the apartment?"

"They took everything."

"The police?"

"The police."

"By everything . . ."

"I mean everything. Furniture, clothes, books. They even took the lightbulbs, the telephones. They cleared the place out like I have never seen an apartment cleared out before."

"Did they take it all at once?"

"They showed up one day in a large truck and cleared everything out. Blocked the street until they got the truck up on the sidewalk."

"May I see?" said Renard.

The concierge shrugged and got the key from inside her door. The apartment was on the sixth which was the top floor. It was bright and spacious, with white walls and high ceilings. A continuous wall of large windows looked out on the rue Jacob. The sun had come out again. Renard gazed down at the doorway across the street where he had waited out the rain. He looked at the light switches and empty light sockets, at the receptacles where the telephones had been.

"Madame, did Ruth Chasen have many visitors?"

"You are the first one to ask me any questions," she said and shook her head. "She did not have many visitors, though she had friends who called from time to time."

"Men or women?" asked Renard.

"Both," said the concierge, a small smile catching the corners of her mouth. "You mean did she have any special friends?" said the concierge, her hands on her hips. She was enjoying Renard's discomfort. "Yes, she did. Men. Well, lately, one man. An American. A handsome fellow. A nice man, too. The last two years, he gave me flowers at Christmas. I did them little favors. That's why he gave me flowers."

"Favors?"

"Little things, you know: taking in their cleaning when it was delivered, mailing letters. Like that. Little things."

"For him too?"

"For both of them. Of course, Madame Chasen always was very generous at Christmas." She patted the pocket in her smock, probably remembering the money she had been given. "But he didn't live here. He often stayed with Madame Chasen when he was in Paris."

"He didn't live in Paris?"

"Oh no. He always arrived with luggage and left with luggage. I'm sure he didn't live in Paris. But he gave me flowers. I thought that was very nice."

"Do you remember his name?"

"It was Robert."

"And the family name?" Renard tried to keep his voice flat and calm. He thought he sounded too eager, but the concierge seemed not to notice.

"It is one of those long American names. It was difficult to understand it, when he said it. It is difficult to pronounce. Perpe . . . Pegga . . ." She tried to remember it.

"Could it be Robert Pendergrass?" asked Renard.

She looked at him sharply. "It could be. I'm not certain, but I think so."

"Madame, do you think this man, Robert Pendergrass, could possibly have been . . . be a relative of Madame Chasen's?"

She studied him again, scrutinizing his face to see what he was getting at. "I don't think so," she said smiling.

"Isn't it possible that they were related?" asked Renard.

"Are you joking with me?" And then immediately: "No, it isn't possible."

"How can you be so certain, madame?"

"You are teasing me, monsieur." She studied his face before smiling again. "I can be certain they were not related to one another, because, monsieur, he is black. Robert Penda . . . Pendergrass is a black man."

By the time he had walked the two kilometers to the boulevard Raspail address, Renard had had enough time to recognize that every possible explanation for what he had just found out led nowhere. For a long moment he stared up at the white enamel numbers—161—as though they might hold the key, as though the one, the six, the one could somehow explain the black half-brother who was a lover, the traveler with a Paris address, the police who had cleaned out the apartment. Hadn't Louis said to him, that investigating this case would only raise more questions than it would answer? That you would know less once it was solved than you had known before? He had said something like that. When he had said it, Renard had thought it was just more of the old man's philosophical ruminations. However, as he stood there at the entryway to 161 boulevard Raspail, he saw the doorway in his mind's eye as the way into chaos and uncertainty.

At that moment, a tall, pleasant-looking man in his mid-thirties stepped quickly through the door and almost ran into Renard. "Oh, pardon," he said with a strong American accent.

"Monsieur Pendergrass?" said Renard, taking a chance.

The man's expression darkened. He glanced up at the building. "No, I'm sorry," he said, this time in English. "I'm sorry, excuse me, I'm late for an appointment," and he hurried away.

"Who came out next," asked Louis, when Renard was telling him about the encounter the next day on the telephone, "the white rabbit?" But Renard did not know anything about *Alice's Adventures in Wonderland,* and Louis did not feel like explaining.

One sixty-one boulevard Raspail was a sprawling modern building made of gray granite, with large plate glass windows. It had shops below—a dress shop, a shoe store, a bakery, and a computer shop—and offices and apartments upstairs. Again, there was a number pad at the door, but there was no bell for the concierge. He asked in the computer shop how to get inside. "The building is managed by an agency," said the woman he spoke to. She stepped behind the counter and handed him a business card with the name of the agency and their phone number.

Renard called Petitot. "Jean," said Petitot, "give me five minutes. Let me call you back."

"Here's the number," said Renard. "I'm at a *brasserie*." Renard ate a sandwich at the bar and waited for the telephone to ring.

"I had to go outside the building," said Petitot. Renard heard the noise of traffic in the background. "Jesus, Jean, what have you gotten involved in here? The files on Chasen and Pendergrass are gone. There were files on both of them, and they were extensive, I know that much, but they've been cleaned out. Paper files and computer files. So there's nothing. In fact, the computer wanted an authorization code just to proceed with my inquiry.

"There's nothing under her address either, but his address, the Pendergrass address, is kind of interesting."

"Don't tease me, Julien. What did you find?"

"The building is owned by some big property management company. So there are descriptions on file in the tax office on all their buildings. Here it is for 161 . . . let's see . . . Constructed 1974 by . . . just a second: square feet . . . plumbing . . . elevators." He read down the page. "Here it is: 'mixed use office-residential; basement; subbasement; six stories.' These reports are always very exact; they're checked and rechecked by the person that files the reports and by the inspectors. Their signatures are at the bottom."

"And?"

"Can you see the building from where you are?"

"It's right across the street."

"How many stories has it got?"

Renard counted. "It's got eight, not six. What does that mean, Julien?"

"It means, Jean, somebody—Espace Enterprises—has a building with two stories that officially don't exist. And whoever is in those nonexistent two stories is somebody with connections in the tax office and in the building inspector's office. In short, it is somebody with influence, somebody very powerful.

"And, wait a second, there's more. Espace Enterprises, which is run, as far as I can tell, as a legitimate property management company, is a subsidiary of Antel Systems, which is in turn owned by the Advanced Projects Group of Rockville in the state of Maryland in the United States. Their telephone there is picked up by a machine. In short, the owners of those missing two floors do not want to be found. By the way, Jean, Rockville in Maryland is right outside Washington, D.C."

Renard stared at the card the computer sales clerk had handed him. ESPACE ENTERPRISES, it said, and gave a telephone number.

"What are you going to do, Jean?"

"I don't know, exactly," said Renard.

"Be careful," said Petitot. "I've got to get back. Be careful, Jean."

"Thanks for your help, Julien."

Renard dialed the number for Espace Enterprises. "I'd like to inquire about the seventh and eighth floors of 161 boulevard Raspail."

"I'll connect you to one of our agents."

"I'm interested in the seventh and eighth floors of 161 boulevard Raspail," he said when the agent came on the line.

"Let me check for you, monsieur," she said. "Those floors are completely occupied."

"Could you tell me by whom?" he said.

"I'm sorry, monsieur, but we are not permitted to give out information about our tenants."

"Is a Robert Pendergrass one of your tenants?"

"I'm sorry, monsieur. I cannot give out that information."

Renard spoke very little while he and Jean Marie ate supper that evening at the small restaurant just downstairs from his son's apartment. Renard had a magnificent view of the enormous white arch of the Defense Building through the restaurant window, and he could hardly take his eyes off it. He had seen it before. But now the sun was setting behind it, and the building darkened in silhouette against the crimson sky. The hundreds of windows disappeared slowly into the shadows. It seemed to Renard as if they were taking countless secrets with them. The great sail inside the arch undulated slowly in the wind.

"Have you ever had a murder before?" asked Jean Marie.

"It turns out to be more unsettling than it is exciting," said Renard. "It is my first." They climbed the steps under the sail.

"Before the building was finished," said Jean Marie, "they discovered that it was like a big wind tunnel. And the wind was so strong in here that they had to put up the sail to deflect the wind and keep people from being knocked off their feet. Imagine, being the architect of such a big building and of such a big mistake. I forget his name, for which he would probably be grateful. I bet he can't even stand to look at the building now. I could help you out, Papa. The customs service has access to lots of information. What's the company called?"

"No, Jean Marie, this is not for you. It could cost you your job. Besides, there's nothing you can do." Was Jean Marie really only twenty-four? Renard took his son's arm as they climbed the stairs. They stood in the wind and gazed out past the blinking semaphores that were, Renard supposed, modern sculpture, into the dark cemetery beyond.

That night Renard slept in Isabelle's arms and dreamt a strange dream. He was swimming in the Dême, which in his dream was broad and swift. However, while Renard could really barely swim, he was a strong swimmer in his dream, making rapid progress even against the swift current. Then suddenly he saw that the water around him was buckling and pulsing as great creatures crowded around him, surfacing and diving into the depths, brushing against him. Their skin was slick and smooth and dark. They were enormous and they frightened him. The water was full of them, and he found himself running across their backs toward the shore. That was all he could remember of the dream when he woke up, and he soon forgot even that.

Louis called at noon. "I have changed hotels. Here is my number. Do not call unless you have to, but if you have to, ask for Mister Twitchell in room 411." Renard told him what he had discovered in Paris, that Chasen's lover had been named or, more likely, had used the name Robert Pendergrass, and that he was a black man. He told Louis about the building with extra stories at 161 boulevard Raspail, and about the Advanced Projects Group of Rockville in Maryland. Louis wrote everything down, including the addresses.

Renard had saved the worst news for last. Solesme Lefourier had just that morning been reported by her husband to be missing. It was probably nothing. This was, after all, not the first time Pierre Lefourier had called the police to report her missing. The old man sometimes panicked when she had only gone out. She would call a cab, or a friend would come pick her up, or she went out to run errands, or to shop. Occasionally she went to Tours. But her husband was accustomed to always having her there, so to him when she was not there, she was missing. Renard would always reassure the old man that she was safe, that they would find her. And she would always turn up a few hours later with a new dress or some rose bushes for the garden.

Only this time she was an important witness to a serious crime. Renard cursed himself for having named her as a witness on the incident reports he had filed and which by now had crossed God only knew how many desks from here to Paris. Louis was silent at the other end of the line. Then he said, "Maybe they want to get to me through her." He paused to calm his voice. Then: "I don't know why else they would have taken her." His voice was nearly steady again. Renard suddenly knew what Louis and Solesme were to each other. He cursed himself yet again, this time silently, for not having realized it before now. He was certain Isabelle would have known all along.

"Or perhaps she has just gone shopping," he said. He did not think this was the case, but he wanted to reassure his friend. He did not know what else to say. "I am looking for her," he added.

"If they have her, you will not find her, unless they want you to. If she turns up, or you learn anything, call me immediately." Louis hung up the phone quickly, without saying good-bye.

At that moment, Solesme was sitting in the backseat of a BMW like the one that had stopped at Louis's driveway that night. For all she knew, it was the very same car. Three men had come for her. They were dark skinned. Two had thick mustaches. All three were dressed in dark suits and spoke in French that was heavily accented with the rolling r's and clipped vowels of North Africa. All three were firm, but polite. They called her Madame Lefourier. They did not blindfold her or make any effort to conceal the direction they were taking.

Once they reached the autoroute, they sped south. Solesme rode in the backseat between two of the men. If they had weapons, she could not tell. She asked them where they were taking her, but they did not answer. She asked why they were taking her, but again they were silent. She asked if they intended to kill her. One of them said, "No, madame." The other said, "Not if you cooperate."

"What do you want?" she asked. They were silent. "My husband will be worried," she said, but then was sorry she had said it. She found it curious that the three men spoke French, even when they spoke to one another.

Solesme had never ridden in such a luxurious car before. The backseat was firm and comfortable, even to her twisted back. The ride was smooth and quiet. A few hours later in Libourne, just east of Bordeaux, they drove straight into a large garage. The garage was empty but for a white panel truck. They parked next to the panel truck and then two of the men helped her into the back of the truck and got in with her. The canvas seats were not comfortable. But they only rode for a half-hour or so. She could not be sure how long it was. Solesme usually wore a watch when she left home. But she had not been intending to leave home when the three men had come for her that morning.

The truck stopped, the driver opened the back doors, and they got out and went into a farmhouse. The men put Solesme in a room on the second floor and locked the door. The room was sparsely furnished with a bed, a small table, and a chair. There were no lamps and no lightbulbs in the metal fixture that hung from the ceiling. She pulled the chair to the window and sat down to look out just as she was accustomed to do at home. If the men below heard her dragging the chair across the floor, they did not come up to investigate.

Looking from the window, she saw only a dirt driveway threading its way through large oak trees. She did not see the panel truck anywhere, or any other cars. She heard birds singing. There were no other sounds. She noticed some neglected roses in the garden below. They needed fertilizing. And they had grown ungainly from not having been pruned the year before. She thought they were pink Anjous, a variety she had wanted to get for her garden. The pink Anjou was a difficult rose that required a lot of attention. But if you put in the effort, you were amply rewarded with large flamingo-pink blossoms that became a peachy golden at the edges.

The door to the room opened, and a man she had not seen before walked in. "What is the point of planting a pink Anjou, and then neglecting it?" she wanted to know. The man looked puzzled. "That rose there," she said. "It needs attention. It is a difficult rose to grow." The man smiled uneasily and shrugged, still not completely understanding what she was talking about. He was larger than the men who had brought her. He had a broad flat face with full cheeks and a heavy brow. His hair was dark and curly and cut close to his skull. He had enormous hands which he kept clasping and unclasping. He smiled again.

"Madame Lefourier," he said, stepping closer and bowing slightly, "I apologize for the inconvenience of having brought you to this remote and inhospitable spot." He swung his hand around to indicate the scene outside the window. "This is not the way we are accustomed to treating women in my country." He responded to his apparent embarrassment with an exaggerated courtliness.

Something in his manner made her stand and step away. "Do you intend to harm me?" she asked.

"Madame, how could you think such a thing?" said the man, looking away from her gaze. He was like a child whose secret intentions had just been inadvertently discovered. The man gestured toward the chair, but she remained standing.

"Very well," he said. "As you wish. I do not want to harm you, madame. But, to be blunt with you, madame, as I see you are a person who prefers plain speaking, I will hurt you if it is necessary to do so, to discover from you what I need to discover. I regret to have to even mention it. What I need from you concerns your neighbor, madame, Monsieur Louis Morgon. Louis Morgon." He said the name a second time as though she might possibly not recognize it.

"Is Louis in some sort of trouble?"

"Madame, I am afraid he is in a great deal of trouble. I am not at liberty to tell you the details of his difficulties. However, I can assure you they are most grave. Now, if you will, madame, where has Monsieur Morgon gone?"

Solesme did not know where he had gone. He had not discussed his plans with her.

"You cannot even speculate where he has gone?"

"I could speculate, but it would be a wild guess."

"And what would be your speculation, madame?"

"I would guess that he has gone to Washington, where he is from. But it is only a guess."

"Was he traveling alone?" asked the man, clasping and unclasping his large hands while he looked at her intently. She noticed that the knuckles were skinned and the nails were broken and dirty.

Solesme did not know whether Louis was traveling alone. She had already said she knew nothing about his journey. Nor did she know when he was going to return, what he had taken with him, whom he had told of his journey. She did not know whether he had gone by way of Paris. In fact she could not answer any of the man's questions to his satisfaction, which caused him to grow increasingly restless. He pulled on his fingers and rubbed his hands. He leaned in close as he questioned her so that she smelled the alcohol on his breath.

The man paced back and forth a few times. Then he asked, "Madame, have you ever seen me before?"

"I do not know. Are you one of the men that stopped on the road outside my house one night not long ago?"

He stopped pacing and asked without turning to face her, "What did you see that night, madame?"

Solesme hesitated. Then she said, "It is as I have already told the police: I saw a car arrive and some people get out of it. Maybe it was the same car that brought me here. I saw them drive off a short time later. I tried to read the license plate but I could not. The car's lights were off."

"Madame, do you know what it was the men did while they were there?"

"I do not know for certain. That is to say, no one has told me. But if I had to guess, I would guess now that it had to do with the body that turned up on Monsieur Morgon's doorstep. I would assume that they carried it up the driveway and dropped it there."

"Aha," said the man.

"Of course, no one expects to see dead bodies carried around, even at night. And it was dark. But I am guessing that is what went on." Solesme looked up at the man questioning her.

"Please, Madame Lefourier," he said, bowing slightly and motioning toward the chair. "Please, madame, take a seat." He raised his eyebrows. He smiled gently as he recognized her terror.

XVIII

*T*HOUGH MILTON HAMSHER HAD LIVED IN THE SAME TWO ROOMS IN Northeast Washington for nearly fifteen years, there was hardly anything about the place to suggest that it might be home to any particular person. There were no photos anywhere, no mementoes. There were no pictures on the faded walls. The furniture resembled worn motel and office furniture, which, in fact, much of it was. The chairs and table, the couch, and the file cabinets had all been bought by Milton at warehouse sales around the city, but only when the particular piece he was replacing had been worn or damaged beyond usability, or, in the case of the many file cabinets, when the drawers of the cabinets he already had no longer held all the clippings, brochures, and files Milton continuously assembled.

There were only two things that made the apartment uniquely Milton's. One was, of course, the file cabinets which now went completely around three walls of the living room and which were in some places stacked on top of each other reaching to just under the ceiling. A stepladder stood ready to allow Milton to get to the topmost drawers. The other thing was the array of locks on the heavy front door. Louis counted six different locks which Milton unlocked and locked each time he or anyone else entered or left.

Milton had picked up the phone as soon as Louis had begun to leave a message. But he had not spoken right away, causing Louis to wonder at first whether Milton's machine was malfunctioning. But then Milton had spoken in that sweet, high voice: "Louis? Is that you?"

"It's me, Milton. It's Louis. I'm in Washington. I'm here. I'd like to see you." Without hesitation Milton had given him the address. "I'll be right over," Louis had said. He knocked and waited while Milton unlocked the many locks and opened the door. Milton's body was old and stooped, his brown hair was thin. His blue eyes were watery and sad. He hardly ever smiled anymore, but on those rare occasions when he did smile, as for example now as he greeted Louis, years of pain and anguish dropped from his face, and he looked like a boy again. "Louis," said Milton, turning to face Louis after he had locked the door. His arms hung at his side. Then he reached out, took Louis in his arms, and pressed his face happily against Louis's shoulder.

The two men had not parted as good friends. However, their affection for one another had remained undiminished. Their careers and their marriages had come apart at about the same time. So, back then just the sight of each man reminded the other of his own failures. The result was that they could hardly stand to be together.

Unlike Louis who had fallen and landed more or less on his feet, Milton had fallen and then had continued to fall. There was a gathering air of desperation about him which made it unbearable for his friends to be around him. Milton's already delicately balanced temperament was increasingly shaken by his suspicions and doubts— about himself, to be sure, but also about the world around him, about his former co-workers at the State Department, about his former wives, about his friends. He suspected nearly everyone of conspiring against him. He had lost his job because of the relentlessness of his suspicions. He had lost both his wives to divorce, Susan and then Tierney, because of his suspicions.

It should not have been too surprising, given his commanding intelligence and his apprehensive and mistrustful nature, that Milton eventually found his way into conspiracy journalism. The first article he wrote in this vein was about the Kennedy assassination. The article was remarkable for its exhaustive detail and elegant arguments. It was picked up by a magazine in New York, and its publication single-handedly revived the then-flagging interest in that terrible event. Milton wrote on Iran-Contra, on the Persian Gulf War, on Whitewater, on the death of Vincent Foster, on Rupert Murdoch and Newt Gingrich, and on less known and more arcane conspiracies as well. His articles were always thorough to a fault. They were exhaustively researched and tightly reasoned. And, like all essentially religious arguments, in order to be absolutely convincing, each article depended in the last analysis on the author's and reader's shared and unassailable faith in the truth of the particular conspiracy being uncovered.

Milton never wrote on assignment. The fact that somebody wanted him to write about a particular subject already aroused his suspicions and made it impossible for him to do so. Rather, he would simply appear one day at the editorial offices of the journal he had selected to receive his next article. He carried a metal attaché case with a thick manuscript padlocked inside. His articles were almost always printed by one journal or another. There were half a dozen journals he regarded as acceptable. The payment they offered, which was usually meager when measured against the time and energy Milton had devoted to researching and writing the article, allowed him to devote his energies to the next project.

Louis listened with growing discomfort as Milton catalogued the apparently endless injustices and injuries he had suffered and continued to suffer at the hands of enemies, known and unknown. This very minute, he was under attack by a cabal of avaricious and unscrupulous editors. Not to mention his jealous detractors, those other conspiracy writers whose viciousness was outdone only by their resourcefulness in finding ways to close off publication outlets to him. Couldn't they see that his work was published where theirs wasn't because his research was superior where theirs was sloppy and less than complete? And, of course, there were his ancient tormentors, the functionaries he had offended in the United States government. They too were continually working to discredit him with the few editors who would still have anything to do with him.

Louis was distressed at his friend's state of mind. He was also startled and disturbed by the thought that he might himself not be so different from Milton. Wasn't his speculation that Hugh Bowes was a murderer just as delusional, just as paranoid, as any of the theories Milton had cooked up? Couldn't Louis be dismissed just as easily? And mightn't he be just as wrong? From the sparse facts of the matter—that a body had been left on his doorstep—he had spun out what must certainly appear to most rational minds to be a preposterous scenario. It had certainly seemed preposterous to Renard and to Sarah.

Louis sat on the battered dining chair and listened while Milton named one malevolent government official after another—names Louis had never heard, others he knew either by name or in person from his own time in government, even some of Louis's old friends and colleagues, including Arnie Muller and Wally Steinberg, who were not in government at all, and never had been. Milton now referred to them as Arnold and Wallace, as though they were names on an indictment. Efforts to ruin Milton's life had failed so far. But who knew how long they would continue to fail, given that his enemies had the full resources and power of the federal government at their disposal? As Milton named each name, he pointed at a file drawer, suggesting by his gesture that all he had to do was pull open that drawer and he could spread the complete and incontrovertible proof of that particular person's corruption and evil on the table before them.

Louis realized suddenly that the name of Hugh Bowes was missing from Milton's list of supposed enemies. It was a strange omission since the list seemed all-inclusive. Moreover Milton had been dismissed from the State Department, as Louis had, at a time when Hugh Bowes's influence had already become pervasive. "And Hugh Bowes?" asked Louis.

"Not Hugh Bowes," said Milton, looking suddenly into Louis's eyes, smiling and laying his hands palm up on the table before him. "Not Hugh." Louis looked at Milton's hands as though they held some writing it was absolutely necessary that he read but whose meaning eluded him. "Hugh is certainly"—he weighed each word—"the reason I am still doing my work today," said Milton. "The reason I am still allowed to work. The reason I am still alive. He is powerful enough to offer me a sort of protection."

"Protection?" said Louis, leaning forward as though he might not have heard correctly. "What protection?"

"Hugh Bowes cannot come right out and oppose the rottenness, the evil, the corruption, the people who are destroying the country. He would himself be destroyed in an instant, like that," said Milton, leaning in toward Louis so that their faces were inches apart. He snapped the fingers of his left hand. "Like that. He is very powerful. But only as long as he operates within the system."

"But what protection?" said Louis, fearful not so much of the answer but of the madness it would signify.

Instead of answering, Milton stood and dragged the stepladder across in front of the file drawers. After a brief search, he found the file he was looking for and placed it in front of Louis.

"What is this?" asked Louis, gingerly touching the cardboard folder in front of him. It was labeled in ink in Milton's squarish hand: H.B., MEMOS.

"See for yourself," said Milton, leaning back in his chair.

Louis opened the folder and found a small stack of typed, unsigned notes, each one clipped to the envelope it had arrived in. The envelopes had been slit open at the top. The notes were on the same ordinary paper, but they had obviously been typed on several different machines. Like the notes, the envelopes were all without any return address or other indication as to the identity of the sender. They were filed in reverse chronological order. The notes had been dated, but not by year, so Milton had carefully added the year in the top right-hand corner of each note. Each note was addressed simply to "Milton."

July 25

MILTON:

A secret meeting between representatives of revolutionary groups from Algeria, Morocco, and Tunisia and American intelligence agents took place recently at the Charles DeGaulle Airport in Paris.

April 12

MILTON:

On August 13, 1993, an executive assistant in the attorney general's office signed a receipt for three boxes of documents from the office of the deceased presidential special assistant Vincent Foster. These three boxes, whose existence has never been made public, contain, among other things, papers with then Governor and Mrs. Clinton's signatures granting tax waivers in exchange for forgiveness of certain loans.

February 1

MILTON:

Papers in the possession of the CIA Office of Middle Eastern Affairs make it clear that a small task force under the direction of Lieutenant Colonel Oliver North met with conservative elements from the Iranian government at the Charles DeGaulle Airport in Paris. The meeting was witnessed by two CIA agents who have documents signed by the participants locating them at Charles DeGaulle Airport.

"These memos?" asked Louis.

"Are from Hugh Bowes," said Milton, taking the folder back. "He has been sending me information for years."

"You're certain they're from him."

"He calls to make certain I've received them."

"He calls in person?"

"He calls in person."

"And otherwise?"

"Otherwise? We never meet or talk, if that is what you mean. He is extremely careful, extremely discreet. As I always advise him to be. His enemies, and mine, are experts at disinformation. They plant lies, vicious rumors, stories, disinformation. I'm only telling you this, Louis," said Milton, leaning forward, suddenly taking Louis's hand gently in both his hands, as though Louis might have been a distraught lover, or a child in need of comfort. Milton's hands were soft and warm. "I'm only telling you this, Louis, because I trust you." Louis wondered why Milton trusted him.

"And his protection of you, Milton? How can you be so sure?"

Milton smiled and spread his arms at his sides. He looked from one side to the other and said: "Here I am. I'm still here. I'm still working."

"The top memorandum in the file mentions a meeting," Louis said, then thought again. "What do you do with the information Hugh Bowes sends you? Is it useful?"

"It is often very useful," said Milton. All the strain had gone from his voice. "Not always, but often. The top memo, for instance, the one you mentioned about the North African meeting? That one? An American CIA agent—I don't know his name—seems to have turned up missing. There may be a connection." Milton rubbed his hands enthusiastically and smiled at Louis.

"It is all about building cases, Louis. Putting things together. Very often Hugh Bowes's memos don't so much give me information as they point me in a direction. I've found that if I follow the lead, I can often find what I need in public documents or from other sources, and a case starts to build itself."

"Why Charles DeGaulle Airport?" asked Louis. "Why does so much go on at Charles DeGaulle Airport?"

"Well," said Milton, rubbing his hands again, "airports are busy places, but with very few regular visitors. They're easy to get in and out of without leaving tracks. And so many places in the world are within eight hours of DeGaulle. You can claim you were far away and witnesses can place you where you claim to have been. Assassins like to work in airports for those reasons. You're in—pop!—then you're out."

"What rumors?" asked Louis. Milton looked puzzled. "You said Hugh Bowes's enemies, and yours, plant rumors," said Louis. "What kind of rumors do they plant?"

"Vicious rumors. The most vicious rumors, Louis. You can imagine what it's like. But, then maybe you can't. You've never lost a wife."

"Rumors about Ruth Chasen?"

Milton looked up sharply. "I can't say any more, Louis." Then: "I don't know what you've heard, Louis, or how. But don't let yourself be fooled. And don't let yourself be used, Louis. Don't let yourself be used for destructive purposes. I can't say any more." And he was silent.

Louis thought for a long moment. "Milton, the rumor I heard about Hugh goes beyond imagination. I'm telling you as my friend . . . and as Hugh's friend." Louis paused. Milton did not try to stop him from continuing. "The rumor I heard is that Ruth Chasen did not die at home. It is that on July twenty-fifth she and her lover, a CIA agent, a black man, were killed together; that Hugh, on discovering her infidelity, had both their throats slit. He is supposed to have had it done at Charles DeGaulle Airport." Milton's face was without expression. He was listening, so Louis continued. "The rumor has it that the lover's body was disposed of in one place and that Ruth Chasen's body was disposed of somewhere else so they could not be connected, and that the reports of her death by stroke were inserted into the record by Hugh Bowes."

The room was silent. You could hear the roar of rush-hour traffic passing outside the apartment, a steady stream of cars in both directions, taking their drivers and passengers home to supper, to families, to lovers, to ordinary lives. "I am telling you this as your friend," said Louis again, "and because you are Hugh Bowes's friend."

Milton looked across the table at Louis. Now there was a slight smile on Milton's face. He looked to be far away in his thoughts. Then he suddenly roused himself and, looking quickly around the room as though someone else might have been there to listen, he said, "I have heard something of the kind, Louis, with somewhat different details. I have heard it in bits and pieces. Your version is worse than what I heard, though not by much. Hugh Bowes's enemies will stop at nothing to destroy him." Will stop at nothing. The words sounded as though they were not Milton's own words, as though they might have arrived in an unsigned memo. "Don't allow yourself to be used, Louis. You have been away for a long time. It is a much rougher game now than it was back then."

Louis had not expected that his improvised rumor would be confirmed in any way. He had combined what he knew, which was very little, with what he imagined or suspected, which was a great deal, and had inadvertently hit the bull's-eye. Nor had he expected that his rumor's confirmation by Milton would lead him to feel the intense sorrow that flooded over him now. Solesme's figure passed through his mind, and he tried not to think of the danger she was in because of him. But the fear remained, like an ache behind his throat.

Milton once again went to the file drawers. The file he now placed in front of Louis was marked RUTH CHASEN, DEATH. It contained photocopies of the following documents: the police report of the emergency call made from the Chasen house at 9:16 on the evening of July 25; the report of the emergency rescue effort begun at the Chasen house that same evening at 9:28, signed with a flourish by Sergeant Phil Reed; the death certificate issued by the coroner at Walter Reed Hospital citing the cause of death as massive cerebral hemorrhage and the time of death as approximately 9:00; and the burial certificate from the Sacred Heart Cemetery in Westhampton, New York, dated July 26. "The family was eager that she be buried quickly, to spare the mother any unnecessary grief," said Milton.

What family? Louis wondered. And, he wondered, aside from the obvious explanations about Milton's penchant for assembling proof of every event whose circumstances were in any way doubtful or suspicious, why did Milton have a file documenting Ruth Chasen's death so soon after the event? And how had he obtained the police and rescue reports? The Walter Reed coroner's report? Louis did not ask.

Louis looked at Milton across the table. Sweet, deluded Milton. If he had, in fact, sent the anonymous memoranda and documents, Hugh Bowes was pointing Milton's nose around the compass at will, and Milton gratefully cooperated by wandering off in the direction he was pointed, happily finding his way into some tangled and utterly harmless conspiracy. Meanwhile, he looked on Hugh Bowes, possibly the one evil person in his entire world, with unfettered and blind admiration.

The next morning when Louis telephoned the Chevy Chase Fire and Rescue unit which, according to the report in Milton's file, had responded to the emergency call at 9:16 that evening, Louis was not particularly surprised to be told that Sergeant Phil Reed had left the service, and no one knew where he had gone.

XIX

*M*ILTON HAMSHER HAD EQUIPPED HIMSELF TO DISCOVER CON-
spiracies—governmental conspiracies, international conspiracies,
military conspiracies. But, like most of us, he was ill equipped to
face the abyss—the mystery, where every answer you arrive at
uncovers larger, even more unsettling questions, where there is no
solution to be found, where order is an illusion, a thin layer cast over
the writhing turmoil to disguise it, to hide it from our own eyes, to
make it seem as though it could somehow support our weight.

Conspiracies are comforting. They offer solace and protection.
Conspiracy implies forces at work which can be sorted out and dealt
with. It implies puzzles to solve, questions which can be answered,
difficulties one can eventually lay to rest. Conspiracies are tangled
enough to seem lifelike, but not so tangled that they will not eventually yield to steady scrutiny and work. If there is a conspiracy, then

there are reasons and motives and explanations which to the patient investigator will ultimately make logical sense.

Conspiracy implies solutions. But who of us can truly bear to look at the bedlam that is life? Life, where human behavior is an unsolvable riddle, where enigma is the rule, where there is no final meaning. To look at that bedlam for long would be like staring into the sun. The heat and the light of it would scar our eyes and make us blind.

"The sordid world." The words sounded almost quaint to Louis now. They were, he realized, a phrase he had used in the same way Milton used his conspiracies. It had helped him keep his intuitive and truer understanding of life's utter chaos from himself. Louis thought of Solesme, lost, doomed for all he knew, and far beyond his meager reach. Then he thought of his children, and then, in almost the same moment, he desired their company—one or the other or both of them—with such unfamiliar and fervent intensity, that he called them both from the first phone he found after leaving Milton's apartment building.

Jennifer was not there. He did not leave a message on her machine. At Michael's number, a young woman answered. She called to Michael, "It's your father." And then again more insistently: "Michael, it's your father."

"Where are you?" asked Michael when he finally came to the phone.

"I am in Arlington," said Louis, regretting that he hadn't told either Michael or Jennifer that he was coming. In fact, at that moment he regretted everything. "I need to see you," he said. He was startled that he had said it. He was more startled still that it was true. The cab driver, a Sikh with a turban, a splendid gray beard, and a wide mustache, found the address with some difficulty. Michael was waiting on the front steps of the building. Despite trying to look alternately stern and worried, he smiled as he stood to greet Louis. He looked taller and stronger than Louis remembered.

Louis held out his hand. But instead of taking it, Michael embraced him. It was an awkward and ungainly embrace. However, when Louis considered it later, when he thought about the time and distance Michael had sought to bridge with that embrace, it seemed to him a brave and exceedingly generous gesture, especially from a son to his persistently absent father. It was the best thing anyone could have given Louis at that moment. It was also the best moment of their visit. Their conversation soon lapsed into awkward and uneasy phrases, which were meant more to help the time pass than to bring them closer.

Louis explained that business had brought him to Washington. He was leaving in a few days. Michael introduced Rosita, a dark, round-faced girl with small, dark eyes and a quick, cheerful smile which, for some reason, Louis found irritating.

Louis tried to talk with Michael about art. He told Michael about his own painting, how he had never meant to be a painter, but how where he now lived everything looked like a painting, so that, at some point fairly early in his life there, painting came to feel like a natural and necessary thing to do. It was almost a way of orienting himself to his surroundings. He did landscapes and still lifes and an occasional portrait because he lacked the imagination to do anything else. He regarded this lack of imagination as a blessing. It spared him the delusion that he might have anything important or even useful to say in his art. Perhaps there were new things to be said in painting, though he doubted it. However, history suggested he was wrong. In any case, he was fairly certain that he had no answers, no wisdom to impart. "There are already too many answers in the world. The best I can hope for in my paintings is to maybe formulate a good question." That had come out sounding pompous and dogmatic, and Louis immediately regretted having said it.

Louis asked Michael about his art, but Michael was cagey and uncomfortable with his father's questions and said little. "Would you show me some of your drawings?" said Louis.

"They're all around you," said Michael, folding his arms in front of him, annoyed that his father had failed to notice them on the walls.

"Will you tell me about them?" said Louis, and stood to examine them.

"They're self-explanatory," said Michael, and then added, "they're about surface and texture." Louis took his time looking. He stepped from one drawing to the next, leaning over the couch where Michael and Rosita sat uncomfortably. He found the drawings tight and overdrawn, just as Sarah had said they were. Michael had the same problem he had, pushing something too far, not letting go of it soon enough. But he was surprised that Michael could draw at all. "They're beautiful, Michael. You draw really well."

"You sound surprised. My gallery has the best ones."

"Where is your gallery?"

"Not far from here. Ten minutes. In Tacoma Park. It's called the Easel Gallery. It's co-op. I may have a show. Next spring. I'll send you an announcement." Michael looked at Louis, then at his own hands, then at Louis again. Rosita held his arm and smiled.

"Send me an announcement," said Louis. The telephone rang. Rosita answered.

"It's for you, Mister Morgon," she said.

"Hello, Louis," said Hugh Bowes. "How nice to talk to you after so many years. I received a message that you wanted to see me, and I certainly would enjoy seeing you. Can we meet tomorrow evening for supper, at seven? That's not too early for you after all these years of late dinners in France?

"Where are you staying? In Arlington? There's a steak house on Wilson Boulevard, just by the Virginia Square Metro station. Bennie's. Was it there when you lived here? I don't think so. I'll see you at seven, then. I'm looking forward to it."

Louis hung up the phone. He fought to regain his composure. "I hope you don't mind, Michael, my getting a call here."

"No big deal, Dad. Who was it? What kind of business brings you back here?"

"It's not very interesting, Michael. I'll tell you about it someday, when it's over. Right now I'm happy to see you, to get to meet Rosita." She smiled at Louis. "And to see your drawings. I'm glad that you're an artist."

"When it's over? What are you talking about, Dad? Are you sick or something? Are you here seeing a doctor or something?"

"I promise you it's nothing like that. It's just not something I can tell you about right now. Do I look sick?" The three of them laughed uneasily.

Jennifer had a similar reaction when Louis reached her the next morning. "Dad, are you sick? Did you come back to see a specialist?"

"I know it sounded urgent, Jenny," he said apologetically as they were having lunch in her apartment. The sun shone on them through the big kitchen window as they ate tuna salad sandwiches Jennifer had made. Louis was able to imagine for a moment that they were sitting together at his old metal table looking out over the sunflowers. "I'm sorry I made it sound so urgent. In a way it was urgent that I see you, but not because I'm sick or anything like that.

I promise you I'm not sick." Jennifer stiffened her back and looked down uncomfortably. She, too, was taller than he remembered, but nothing like he had imagined her. She was thin. Her blond hair was pulled back loosely. She wore a flowered dress. She was pretty.

"I'm glad to see you too, Daddy," she said in a tone that suggested more reluctance than gladness.

"Tell me a little about your work, Jenny," said Louis.

"Well, you know what I do, don't you, Daddy?" she said.

"No, Jenny, I don't really. I know that you work on the Hill, but . . ."

"I'm an aide to a congressman, the agriculture committee chairman, so I do some research, some word processing—typing—some public and press relations. I get to travel a little, but it's mostly to the Midwest. Not to France. It's pretty interesting really. I'm sure I wrote you all this. Only I'm thinking of going back to school."

"What do you want to study?"

"Promise you won't laugh. I think I want to be a nurse."

"I think that's wonderful, Jenny." Seeing her uncertainty, he added, "I really do. I think that's wonderful."

She looked down at her unfinished sandwich and jumped up to clear the table. "Can I get you anything else?" she asked.

"I'm leaving tomorrow," said Louis. "Somebody I care about is in trouble, and I need to get back."

"Tomorrow? Already?" He thought she sounded both hurt and relieved.

Louis invited Jennifer to visit an art museum with him, but she had to go back to work, she said. She had to type some reports. She was glad he had called. She really was glad, she said. When would he be back in Washington again? Would he write to her when he got home to France? She would love to go to France. She had never been to Europe at all. She would love to go. But if she went back to school, well, it would be a while before she could visit him in France.

Louis stood in the museum alone and tried to make himself think only of the paintings in front of him. It seemed to him as though viewing these paintings and thinking about how they were made was a crucial thing for him to do right now. It was as though Solesme might turn up in their broad sunlit gardens or along their sunny paths, as if the light dancing off the sea, the girl at the piano, the woman with the teacup, could yield up clues and insights that would render him invaluable service in his meeting with Hugh Bowes. But no matter how hard he studied them, the paintings gave back only joy and melancholy, color and light.

He found a phone. "There is nothing new on Solesme," said Renard when he heard Louis's voice. "I have reported her missing and have searched where I could, but there are no leads, no clues. Pierre did not see or hear anything that might be helpful."

"I am having dinner with Hugh Bowes this evening," said Louis after a long silence. "And I am leaving tomorrow, arriving in Paris Friday morning. Air France, flight twenty-three from Washington Dulles Airport to Charles DeGaulle. Can you meet the flight? It arrives at eight Friday morning."

"I can," said Renard.

Louis heard the question in Renard's answer. "I will feel safer if you meet the plane," said Louis. "I believe that the person whose body was found on my doorstep—who could be a missing American intelligence officer who was also Ruth Chasen's lover—and Ruth Chasen herself, were killed at the airport. See if you can discover whether Ruth Chasen or possibly Robert Pendergrass were on flights arriving at Charles DeGaulle on July twenty-fifth."

"It might be just one more coincidence," said Renard, still hopeful that it might all turn out to be his friend's imaginings.

"It doesn't matter," said Louis. "It isn't my purpose that anyone should be arrested or convicted. I know that is your purpose—a crime has been done. In any case, I doubt that there will ever be sufficient evidence to arrest anybody. I only want them stopped. To that end, coincidence is more than sufficient. My scenario does not have to be true. It only has to be believable."

"Your dinner with Hugh Bowes?"

"Mainly curiosity. Meeting him again was not my intention. I never imagined he would see me. But when he called and offered to meet, I couldn't refuse. Incidentally, he found me with startling ease. He called me while I was at my son's house, to demonstrate, I suppose, that changing hotels and names as I did was a ridiculous exercise on my part, and that he could always find me if he wanted to. Don't worry. There's nothing dangerous about meeting him. We'll be at a restaurant. A public place."

"Charles DeGaulle Airport is a public place."

"Which reminds me," said Louis, ignoring Renard's concern, "do you think you could arrange for Jean Marie to meet us at the airport Friday?" Hearing Renard's silence, he continued: "There is nothing dangerous or untoward about it. I just want to ask him some questions about the airport. Maybe get him to show me around. That's all. I want to get some idea of how it was done. Where it was done, and so on." Louis thought for a moment, then added, "I saw my children, both of them, Jennifer and Michael. They both seem to be doing well."

Renard waited for more in light of this uncharacteristic loquaciousness on Louis's part, but the telephone was silent.

XX

*W*HEN LOUIS RETURNED TO THE PAINTINGS, THEY HAD LOST THEIR hold on him. He was disturbed by thoughts of Solesme. He then found himself engaged in imaginary conversations with Hugh Bowes, in which Hugh confessed that he had deposited the body at Louis's door. Had Louis wounded him so deeply back then, that after all these years he had placed everything in jeopardy for the sake of a vicious prank? Louis imagined formulating just the right questions to reach the bottom of Hugh's soul. Of course there were no such questions.

Louis left the museum and walked toward the Metro station. But when he reached it, the escalator down into its yawning tunnel repelled him, and he walked on past. He was certain he still remembered the way to Wilson Boulevard. He could follow P Street to Georgetown and then cross the river to Roslyn. Once there, he could simply walk along Wilson until he found the restaurant. The prospect of a long walk through half the city comforted him. Setting out on foot might once again be the way to find solutions to what seemed to be intractable problems. It might draw things out, put them in order, settle the logic of things, give them clarity. Walking had led him to solutions once before.

The day had turned uncommonly beautiful for a summer day in Washington. Crisp, dry breezes riffled shop awnings and people's clothes. Brushing their hair from their faces, two young women smiled at him as he passed, as though he had been the subject of their conversation and now had suddenly appeared before them.

Here in Washington after so many years, Louis was more a stranger than ever. Even though his children still lived here, Washington claimed only a small corner of his consciousness. Perhaps, he thought, because he had never painted or even drawn anything while he had lived here, he now had the sense that he had never really seen the city. It had never been as vivid a place for him as Saint Leon had become. His brushes were like a blind man's stick, tapping here and there until he had formed a picture in his mind which, if it was not accurate—and who could know whether or not it was—was at least detailed and thorough.

He was walking, he reminded himself, to meet Hugh Bowes who had, if not absolute power, then the illusion of absolute power, which was, to all intents and purposes just as effective, and which, Louis was certain, Hugh had never hesitated to exercise when he felt either the need or the desire.

Louis stopped in the middle of the Key Bridge and looked down the river at the city. Traffic roared past behind him. A panhandler appeared as though out of nowhere, and when Louis ignored his pitch, he began ranting before finally moving on. With a terrible whine, an airplane passed low overhead on its way to land at

National Airport. Several skaters raced past in their bright spandex, their helmets gleaming. The sun behind him reflected off the windows of the tall glass buildings in Roslyn and into his eyes.

Not long after Louis had bought and moved into his house in Saint Leon, he had stood one morning on his terrace unpacking books which had just arrived from Washington, trying to decide whether to put them in the house or the barn. Why had he brought them? They were mostly about politics and cybernetics. He knew he would never read them.

His steep driveway had been a difficult climb for Solesme even then. He saw her approach taking small steps on the balls of her feet. She turned with each step and pitched forward slightly, her head held back, her arms out slightly, one hand held palm down with the fingers extended parallel to the ground. She held a small cloth sack in the other. The breeze fluttered through her dress. She looked as though she were about to begin dancing. She smiled as she noticed him looking. She introduced herself as his neighbor and reminded him that they had met once before on his first visit to Saint Leon.

She had brought an onion tart which she had baked. Since it was lunchtime, Louis invited her to eat the tart with him and share a bottle of wine.

"I told Pierre I would only be gone a short time," she said. "Just to say hello and welcome."

"It was very kind of you to come," said Louis. "It is nice to have neighbors I have already met once before. It makes me feel at home." He offered to drive her back down the hill, but she declined. He watched until she disappeared over the crest of the hill.

A week later, she telephoned to invite him to have dinner with her and her husband. He put on a clean shirt and cut some flowers from his garden, although he knew from passing it every day that the Lefourier garden was overflowing with flowers of every imaginable kind. But what else could he bring? Madame Lefourier— Solesme—and Louis exchanged kisses on the cheek as is the French custom among friends. She introduced Pierre who seemed to have grown even wider and more substantial than Louis remembered him from the earlier summer. Pierre and Louis faced each other silently across the table as Solesme served the cassoulet. Louis helped her carry the dishes from the table, while the great pyramid sat in his place, looking across the table as if Louis were still seated there.

Louis invited them to come up for lunch. Solesme came walking up the driveway alone. He watched from the door as she approached. When he asked where Pierre might be, Solesme smiled and kissed his cheeks. She steadied herself with her hand on his arm. Every affair begins differently, and yet there are always not-so-secret signs future lovers give each other by which they can discern that it is beginning, is about to begin, or will soon begin. Once the signs begin to appear, like the first tremors of an earthquake, or the breeze that signals a storm, the affair becomes all but inevitable. Solesme and Louis had undoubtedly given each other signs, even when they had danced at the *fête*. But Louis could not remember any such signs. He seemed surprised the first time they kissed on the mouth, so that Solesme leaned away from him and looked in his face with curiosity. She laughed as she recognized his obliviousness.

He looked with curiosity at her body lying tangled in the sheets of his bed. It did not look deformed. He was surprised at the beauty of its proportions. Solesme was slight. And though she moved in sex as she had danced and as she walked, with care and with an air of delicacy, she was not restrained or guarded, and she laughed and shouted with passion and abandon.

She stared back at Louis with equal curiosity. "I am thinking about our differences," she said, leaning on an elbow, her other arm draped across her white stomach. Whatever her ideas about their differences, she kept them to herself. From the very first, they were intense, devoted, and discreet lovers. They were careful to be certain that no one else knew.

Louis did not ask Solesme about her marriage to Pierre. And Solesme made no attempt to explain it. The love affair between Solesme and Louis was about sex and affection. "Do all Americans have such peculiar notions about marriage and love?" asked Solesme one day, after Louis had wondered aloud where things between them might be leading. "You seem to imagine that every passion must eventually become public, that it must be officially sanctioned. In fact, everything always seems to have to lead somewhere for you. What a busy and purposeful people you are. This has already taken us where it is taking us. The fact that it might not be going anywhere else, does that frighten you?" It did frighten Louis, but only a little. And whatever fears he had, disappeared altogether when Solesme stepped out of her dress.

Louis was enraptured by her body which was twisted to a considerable degree at the base of the spine. With his hand, he would trace the asymmetry of her back. The muscles on one side were more developed to compensate for the distortion in her bones. She lay on her stomach as she explained exactly where the bones were fused and misshapen. Then he kissed her back from top to bottom which excited them both. She also studied his body. Louis was nervous lying on his back while she looked at him, touched him, kissed him. He tried to roll onto his stomach.

They met when they could, somewhat less frequently as time went along, but always, even in recent years, passionately and happily.

The twist in Solesme's spine became more pronounced. And while her face, hands, and arms were brown and wrinkled from the sun, her body still curved and moved in a way that excited Louis. The white skin under her dress still drew his hands and lips like a magnet. Sitting on a bench there on Wilson Boulevard facing Bennie's Steak House, Louis thought of Solesme with desire and trepidation.

Bennie's Steak House was in a large, low building made of dark brick. Narrow windows ran the length of the front. People poured out of the Metro station behind where Louis sat. He heard their steps as they scattered in every direction on their way home. From time to time someone went into Bennie's or someone came out. It was not yet even six o'clock. Louis sat and watched and waited.

At seven fifteen, Hugh Bowes stepped from a limousine and walked quickly into the restaurant. Louis got up from the bench, crossed the street, and followed him inside. But Hugh was nowhere to be seen. "I'm meeting Hugh Bowes for dinner," he said to the smiling young man at the podium. The young man's smile disappeared suddenly. Perhaps he thought he was part of some momentous event of state. "This way, sir," he said in a low voice and escorted Louis around the bar to a door in the dark paneled wall. He knocked on the door and opened it.

Another man wearing a dark suit and glasses stood inside the door. Hugh Bowes was seated at a table in the center of the small room. The table was set for two, with a white, heavy cotton cloth and a vase with a single red rose. Hugh looked at Louis as the young man closed the door. "Security," said Hugh, smiling apologetically, as the man with the glasses stepped forward and patted him down. That done, the man left. Hugh smiled, got up from the table, and offered Louis his hand. "Louis," he said, "I'm delighted to see you. Delighted we could meet. I hope you don't mind," he said, gesturing at the room which would be theirs alone. "We won't be bothered." A waiter appeared briefly. "How does steak sound? And a nice California red. You drink California wine, I hope," said Hugh and parted his full lips to laugh. He was heavier than he used to be. He wore glasses with thick gold frames. He had little hair, but he still parted what he had. His face was jowly and pale. He wore a dark blue suit, a white shirt, and a red-and-yellow striped tie. He had heavy gold links in his cuffs. His thick fingers were curled at the edge of the table.

"You look as though life in France agrees with you," said Hugh. "I get to France often, but rarely outside of Paris."

"You should get out in the country if you can," said Louis. "It is wonderful there." He thought his voice had sounded tenuous and uncertain.

"I know it is, but," said Hugh Bowes, and he raised his hands in a shrug to indicate that his time was not his own. "Forgive me, Louis, for appearing brusk, but what is it you wanted to see me about? Is there something I can do for you?"

"I was sorry to hear about Ruth's death," said Louis.

"Thank you. She was struck down so unexpectedly. She had so much life left in her. It was a terrible loss." Hugh rested his hands on the edge of the table and frowned at the dark hairs curling up over the edges of his cuffs. He looked up. "Thank you for mentioning it."

"Are you doing all right?" Louis asked.

"Of course, it was an unbelievable shock. I simply couldn't grasp it at first. I was devastated. Her loss will always be with me. Again, thank you for asking." He looked at Louis. "You'll appreciate that I can't stay long, Louis. I have a meeting in my office in less than an hour. I was just able to take some time for supper. Tell me what I can do for you."

"There was, on the day after Ruth's death, as it happens, a dead body deposited on my doorstep. He was a black man; his throat had been slit."

"Good heavens," said Hugh putting his hand to his cheek. "Who was it? Why was he put there? What have the French police found out?"

"He had the appearance of a North African . . ."

"Some connection with the work you did at the agency, you think? You were involved with North Africa, weren't you?"

"The Middle East, mostly," said Louis. "Anyway, I can't imagine how there could be any connection. That's all ancient history. But still, it does have that appearance. Or," he paused. "Someone wants it to have that appearance."

Hugh rubbed his chin, musing. "The Algerians are very active right at this moment. In fact, they're very busy in France right now. You know, there were those bombings in Paris a few years back. Of course you know. Algerian rebels were responsible. We know who they are and where they are. They were never arrested. For reasons I am not at liberty to offer. Still, I can't imagine why you might have been brought in. I suppose they could think you're still connected with us in some way. They could be trying to send us a message, although it's a strange way to do it."

The door opened and their dinners were brought in by the young man that had shown Louis into the room. He set the plates down without looking at either of the men. "Please be careful," he said. "The plates are very hot." He left the room as quickly as he had entered.

Hugh had already swung the napkin across his front. He poured them both wine and began to eat. He cut small pieces of steak rapidly and deftly. As he was chewing one piece, he was cutting and picking up the next one to be eaten. He ate efficiently, and without apparent pleasure.

"Thank you for bringing this to our attention, Louis. It could be something. We'll look into it. We'll check with our French police connections. Of course, we'll let you know what we discover as it concerns you. I'm sorry about this, Louis. I'm sure you thought you were rid of politics from your life forever."

"This is more than politics," said Louis. Hugh did not look up from his plate but continued cutting and chewing. "It's murder," said Louis, speaking a little louder, leaning forward slightly, as though it might be difficult for Hugh to hear through his eating. He seemed voracious and indifferent at the same time. It was as though eating simply occurred in one's life as a natural physiological event, like breathing, and just as with the air one breathed, what you ate, how it might taste, didn't matter at all. Louis had the impression that Hugh ate steak for the sole reason that he *always* ate steak. "And Hugh," said Louis, "what do you make of the fact that this murder happened the same day that Ruth died?"

Hugh stopped chewing and he stopped cutting. He weighed the fork and steak knife in his hand, looking at one, then the other before he looked up at Louis. His face was blank the way practiced diplomats' faces can be. If anything, he looked bored, as though what Louis had just said neither interested nor affected him in the least. "I'm afraid I don't follow your thinking, Louis. What connection do you see between my wife's stroke and the death of this North African . . . ?"

"I don't think he was a North African," said Louis.

"I thought you said he was North African," said Hugh, turning his attention back to his plate.

"I said he *appeared* to be North African. I wondered about Ruth's death and this man's death being on the same day and whether that implied some connection."

Hugh studied the last small piece of steak on his plate. "Go on," he said. But then he continued himself. "Do you mean to say that this dead man, whoever he might be, was killed when my wife died to somehow attract our attention? That seems very far-fetched, Louis."

"Excuse me, Hugh, but what I was suggesting is even more far-fetched. But leaving that aside for a moment—"

Hugh had finished eating. "Louis," he said, pushing the plate aside. "You think politics is nothing but intrigue, don't you? That policies are formulated and decisions are made primarily so that those involved can pursue their own ambitions? Doesn't that fairly state your idea of how we operate? And that political events, and you apparently include this murder among political events, are not what they seem to be, that their occurrence is not the main event, so to speak, but a subterfuge, a distraction, designed to hide what is really going on? Doesn't that fairly state your opinion? That's what got you in trouble when you were in government, isn't it?"

Louis did not know what had gotten him in trouble when he was in government, but he did not answer. Hugh examined the knuckles of both hands. He turned the wedding ring on his left hand between his fingers. "I'm going to speak plainly to you, Louis, about things you ought to consider carefully before you do any further speculating about events you know nothing about, speculations that will almost certainly embarrass and humiliate you even further. I was going to say that your speculations could ruin you, but of course you were ruined long ago.

"Whatever illusions you may harbor, Louis, the world is in actual fact a more or less orderly place. Moreover, its orderliness is apparent. Or rather, when one behaves in accordance with its orderliness, its orderliness becomes apparent. Furthermore, whatever its design, the orderliness of the world exists to our, to mankind's, benefit. That is not to say that we don't make mistakes in our perceptions and hence in our actions. Despite its clarity, the order of things sometimes eludes us, usually because we are distracted by our own delusions. But the appropriate response to such mistakes is not to deny the order. It is not to reject our own capacity to change things, to make things better. It is to discover the deeper order we somehow missed, it is to find out what might have allowed us to make a mistake in the first place. And to use our new understanding of things for the benefit of mankind.

"It is not only fallacious, but it is also dangerous to conclude that things are other than they appear to be. You may recall, Louis, from your own abbreviated time in government—this is particularly true when dealing with the decision makers of other countries—that it is fallacious and dangerous to assume duplicity and dishonesty, where one can discover honor and virtue. Of course duplicity and dishonesty exist everywhere in the world, and in everyone. But they are aberrant, they are abnormal. I believe honor and good will are the norm. All progress that is made toward a peaceful world, a prosperous world, comes about when one is able to assume about others, even one's adversaries, that they are essentially and despite all appearances people of good will and of honor."

Louis interrupted. "Is that an assumption you make about me?" Though he had asked the question with the intention of putting an end to Hugh's speech-making, for he was certain this was a speech Hugh had delivered many times before, he found that he was genuinely curious about the response.

"It is an assumption I *made* about you, Louis, when I knew you before, and when you recently expressed the desire to see me. Had I known that you had already been infected by rumor and innuendo, had I known of your malice toward me, though I am at a loss to explain it, had I known these things about you, I would certainly have declined to see you.

"Don't get me wrong: the fact that I assume honor and good will, does not imply that I am naive about evil and malice. I know the world is filled with malice, filled with evil, that people are duplicitous, that they do not act in an honorable way. I simply do not begin with the presumption that they are that way. I respond to evil as I find it. I should say Louis, that I find your suggestions about Ruth's death to be evil. And shocking. You should stay away from Milton Hamsher."

"Milton Hamsher is your strongest champion, Hugh," said Louis. "Whatever suspicions I may have, are my own."

"Then you are even more lost than I thought you were," said Hugh. Louis expected him to slide his chair back and stalk indignantly from the room, but he seemed in no great hurry to leave. In fact, it seemed as if the conversation had come to interest him. He filled his wineglass and gestured toward Louis's plate, saying "You haven't touched your food." It was as though they had been having a friendly argument about the nature of being and not a debate— albeit a veiled one—about whether or not Hugh had murdered his own wife.

"You have told me your view of the world, Hugh," said Louis. "May I tell you about mine?"

Hugh Bowes leaned back in his chair and crossed his legs. He studied his arm at rest on the table's edge. His expensive suit, the crisp shirt, the silk tie, the polished shoes, the presidential cuff links, the wedding ring, all these things stood for the man he saw himself to be. They contrasted dramatically, Hugh thought, with the blatant failure who sat facing him.

And yet, despite his best efforts—perhaps because of his intense desire that his carnal self not exist at all, maybe because of the urges and passions which just now seethed inside him, and most certainly because of his acute awareness of the flaccid, pale flesh which he knew that Louis knew to hang beneath his clothes—his shame was all but unbearable. He raised his eyes and looked across at the man looking back at him. And because he wanted nothing more than to be somewhere else, he spoke slowly, casually, with a languid look, and a light wave of his hand. "I would be curious to hear your view of the world, Louis."

Louis sat with his hands folded on his lap. For a long moment he imagined Solesme, frightened or dead. "It is not surprising to me, Hugh, that you would choose to see the world as you do. After all, your view carries with it an implicit justification of the life you have chosen to live, by which I mean a life of public service and devotion to the greater good. You believe in this greater good, and, more importantly, you believe in your own capacity, your own *superior* ability to discern and serve it. You believe that you are uniquely suited to know what the world needs and how to accomplish it."

Hugh kept his eyelids lowered, but his eyes were fixed firmly on Louis. He watched as each word formed on Louis's lips and emerged softly into the room. Instead of the tirade he had hoped for, instead of conspiratorial rantings, what he heard Louis say was perceptive and true. What Louis said that Hugh believed in, was what Hugh believed in, and, although there was nothing startling about what Louis said, it was disconcerting to be accurately summarized in this way, and doubly disconcerting for someone whose professional achievement and success depended on his maintaining a large degree of inscrutability. Moreover, Louis did not seem cowed or intimidated. Despite's Hugh's best efforts to reveal nothing, Hugh felt his body grow tense as though he were in the presence of an approaching danger.

"The world"—Louis thought of the night sky over France— "and, if the world then the universe, *could* be, *might* be orderly, but I do not believe, as you do, that the order of things is apparent or even available to us. Nor do I believe that anyone, not even you, Hugh— and I do not mean that 'not even' ironically—can perceive and understand the workings of things, even things much smaller than the world, like American foreign policy, or things that seem even smaller than that, like marriage, just as an example. I do not believe one can understand these things with a thoroughness and detachment sufficient to recommend one as life's designated engineer."

Hugh objected to marriage being made in any way analogous to foreign policy. "Fine," said Louis. "Leave marriage out. Foreign policy, then, since that is your chosen arena. You imagine yourself sufficiently versed in the ways of world politics to know what to do to make things better. But that is an illusion born of your shame, or your own deep sense of your own insufficiency, of your ultimate powerlessness, which thought, I believe, is all but unbearable to you. I have been a witness to your shame, you will remember, as you have been a witness to mine. But your shame, I believe, which is all but unbearable to you"—Louis repeated the phrase—"has driven you to do things which, but for your arrogance, you too would see as more than wrong. It has driven you to do evil, to use your word. I am still leaving marriage aside."

Hugh looked at Louis through narrowed eyes. He did not move. Even his breathing was shallow and imperceptible. It was not possible for Louis to tell whether Hugh had been listening. Hugh continued to practice his studied diplomatic indifference. But some faint tremor—did his eyelid flicker?—betrayed the uncertainty and fear which had begun to emerge from deep in the heart of his being.

Louis had found him out. And what was far more shocking: he had, for the first time, made Hugh known to himself. In all his years of thinking and reflecting about the political and social world, Hugh had, of course, thought about his own role on the world stage. But he had never once actually reflected upon his own weakness. How should he have? There was no place for weakness in his life. He had put his life together, managed and arranged it as though it were something apart from himself, something that existed on its own, as though it truly might have been that work of art Louis had spoken to Renard about. Its construction was Hugh's only sustained and sustaining passion.

If Hugh had other passions, he was unaware of them. But in fact he did. His humiliation by Louis many years earlier had caused him to experience a violent and passionate reaction. The discovery that Ruth, his wife, had taken a lover had caused him to have another. In Hugh's peculiar psyche, such moments of extreme feeling almost immediately gave way to his rational self, which he regarded as his true self.

Hugh treated the murderous moment as though it might be a natural or, better, political event, like a war, for instance, or a famine. It was something outside himself which had occurred and had to be reckoned with, but which, except that it had occurred within his range of knowing, had nothing to do with him. He did not deal with or even acknowledge these passions as belonging to him, so that it would not have occurred to him to feel either remorse or sorrow. They were simply things which had happened and which, therefore, had to be disposed of.

Hugh's disposition of these events was, of course, in large part, designed to conceal his part in them. One could, therefore, argue that he recognized his own wrongdoing. But, in fact, the concealment was no different in his mind than any other political strategy. He sought to conceal his part in the death of Ruth Chasen and her lover, and the subsequent taunting of Louis, not to protect himself, but rather to protect that work of art—his life of service to the greater good—which he had been working on for as long as he could remember.

The carefully planned murders had obviously not been executed in a moment of passion. Neither had dumping the lover's body at Louis's door. But this malevolent prank had certainly sprung from Hugh's passionate hatred of Louis. Hugh's hatred had begun, as Louis correctly surmised, at the time of Louis's early and rapid successes in the State Department and had reached its culmination on being found in bed with Sarah. Perhaps Hugh's affair with Sarah had been meant as a similar prank. Perhaps Hugh had simply intended to reassert his superiority, and then Louis had inadvertently turned the tables on him.

But why, Louis wondered, had Hugh risked everything this time? Why had he gone to such elaborate lengths to conceal his part in the murders, and then turned around and foolishly jeopardized his efforts? If the body had not been deposited at Louis's door, Louis might never have even known about Ruth's death. Hugh must have known that Louis would eventually think of him, despite his elaborate ruse to implicate the Algerians.

It is a truism, Louis thought, that all criminals yearn to be caught, and that the cleverest desire it most deeply. For, without being discovered, their cleverness remains undiscovered and unappreciated. And their hatred remains incomplete. It needs to be perceived by others, especially by those against whom it is directed, in order to be real. But hatred also has its own reasons beyond explanation. It was not Hugh's hatred of him that puzzled Louis. It was the depth, the murderous force of Hugh's hatred which he could not fathom. Louis leaned forward slightly and looked into Hugh's face in search of an explanation. But Hugh's face remained mask-like, his half-closed eyes glimmered.

Then with an exaggerated gesture, Hugh looked at his watch. "I'm sorry Louis," he said. "Your ruminations are fascinating. Unfortunately, there are real and important affairs of state that require my attention." He removed the napkin from under his chin. He stood without haste. Then without looking at Louis again, he strode from the room.

XXI

*G*OETHE ONCE SAID — WAS IT IN HIS CONVERSATIONS WITH Eckermann?—that he could not imagine a crime which he could not himself commit. Louis pondered this as he stared at the cold steak on the plate in front of him. It glistened under a film of congealed fat. The baked potato beside it was still wrapped in its foil. His wineglass was full. Louis felt the emptiness of the small room, sensed the door behind him, sensed the restaurant dining room, the street, the city beyond that, and felt afraid for his life.

The reasons for Louis's exile from the United States, which had gradually become less distinct in his mind over the course of the years away, now came rushing back to him with alarming clarity. Of course, the principal reason had been the desire, no, compulsion was the better word for it, to flee from the remnants of his disintegrated life—his failed marriage and career. He had, at the time, regarded Sarah and the children as the detritus of his failure, the floating wreckage of who he had once been or, rather, who he had considered himself to be.

Despite his fears, Louis waited until fairly late the next evening to leave for the airport. A man with an American flag on his baseball cap was driving the cab. The man opened the trunk without getting out from behind the wheel, and Louis lifted his bag in. "O.J. done it, sure as shit," said the driver as soon as they had started down the road. Louis knew very little about the trial of the famous football player who had just been acquitted of murdering his estranged wife. The man was looking at him in the rearview mirror. "But what do you expect when you get a bunch of niggers together on a jury?" Louis turned his gaze out the window and watched the highway pass.

The sense Louis had of himself as someone with a powerful enemy was of little use to him. There were no precautions he could take. He had decided not to call Sarah again, not to speak to the children again either. It allowed him the illusion that he was protecting them by keeping them out of it. Moreover, they would have immediately detected his uneasiness. He was relieved to have the day to himself, to think his own thoughts, to allow the feelings that his visits with Sarah, Michael, and Jenny had stirred up in him to settle. Sarah, Michael, Jenny.

At the Air France counter he was the last passenger. Everyone else was already at the gate. The young attendant typed the information from his passport into her computer and assigned him a seat in the middle of the plane just adjoining the smoking section. "I'm sorry, sir," she said, "but the aircraft is very full."

He stepped through the metal detector. As he approached the gate, he heard his name over the public address system. "Louis Morgon. Louis Morgon, please pick up a white courtesy telephone." Louis found a phone near the gate. The last passengers were boarding.

"Hello, Louis," said Hugh Bowes. His voice was casual and light, almost friendly. "Just a word. I won't let you miss your flight. In the matter we spoke about, I wanted to bring you up to speed. Your neighbor was kidnapped, we think, by Algerians, probably because she saw the body being left at your home. We'll continue looking from here, and I'll let you know when I have something more. I have your number in . . . Saint Leon sur Dême is it? Pretty name. We'll talk soon, Louis. Bon voyage."

"Thank you, Hugh," said Louis. "I appreciate your help."

"What are friends for?"

Louis hung up the phone and hurried onto the plane.

He was glad when he spied Renard and Jean Marie waiting for him in Paris just beyond the customs booth. It was eight o'clock in the morning. The flight had been smooth, but Louis had not slept. He had tried to read, still *Anna Karenina*, but couldn't concentrate. When the lights were turned down and the other passengers pulled the little blankets over their heads, Louis had stared into the darkness.

The three men shook hands. "Thank you for coming, Jean Marie. How is your work going?" Jean Marie was handsome in his blue customs uniform. He looked like Renard, but was taller. He had his mother's bright eyes. They stopped in a small airport cafeteria for breakfast.

"Neither Robert Pendergrass nor Ruth Chasen went through DeGaulle, according to airline records, or according to customs records," said Renard, sipping his coffee. He noticed that Louis's eyes had dark circles under them.

"I am not surprised," Louis said, buttering a piece of baguette and then spreading marmalade on it from the small foil box.

"But," said Renard. "Everyone leaves tracks. It was Jean Marie's idea," he said, covering his son's hand with his own for a moment and smiling.

Louis looked from Renard's face to the son's and back again. "Tell me," he said.

"It was Jean Marie's idea," said Renard again. "Look at this." He pushed a paper in front of Louis.

"What is it?" said Louis.

Jean Marie spoke. "It's a photocopy of a page from the logbook at the lost and unclaimed baggage office at Air France. Customs goes through the logbook all the time. It's one place we look for contraband. So I thought, let's have a look. Anyway, when baggage is reported lost by a passenger, the information is entered into the computer. It is also entered into this logbook. There is a description of the missing article—in this case, 'large brown Louis Vuitton suitcase containing personal effects. Suitcase has name tag with name and address of passenger: Ruth Chasen; sixty-six rue Jacob; Paris, sixth arr.; telephone, etcetera.' There's the flight number: AF 415. And look here: the claim is signed and dated: 'Ruth Chasen, July twenty-fifth.' She was on the flight arriving from Washington, July twenty-fifth."

"They cleaned out the flight and the customs records," said Renard. "But they didn't know she had reported a lost bag. The lost bag report is still in the computer too."

"Chaos wins over order," said Louis and smiled. Neither Renard nor Jean Marie knew what he meant, and Louis did not elaborate. "Jean Marie," Louis asked when they had finished eating, "can you give me a short tour of the electronics in the airport?"

"The electronics?" said Jean Marie.

"The loudspeakers, the telephones," said Louis, "who operates them, where their centers of operations are located. I believe that these murders might have occurred in this airport. That's why I wanted you to meet me here. You know the airport well"—Jean Marie nodded—"and I hoped that your explanation of how the airport works, where things are, anything you could tell me, might somehow offer a clue as to how they had been committed. Then, last night, just as I was about to get on the plane, Hugh Bowes gave me the clue I needed. So, now I want you to tell me specifically about the telephones, who controls them, and from where?" The men sat for another hour, with Jean Marie talking and drawing diagrams while Louis listened. Louis did not understand electronics, but occasionally he would ask a question. Could one part of the system be isolated from other parts of the system? Could the public telephone system be connected to other systems, that is, could the isolated system be temporarily wired to broadcast over airport loudspeakers?

Later in the car, Louis leaned against the door and slept. Renard glanced over at the old man. Louis's body sagged. His mouth hung open. Renard wondered, what happened to your spirit after you had been batted around by life the way Louis Morgon had? As you got older, Renard's own mother had told him, a cosmic sort of tiredness invades your life and teaches you resignation. Death becomes less of a stranger, less of an enemy, as it takes your friends and acquaintances, or your husband, as it had in her case. And life becomes more of a struggle, less easy, less natural, so that at some point it becomes easier to die than it does to live. Louis was nowhere near that point, of course, but in the last months he had begun to seem his age. He was dispirited, seemed distracted sometimes, lost in thought. Renard looked over at his passenger. Louis was looking back at him with those bright blue eyes, alert, unblinking. Renard could have sworn Louis had read his thoughts.

Louis knew that Solesme was still missing. Hugh Bowes had told him so. This gave him comfort. Hugh Bowes, he reasoned, was a careful killer. And since Solesme had been a witness to the Algerian diversion Hugh had cooked up, she would be more useful to him alive, at least as long as the fiction that the murdered man was an Algerian insurrectionist and not Ruth Chasen's murdered lover continued to be at all even remotely plausible.

"Plausible?" said Renard angrily. "What you say happened is the least plausible thing of all. It is supposition heaped on supposition. And even if I believe things happened as you say they happened, and I admit that I am inclined to, there is no evidence for any of it."

"And there never will be," said Louis, looking at the policeman, "beyond the few scraps we have."

"These scraps of what you call evidence are beyond circumstantial. This case is a string of suppositions. And nothing links it to Hugh Bowes but more suppositions, different suppositions."

"It is not a case at all," said Louis, sounding weary again. "You are quite right. It is not the kind of truth a policemen needs. You look for evidence, and all we find is where the evidence once lay. If we are lucky. Our evidence is the absence of evidence, a collection of negatives. It isn't much."

"It's nothing," said Renard, still angry. "What can you do with nothing?" Their exit came up and they left the autoroute. Only when they had driven away from the tollbooth did Louis respond, and then in such a curious and troubling way that Renard stopped the car and stared at him. That is, Louis began to sing. He faced straight ahead, sat very erect. His eyes were closed and he sang in a surprisingly light and clear tenor. Renard thought he might have heard the song before. He couldn't be certain. In any case the words stayed with him, though he couldn't say why. They were nonsensical. And they certainly had nothing to do with Louis or Hugh Bowes or anything they had been talking about.

> *"Charles the great has come at last,*
> *Come at last to stay.*
> *He knows not where he's going, though*
> *He thinks he knows the way.*
>
> *Charles the great might disappear*
> *While thinking you can see him.*
> *But life is short and art is long,*
> *And she can live without him."*

XXII

ONE PART OF BEING HUMAN IS THAT WE ARE ALWAYS WAITING FOR something, though it is usually something so vague and ill-defined that we cannot feel our own waiting. So we do not even know we are waiting, except somewhere in our inner souls. As far as we can realize, we are merely living in time or, more likely, living *out* time as it passes. But now Louis knew he was waiting, and he knew what he was waiting for. He was waiting for Hugh Bowes to kill him. "It is his only possible course of action," Louis would maintain over Renard's angry reaction. He insisted Renard was powerless to stop his murder, that Hugh Bowes could accomplish it at will, when he desired, how he desired.

Renard knew Louis was right, that if Hugh Bowes wanted to have him killed, he would have him killed. In the face of that knowledge, which was, for Renard, the knowledge of his own helplessness, it was not surprising that he began to keep his distance from Louis. He found routine police business that needed attending to. He regularly called his superior at the prefecture to inquire about the disappearance of Solesme Lefourier. "There is no news, Monsieur Renard," his superior would say each time. "We continue our investigation and follow leads as we receive them." But there were no leads. Weeks had passed since her disappearance, and Renard was certain that whatever trail the kidnappers had left had grown cold. "The trail is not cold," his superior assured him. "Her kidnappers are Algerian extremists who believe she witnessed them committing a crime. We have a good idea who they are. We need for them to make some kind of a move."

"She *did* witness them committing a crime," said Renard, trying unsuccessfully to contain his exasperation.

"We will let you know as we develop any leads," said his superior. "And, of course, you will notify us should anything develop where you are."

"They probably know less than you do, Renard," said Isabelle. That thought did not comfort him.

Louis, meanwhile, to his own surprise, began to spend time with Pierre Lefourier, the great pyramid, whose grief seemed no less colossal than his size. Pierre seemed enshrined in gloom and despair. And yet he was also able, again to Louis's surprise, to converse with Louis as he had never done when Solesme had been there. He talked about his youth in Russia, the years he and his sainted mother, bless her long departed soul, had lived in Paris where he had worked as a journalist and, for a brief period toward the end of the war, as a spy, first for the Germans, then for the resistance. His mother had died during the war. During the chaos that immediately followed the liberation of Paris, Pierre had left the city forever. He waved his hand vaguely when Louis asked the reason for his leaving.

There was nothing there for him but the apartment he had lived in with his mother, and bad memories. So he left.

He went first to Orleans, then to Nantes. He thought he would like it near the sea. Eventually, though, a friend from Paris, who had gone back home to Saint Leon after the war, invited Pierre for a visit. He came on the train from Nantes. The small town appealed to him. He found a job in the fish market. Then he found a job at the bank. He and his Paris friend bought the small Hotel de France which they sold a few years later when the friend moved back to Paris. They sold out to Didier LeDru who later sold the hotel to the Chalfonts. It was while Pierre had owned the Hotel de France that the British racing teams had begun staying there each year during the Le Mans races. Pierre had sold his share in the hotel for enough to buy a small share in the mushroom caves. Solesme was his Paris friend's youngest sister. She was four when Pierre arrived from Paris. They married when she was twenty. As he repeated the story yet again to Louis, Pierre began to weep silently, tears pouring from his closed eyes, his great, ancient body heaving in the chair.

Mostly, Pierre talked and Louis listened. Louis had the feeling that Pierre had never talked like this before, that he had been gathering and saving his life story, as one might save money for retirement, investing it and watching it grow until the moment comes to start spending. He did not ask Louis anything. He always seemed glad when Louis knocked at the door. As soon as Louis came inside, Pierre began to talk.

He stopped talking to Louis, stopped his story in midsentence, so to speak, the day Solesme reappeared. It was October. Pierre called Louis. The police had called from Tours. She had been put out of a car near the train station in Tours early that morning after being driven from somewhere near Nantes. "Nantes," said Pierre. He said it again like it was the answer to the entire riddle: "Nantes."

According to the police report Renard received by telefax that evening, the missing person, Madame Solesme Lefourier, had been freed by her kidnappers without ransom or other demands having been made. She had been beaten repeatedly. Two fingers and the thumb on her left hand had been broken. Several ribs had been cracked. Her jaw had been broken. She was immediately taken to the hospital. She was examined and her injuries were treated. She was given a thorough physical and psychological examination. It was determined that she was in good physical and emotional condition, considering the severe and continuing hardship—torture was not too strong a word—she had experienced for the last seven weeks.

Louis drove Pierre to the hospital in Tours where they sat at Solesme's bedside. Her face and arms were bruised. Her jaw was bandaged, so was her hand. "They threatened to cut off my fingers. They came in with a bolt cutter. But they broke them instead," she said. "It was the large one. He did it with his hands. I heard the bones snap like twigs." She began to cry at the memory. Pierre sat caressing her arm. She fell asleep.

A week later a police ambulance brought her home from the hospital. Louis and Renard sat with Solesme at her kitchen table. Pierre sat nearby in his chair. He might have been listening, but you could not tell. He had retreated back into himself. "It was the people I saw that night carrying the body to your house. I saw eight different people altogether while they held me. Four different people interrogated me. Two men I had never seen before drove me back from Nantes.

"When they first took me, it was to somewhere near Libourne. They moved me three times. They threatened me. Then they hit me. They broke my fingers at the same time. It was the big one. He did it with his hands."

"Madame," said Renard, "were they all North Africans?"

"Algerians," said Solesme. "Liberationists. The Algerian Liberation Front."

"How do you know?" said Renard.

"They told me so," said Solesme, brushing a strand of hair from her face. She looked uncertain.

"Do you think it was true?" said Louis.

"I do not know," said Solesme. They had asked her questions about Louis, about his trip, about her own politics, about Pierre, about things she couldn't imagine could be of any interest to them.

"What things?" said Renard.

Her life in Saint Leon. What she knew about Louis. What she knew about his earlier life. "They did not interrogate me often, but when they did, I got the impression that they were asking questions for the sake of asking the questions. They did not seem interested in the answers I gave them. That is, when I was able to give them answers. They did not follow any direction in their questions. They just asked questions. What I said didn't seem to matter. Their beatings seemed random too. My answers didn't matter. Until right before they released me, that is. It was strange."

"What happened?" asked Renard.

"It was the first man again, the large one, the one who broke my fingers. He threatened to break the fingers on my other hand. But now the same answers I had given before seemed to satisfy him. No matter what I said. Whether I knew the answer or not."

The man had rubbed his hands together eagerly, energetically, and with each answer, whatever the answer, had taken a small step toward Solesme, apparently more out of relief than for any other reason. Leaning very close, he asked her more questions—when Louis had first arrived in Saint Leon, how long she had known him, questions she, or anyone else in Saint Leon, for that matter, could have answered. She answered every question she could answer.

Finally, the man had looked at his watch. He had smiled at Solesme. " 'Madame, I want to congratulate you on your good sense. It was most wise of you to cooperate.' Those were his exact words," said Solesme. "I remember, because they seemed to make no sense at all." The next morning, two men she had never seen before put her in the back of a truck and drove her to a warehouse near Nantes, a drive of an hour, she guessed. She could tell it was on back roads because of all the stopping and turning. Inside the warehouse, they put her in a waiting car, a large Peugeot. They sped east on the autoroute. No one spoke. After an hour and a half, they reached Tours.

"They kidnapped me, hurt me, asked me stupid questions they could have asked anyone, and then brought me home. The whole thing makes no sense at all. It was like a terrible charade."

"It may have been just that, madame," said Renard, leaning back in his chair and looking over at Louis. Louis was watching Solesme intently, but his face was without expression.

She continued. "It was as though they wanted me to believe I had been kidnapped by Algerians. Of course they were Algerians," she said. "I'm quite certain they were Algerians."

"Yes, madame, I'm sure they were Algerians. But whose Algerians were they? That is the question."

That evening Solesme and Louis lay in each others arms. "I am sorry," said Louis, "for the trouble I have brought into your life."

"Are you feeling sorry for yourself?" asked Solesme. Louis admitted that he was feeling sorry for himself. "And why do you think I was kidnapped?" said Solesme.

"I think you were kidnapped to throw us off the track," said Louis.

"Who was murdered?" asked Solesme.

Louis was tempted to say, I cannot tell you. For your own protection I cannot tell you. But instead he held her tightly and told her everything he knew and everything he suspected.

Solesme's injuries healed. Her recovery coincided with the return of a certain equilibrium to Louis's life. He painted again. He ate meals on his terrace, watching the Virginia creeper leaves turn red and then drop to the ground. They swirled around him in little whirlwinds and settled under the laurel bushes. The days were short, the nights frosty, and the mornings thick and moist with fog.

Louis wrote long letters to Jenny and Michael describing what he was doing. And they wrote back.

La Frenellerie
Saint Leon sur Dême
October 23, 1995

Dear Michael,
Thank you for your last letter. I am glad to hear that you and Rosita are thinking of getting married. Are you surprised that I am for marriage, given what a mess I made of my own? I am somewhat surprised by my own sentiments. It is true that I think of marriage as a dangerous and, at best, sloppy business. For two people to get along is difficult enough without hanging the millstone of society's expectations around their necks. But I have come to believe that marriage is the beginning, the basic atomic unit, of the larger civilization—if that is what you can still call it—in which we live. By that I mean that in the insti-

tution of marriage one finds the things that are necessary in order for us to have a prospering and healthy society: commitment to something outside ourselves and to someone other than ourselves. Love, consideration, and the recognition that these things are important. I'm sorry to go on this way. I hope it doesn't feel like I'm weighing your plans down with lofty concepts. It's just my convoluted way of saying I'm happy for you and wish you the best.

Any word on your show? If and when? Let me know. I would love to see it. Do you ever paint with oils? I started with acrylics, and for a long time they were right for me. But sometime about five years ago, I found that I needed to slow things down, so I switched to oils. I'm still fiddling with underpainting, but it has gotten more complicated. In effect I'm doing several paintings on top of each other. They're mostly landscapes, and not very good. They're usually either overworked, or overcalculated, which amounts to the same thing.

My friend and neighbor, Solesme Lefourier, continues to recover from the ordeal of her mysterious kidnapping, though the experience has changed her. I hope it is only for the moment. But it is as if the kidnappers released everything but her trust. She is more withdrawn than she was before, more guarded somehow. I passed her standing in her garden recently. I was coming back from a walk. I spoke, and she looked at me as if she didn't know me, just watched me walk by. We still have a glass of wine together, or a cup of coffee. Maybe it is not just the kidnapping. Something happens when you get to be sixty, and you imagine the end to be in sight. Being treated the way she was steals something precious from you. It makes me loathe the people who did this.

I'm sorry to have gotten somber again. I hope you will come visit someday, with Rosita, of course, to meet Solesme, my friend Renard, the cop, my other friends and neighbors. I would, in fact, be glad to buy you a ticket. Say you'll come.

Love,
Dad

112 Hillburton Street
Tacoma Park, MD
November 18, 1995

Dear Dad,

Thanks for your letter. I'm sorry it took me so long to get back to you. No word yet on the show. It may come off. It may not. I'm trying not to care too much about it. But I find myself wanting it. Even if it is a co-op gallery. I don't know how much you know about the gallery scene, but it could be a step to a major gallery. The owners watch these shows for stuff with promise. Anyway, I'll let you know.

Sorry to hear about your neighbor. It must have been rough for her. Any idea who did it or why? Did they want money or what? Is she married?

I'd love to visit you someday and so would Rosita. It's not going to be soon though. She can't get away from work that easily, and neither can I. She has actually been to France. She was a little girl, and her parents took her. They were mainly in Paris. She doesn't remember it very well. She remembers riding a pony in a big park. Was that the Tuillery (sp.)?

Yours,
Michael

XXIII

*I*T WAS RAINING. IT HAD BEEN RAINING HARD ALL DAY, CLATTERING on the slate roof. Zorro, the cat, was curled on the tile hearth not far from the woodstove. Louis sat nearby at his long table, reading, and eating hot soup. He was having an early supper, as he sometimes did in winter. It was six o'clock. It seemed as if the day had never really begun. It had been twilight all day, and then what little light there had been had disappeared two hours ago. The telephone rang and, after hesitating, Louis decided to answer it.

"Louis, this is Hugh Bowes. How are you? I hope I am not disturbing you."

"You're not disturbing me, Hugh," said Louis. He stepped to the door and checked that it was locked.

"I told you I would call when I had something to tell you about the situation we talked about. I'm glad your friend is all right, that she was released unharmed. I was able to exert some pressure there, and it may have done some good. Anyhow, I'm glad of the out-come." Hugh paused. Louis waited.

"I can't tell you anything over the phone, Louis, but I'll be in Paris in a few weeks for a meeting. On the fourteenth. December fourteenth. Can you come to Paris then." It was not really a ques-tion. "I'm sorry to inconvenience you this way, but some very sensi-tive information is involved that could damage French-Algerian relations. Not to mention French-American relations, which, as I'm sure you know, Louis, do not need any more stress at the moment."

"I can come to Paris, Hugh. Shall I come to the embassy?"

"No, no, no, Louis. The embassy is out. This is *very* sensitive, Louis. Extremely sensitive." He paused for a moment, then said, "How about the airport? Charles DeGaulle Airport? We can meet on my way home. *Aerogare* Two-B. Terminal Two-B, by the arrival gate for international passengers. December fourteenth at six in the evening. I'll be there as soon after six as possible. I might get held up though, Louis, so please wait. Of course, I don't need to ask you not to tell anyone and to come alone, do I, Louis. That goes without saying."

"Of course, Hugh. That goes without saying," said Louis.

Louis drew the curtains tighter and checked the door yet again. He pulled his chair to the stove. He put Zorro on his lap and scratched his head. The cat purred, but jumped off when the phone rang again. When Louis answered, there was no one there. It rang twice more that evening, but there was no one there.

"And you didn't call me immediately?" Renard was furious. Louis had come into his office the next morning and invited him for a cup of coffee at the Hotel de France. They sat in the bar under autographed photos of the British racing teams.

"I did not call you," said Louis, "because five minutes later he called back to make certain I was not on the phone. Besides, Jean, what could you have done?" Renard was startled to hear his first name and he looked up. Louis was smiling at him. "Could you persuade Jean Marie to come visit next weekend?"

"You are actually planning to go through with this meeting at Charles DeGaulle Airport with someone you believe intends to kill you, or have you killed, and who, as you have repeatedly pointed out, has the power to do it easily?" said Renard.

"It is a public place; what could possibly happen?" Louis said and smiled again. "Besides, you will be there . . . at a discreet distance. I have laid a trap for him and he is walking right into it." Renard stared at Louis as though he were a madman. Louis just looked back at him and smiled yet again. For the first time in months he felt free. It was liberating to finally know the date and time of his intended death. And, if things worked out as he hoped they might, he would not be killed. Instead he would be free of Hugh Bowes. The peaceful existence he had built for himself over the last twenty years would be restored.

Of course Louis already knew in the back of his mind that that was not possible. What he had built over the last twenty years was the *illusion* of tranquility, an illusion that could never be restored. In creating a "sordid world," and then cutting himself off from it, he had done nothing so much as try to amputate his past. One day much later, after Solesme had died, after Renard had left Isabelle and then come back again, after Jenny had visited, in short after everything had changed and nothing had changed, he realized that the operation had been a failure. After the amputation of a limb, there is often what is known as phantom pain. A combination of damaged nerves and mysterious psychological stirrings brings about pain that seems to come from the limb that is no longer there. Louis thought for a long time that the year which began when he found the dead man on his doorstep was a year of something like phantom pain. But it wasn't. How could it have been? His past had never been cut off to begin with. It was still there, still his past.

Louis invited the three Renards for dinner that Saturday. He prepared a lamb stew he knew Renard liked. He had gotten the recipe from Isabelle, but had embellished it. He served the stew over couscous with a sliced beet and onion salad.

"Louis thinks he can buy Jean Marie's help with a serving of lamb stew," said Renard, mopping the last sauce from his plate with a piece of baguette.

"It was delicious, Louis," said Isabelle. "What did you add besides the black beans and red pepper?"

"Cumin," said Louis. "And I am not buying anyone. I am asking Jean Marie for his help. I wanted you both to hear what is involved so you could assure yourselves that what I am asking him to do is not dangerous. It involves electronics, Jean Marie, which is your specialty." Jean Marie nodded. "It involves coming up with a method, or a device, to connect the public telephone system, the one for internal communication within the airport, the so-called courtesy phones, with the loudspeaker system. What I need is to be able to broadcast a telephone conversation over the loudspeakers and to control the broadcasting of the conversation from a courtesy telephone. Then the connection should be quickly removable so that airport communications can be returned to normal, and, of course, so that all traces of your involvement disappear."

"A plug-in circuit and a switch or two would do it," said Jean Marie, brushing his pale mustache with the back of his hand and smiling proudly at his mother and then his father. "There's nothing to it. The tricky part is the switching back and forth, but I could do that from the central panel. I can get the key. It is not a high-security situation."

"He could lose his job," said Renard.

"If he is caught," said Isabelle. "But Jean Marie is clever, and he won't be caught."

"The choice is yours, of course, Jean Marie," said Louis, astonished at the unexpected support he had gotten from Isabelle. "It is, as you see, not dangerous to you, but, as your father points out, it might be dangerous to your career."

"When you put it like that, Louis," said Jean Marie with a laugh, "how can I possibly refuse?"

"Jean Marie, you're just like your father," said Isabelle with a laugh, and kissed her son and then her husband. Then she leaned across the table and kissed Louis on the cheek.

Louis had always been a reticent man. His Washington experience had made him all the more loathe to share confidences with even his closest friends. Which made it doubly strange that he chose to tell Solesme what he had in mind. True, he spoke in generalities, keeping the specifics vague, concealing the place, the date. But even so, he wondered later, what could he possibly have been thinking? He knew Solesme was protective of him and that she was stubborn and resourceful. He should have known she would find a way to be there.

So, as Solesme lay in his bed one gray morning late in November, he told her he planned to meet the murderer. On arriving at Orly—he changed the airport—he expected to be summoned to a public phone to receive directions to the site of his own execution. He intended, by means of electronics he could not himself begin to understand, to record and, more importantly, to broadcast the murderer's summons along with whatever incriminating evidence he could entice from him, so that all the passengers, airline personnel, visitors, bus and cab drivers, the hundreds of people in the terminal would suddenly hear an English conversation between two men—discussing what, had it been murder?—coming over the airport's loudspeaker system. Most of the people who heard it probably wouldn't notice, and those who noticed wouldn't understand, but some would understand what they had heard, and they thus became unknown and anonymous witnesses to the crimes that had been committed and to the one that was about to be committed.

Moreover, their witness would prevent its occurrence, that is, would keep Louis alive. And if Louis was correct in his calculations, their witness would put a stop to the murderer. The exposure of Hugh Bowes would be tentative, that is, Hugh could never be certain who had even heard, but he could be reasonably certain someone had heard something. But what? In this case the uncertainty worked in Louis's favor. Just the *possibility* that someone might have heard something incriminating seemed to Louis to be a more powerful deterrent than any certainty could have been.

Solesme did not express astonishment or concern. Did she approve or disapprove? Louis could not tell. She merely drew back from him, as she sometimes did, and watched him as he spoke. When he had finished, she asked him when this was to happen. It did not seem to matter to her that he refused to tell her.

As a girl of sixteen, Solesme had been in love with a boy named Julien Trignet. She had lived then on her father's farm outside Saint Leon. Julien lived in the village of Dissay where his father was the butcher. Solesme and Julien went to the same school. They were in classes together and both sang in the school choir. Julien was a thin boy with a narrow chest, but he had a deep and beautiful baritone voice which, despite his lack of training and singing experience, was lovely to hear. The first time Julien visited Solesme at her home, she begged him to sing. He refused at first, but when she continued to plead with him, he sang a ballad, his cheeks flushed with excitement and embarrassment while Solesme's mother, father, and the two sisters who were still at home all listened in silent amazement. They clapped enthusiastically, and Solesme beamed with pride.

Solesme could not ride a bicycle, except with the greatest difficulty. So Julien visited her home frequently, while she remained pretty much a stranger at his parents' home in Dissay. After another year both left school. Solesme found work as a seamstress. Julien worked in his father's shop as an apprentice. Julien continued to visit when he could, but his work kept him away more and more, and one day he stopped coming altogether. Solesme called on the telephone, but he did not come to the phone, or when he answered and heard her voice, he simply hung up the phone. She wrote him anguished letters, wondering why he had stopped coming, why he didn't call, what had happened between them, were his parents keeping him from coming, from calling, had she done something wrong?

"Where is Julien?" said Solesme's mother.

"He had too much work to come over," said Solesme.

But a mother who has two sons and five daughters knows things without being told. She knew that the fault lay with Julien, that he had decided not to tie his fortunes to those of a girl with a crippled back.

Two years later word came of Julien's engagement to a girl from Dissay, a pretty blond girl who worked as a cashier in the grocery store. Their wedding was on a bright Saturday in June in the church in Dissay. After the service, the reception was to be at a small country inn a few kilometers down the road. The procession to the inn was to begin in the small square in front of the church and proceed through the whole of Dissay, then out into the fields. The cars that were to carry the bridal party had been parked in front of the church facing in the proper direction. The road through town was so narrow that turning a single car around, let alone a wedding procession of cars, would have been out of the question. The car which would carry Julien had been decorated in the traditional way with flowers, a broom, dolls, and a baby carriage, and lots of gaily colored streamers.

At the end of the service the wedding party came through the ancient wooden doors and stopped on the top step. Solesme stood in front of the decorated car. She was wearing a black dress that was cut low in the back. Her skin was pale, her face was beautiful. As the bridal party nervously piled into the cars and started their engines, the wedding guests watched from the stairs. Except for a few indignant whispers, everyone was silent. As the cars began to inch forward, Solesme started down the middle of the street. The procession moved at a funereal pace, for Solesme could only walk slowly and with difficulty, and she walked in the middle of the street so that no one could pass. She may even have exaggerated that strange twisting motion of hers which was both disconcerting and beautiful to watch.

Dissay is a small town, but the procession to the edge of town took many minutes. Julien sat slouched in the backseat, not wanting to look out the front of the car, but unable to look anywhere else. His cheeks were red with anger. His pretty bride was in tears. At the edge of town where the buildings ended and orchards began, Solesme stepped to the side of the road and let the cars pass. They raced off to the inn as fast as they could.

Of course there was music and dancing at the reception. There was champagne and lots of food prepared by the bride's mother and the groom's mother. The bride and groom were presented with funny gifts that made everyone laugh. Glasses were repeatedly raised to the happy couple. The guests all danced and drank. They seemed to have put the strange wedding procession out of their minds. But, to everyone's surprise, when Julien was asked to sing, he refused.

XXIV

$\mathcal{D}$ECEMBER FOURTEENTH. IT WAS COLD. THE SUN SAT PALE AND low in the sky. The countryside was silvery with frost. Wood smoke hung in low clouds over the roofs of the village. Ice was forming along the edges of the Dême. "I will be back tonight," Louis said as he stroked Zorro's head. He did not know whether it was true. Louis put on a gray suit, his only suit, a white shirt, and a dark tie. Why, he wondered. It was as though he were attending a solemn ceremony. He put on his gray overcoat. He looked in the mirror before he left and was alarmed, as he almost always was these days, at what he saw. He smiled at himself.

Louis drove to Le Mans and waited on the platform as the train sped into the station. Inside the train, he took his seat and was immediately lost in his thoughts. What do people think about when their death is imminent? What do they think in the morning, when they know they will die that evening? Louis wondered who would take care of the cat. He wondered how long it would take before his old car would be discovered and towed from the train station parking lot. How long it would be before it was noticed that the car no longer had an owner.

Louis wondered whether Milton Hamsher would learn of his death and somehow weave it into the conspiracy to discredit Hugh Bowes. Maybe Hugh would already have sent him a note:

December 14

MILTON:

Louis Morgon, who was formerly employed at the Department of State and the CIA, and who was dismissed under questionable circumstances, was seen today meeting with known Algerian revolutionaries at Charles DeGaulle Airport in Paris. They then boarded Air Tunis flight 1221. After leaving the plane in Tunis, they got into a black Mercedes which was waiting for them and left the city.

Louis wondered whether his life had had some logic to it, whether he had moved consistently through it in a direction which, while it eluded him, might be discernible to others. To him his life's patterns and themes were invisible, swallowed up in its overlapping events, its pleasures and celebrations, its dilemmas and confusions, the realities and the illusions, the day by day that had gradually accumulated over the sixty years. He could not see the sense of it. He remembered a story—was it by Chekhov?—about how quickly the traces of your existence disappear after you die.

"Excuse me, are you all right? Can I do something for you?" It was the young woman sitting next to him. She spoke with an American accent. "Are you ill?" she asked. "You were breathing heavily."

Then: "I thought you were sick. I'm sorry if I bothered you." Louis's mind had flooded with memories from his life. That is supposed to happen when you are dying, he thought. But now he felt as if he were coming alive again. It was as if his own death had entered his life, laid its cold hands on his innards. Then, before it had gotten a grip, this woman's inquiry, this stranger's quite ordinary and understandable concern, had driven it from him. He took a deep breath, and then another, as she watched him with a mixture of curiosity and concern.

"No, I'm fine," he said then. "I'm sorry if I alarmed you." Then, in a gesture so uncharacteristic that it surprised even him, he began a conversation with her. "You are American, aren't you?" She was perhaps forty, and pretty. She wore blue jeans, boots, and a black sweater. She had a parka around her shoulders.

"I am an American," she said. "From California. But I have lived in Paris for the past three years." Then she added with enthusiasm, "I adore your country. It is a spectacularly beautiful country. It is so varied."

"Have you seen much of the rest of France?" Louis asked.

"I visit different parts whenever I can," she said. "I am just returning from a few days in Normandy, the coast, near Honfleur. I rented a car. Do you live in Paris?"

"Saint Leon sur Dême," he said. "A village between Le Mans and Tours."

"I have been to Tours. In fact, I spent two months there as a student learning French. And I was there again last summer."

"But north of Tours," said Louis, "where the Touraine ends and the Sarthe begins, the river Dême, an insignificant stream, empties into le Loir—not la Loire, which has an e. The Dême and the Loir are fishing streams with plenty of trout and other fish. Saint Leon is a farm town right on the Dême. I live in an old house made of tufeau, the soft chalky stone." He talked on and on. He relished the sound of the words in his mouth, as if each word were a new breath. He savored the feeling as they left his lips. He watched his hands moving through the air in front of him as he described the hill on which his house sat, where Saint Leon was situated, the Dême winding through the valley, Vauboin across the valley, the rows of poplars he had watched grow tall. He looked at her sitting next to him, smiling, her legs crossed, her hands in her lap. "I'm sorry for talking on and on, like an old man," he said.

"No, not at all. You make it sound absolutely lovely," she said. "Are you a poet?"

"I am a painter," he said. "But, don't worry, it's nothing serious." They both laughed. "I am going to give you my name and address," he said and took a pen and scrap of paper from inside his suit coat. "I would like you to come visit some time, to see for yourself." Louis had never done such a thing before. "You can stay with me."

She took the paper. "Louis Morgon," she read. "I'm Janet Dryer," she said and held out her hand. It was small and strong. "Thank you for the invitation. It is very generous. I would like to take you up on it sometime." She tilted her head in such a way that it made him think of Solesme.

Renard had left for Paris earlier. He had decided to drive. Isabelle had packed a sandwich and a thermos of coffee. "Keep an eye on Jean Marie and Louis," she said.

"And who is going to keep an eye on me?" he said.

"Would you like me to come?" She laughed.

"No, thank you. That is all I need," he said. He kissed her on the mouth, and they held each other tightly for a moment. He promised to call her as soon as . . .

"I'll wait for your call," she said.

By the time Renard arrived at the airport, Louis and Jean Marie were already going over what was to be done. Jean Marie was in uniform. *He is handsome,* thought Renard, as he did whenever he saw him. *I keep forgetting he is a grown man.* Jean Marie explained that he had arranged everything so that it was quite simple. There was very little that could go wrong with the plan. Louis would wait where he had been instructed to wait. There was a telephone nearby with an OUT OF ORDER sign which Jean Marie had placed there this morning. That was the phone Louis was to answer if he was called to the phone. "There is little doubt," said Louis. He seemed so certain.

Jean Marie would be inside a nearby electronics closet—Louis would be able to see the closet across the vast hall—where he would make the switches manually, and from where he could watch Louis. As soon as the announcement paging Louis was made, Jean Marie would remove the old card and insert the new card—he held up the manilla envelope containing the electronic circuit card he had constructed—so that any conversation from that phone could be broadcast throughout the terminal. Louis could start the broadcast himself by depressing and quickly releasing the receiver mechanism. When the conversation was over and Jean Marie had replaced the new card with the original card, which would return the circuitry to normal, he would leave the closet. Did Louis understand? Louis nodded. There were eight such closets throughout the terminal, so that even if the men on duty responded immediately to the malfunction, it would most likely take them a while to arrive at this closet, by which time Jean Marie would have left with the new card and without leaving a trace. Everything would have returned to normal.

"And what am I to do while all this is happening?" said

Renard. Of course he knew the answer. "I don't like just watching and waiting."

"It is the most important part. If things go awry, I am depending on you to save my life. You have your pistol?" Renard patted his side.

It was nearly six o'clock. Louis got on the shuttle bus alone. The bus made several stops before it reached terminal two. Confused travelers leaned in the door to ask in broken French if the bus stopped here or there. With each stop, Louis's heart beat faster. He tried not to look at his watch. But when he finally did look, barely a minute had passed since the last time he had looked.

Louis walked through the terminal's great hall. His steps echoed against the marble floor. This part of the terminal was nearly empty of passengers. A woman in a yellow smock pushed a cart with a trash can and brooms. Louis had not taken into account the fact that most international flights arrived and departed early in the day. There were a few passengers seated here and there, and airline agents were busy behind some of the counters. But he would not be surrounded by crowds as he had hoped. And, as the evening passed, there would be less and less people. He was certain that Hugh meant to keep him waiting. He sat down in the middle of an empty row of white plastic chairs not far from the out-of-order telephone. He looked at his watch so often that he finally took it off and put it in his pocket.

After a while he saw Jean Marie walk across the great hall and enter the closet. He closed the door behind him. Louis looked around the terminal. The windows were black. It was night. The ceiling lights reflected on the wet floor where the woman in the yellow smock was mopping. Louis followed her progress as she worked her way past him. He did not see Renard but he knew Renard could see him.

Louis waited. He sat beside his folded overcoat, his hands resting on his thighs, his eyes closed. He listened to his own breathing. He tried to empty his mind of everything, but of course he couldn't. He thought of the pretty American, Janet Dryer. He was pleased that he had been attracted to her. "Not dead yet," he thought and was startled by his own frivolity. He wondered whether Janet Dryer would come to Saint Leon and whether he would be dead.

Announcements for flights came less frequently. The airline desks closed and their attendants disappeared. The customs desks were empty. There would be no more flights tonight. A few travelers dozed in chairs across the way. Perhaps they had early morning departures. Two men were engaged in animated conversation and their voices echoed through the terminal. The sound of their voices became a roar, like a great airplane passing low above their heads.

Louis dozed and dreamed he was sitting alone on a canvas seat in the great empty plane. The only light came from a dim green bulb across from where he sat, so that the area around him was bathed in eerie twilight and the back of the plane disappeared into darkness. It was cold, and the roar of the engines came through the thin metal skin of the aircraft and filled the emptiness with sound. The plane's frame creaked and groaned as it plowed through the air. He was alone in the plane. There was no one in the cockpit.

Then he was on a bicycle riding across a vast field of milk. The sky above the milk was a smooth dark gray as though it were made of a sheet of steel. Louis was riding on the tender skin which had formed on the surface of the milk. He had to pedal with exquisite care and absolute concentration so as not break through.

Louis awoke to the announcement calling him to the phone. The lights inside the terminal had been lowered. The lights outside were surrounded by haloes. Fog had settled in over the airport. The closed door across the hall was still closed. A few passengers dozed in a twilit corner. They had managed to lie down around the armrests of adjoining seats, their suitcases on the floor in front of them. Instead of pointing at numbers, the hands of the large clock on the wall opposite where he had been sitting pointed at dots to indicate the time. This made Louis uneasy, as though time were no longer specific, as though any time could be any other time. He looked down half expecting to see that he was standing in milk. He looked up at the clock again. It was ten thirty.

"Were you asleep?" said Hugh Bowes. "I'm sorry to have kept you waiting. I assure you it was unavoidable. I've just come from Élysées. I think I can put your mind to rest about the matter we discussed in our last conversation."

"The murdered man," said Louis.

"Not on the phone, Louis. I'm certain you understand." Hugh's voice was calm, not scolding. "Just walk toward the doors right behind you, do you see them? One of my people will meet you inside and escort you to a room where we can talk openly. As you can imagine, this is a matter of the utmost delicacy." Louis saw the doors Hugh was talking about. They were windowless double doors with a sign forbidding entry to anyone but authorized personnel. "Go ahead, Louis. They are unlocked." It was as though Hugh were watching him from somewhere and could read his thoughts.

Louis looked to the left and the right of the doors for mirrors or openings from where he might have been observed. He did not see any. He looked up for security cameras, but they were hidden in the dark ceiling. "I can't go through the doors, Hugh," said Louis.

"You can't?" Hugh sounded genuinely puzzled.

"I am alone, Hugh. And I don't trust you." There was silence at the other end of the line. Louis waited. There was no response. "Hugh?"

"I'm still here. It seems to me, Louis, you are the one not to be trusted, given your history of instability, your well-documented efforts to make unauthorized visits to me at the State Department, your association with Milton Hamsher, a man who is also known to be unstable. That is not to mention the preposterous and reckless suggestions recently made by you to me and to Hamsher. I would be foolish to have a serious conversation with you over an insecure telephone line, wouldn't I?" Hugh's voice was calm, as though he were a patient father dealing with a recalcitrant child.

"I see your point, Hugh. What do you suggest?"

"What do I suggest. I suggest, Louis, that I was wrong to even imagine you could be trusted with the information I was about to offer you. I suggest I was blinded by our earlier association and by my lingering feelings of friendship for you. I suggest that we each go our separate ways. I have had a long day with the foreign ministers of France and Germany, and I now have a long flight home. As for you, Louis, your suspicions about me are as unfounded as your life is pathetic." Hugh's voice had begun to rise, his patience had given way to indignation. Louis quickly pushed and released the receiver cradle. "You have returned my generosity and affection with disloyalty and malice."

The sound of Hugh's voice echoed through the great hall. The amplification emphasized his impatience. His voice had a hard metallic ring to it as he unwittingly announced his indignation to the entire passenger terminal. The two passengers opposite Louis, who had been jolted awake by the unexpected sound of the loudspeakers, sat up slowly, smoothing their clothes as they did. They leaned forward trying to tell whether the announcement concerned them or not. Louis noticed that the closet door where Jean Marie waited had opened a crack. Two men, airline mechanics judging from their blue overalls, paused by an exit far across the hall, listened, then looked at one another, then left.

"I am still willing to help you, Louis." Hugh had regained his composure. Louis stood with the telephone receiver in his hand, but he listened to Hugh's voice coming over the loudspeakers. "Please appreciate my position, Louis. You will be perfectly safe. My people will escort you."

Two men wearing dark suits stepped through the doors which Hugh had invited Louis to enter. They moved quickly but then stopped. They looked up as they recognized Hugh Bowes's voice coming through the loudspeaker. The awakened travelers stood by their suitcases now. They strained to understand what was being said, thinking it might be information about their flight. Except this announcement was not in French. And it sounded more like a conversation than an announcement. The voice that boomed across the terminal was obviously talking about something important. He was not simply giving flight information. And Jean Marie had turned up the volume. Hugh's impatience, then his solicitousness were being amplified, were ringing through the terminal. Louis could see the airline mechanics outside the window across the hall. Were they listening to the outside speakers? A shuttle bus driver stood nearby.

One of the two men who had just come through the door spoke urgently into a small telephone as they began again to move quickly toward Louis. Louis dropped the telephone receiver and turned to run toward Renard, who was running toward him from across the terminal. But Renard was too far across the terminal to reach Louis before the two men did.

"What the fuck are you talking about?!" Hugh Bowes's voice

roared from the loudspeakers and echoed through the terminal, his anger crashing about them like a storm. The passengers gaped in astonishment and listened. The mechanics and the bus driver had come into the terminal. After a brief pause during which the man coming toward Louis spoke excitedly into his telephone, Hugh shouted, "Well, stop the son of a bitch. Stop him!" He realized too late that he still had the telephone from his call with Louis in his other hand. Louis turned to see the two men twenty feet from him, the larger of the two with a small automatic weapon pointed at Louis's chest.

Then Solesme stepped between Louis and the killers. She stood and faced the two men. Where had she come from? No one had noticed her approach. The two men skidded as they tried to stop on the slick granite floor. The large man recognized her first, then the other one did. Seeing that they knew who she was, Solesme slowly, one could almost say ceremoniously, turned and faced Louis. She was wearing a long black coat and a hat, as though she had known what Louis was wearing and had dressed to accompany him. She smiled at his astonished face. Louis raised his arms toward her.

Solesme took several steps toward him. She walked slowly and deliberately, her shoulders twisting with each step, walking in her unmistakable way, her body pitching in a way that was both painful to watch and arresting. She was taunting the two killers just as she had taunted the wedding procession in Dissay. The big man aimed his gun at Solesme's back.

When Solesme had almost reached Louis, she turned to face the men again. No one spoke. No one moved. There was silence from the loudspeakers, as though the great voice were now watching and listening too. The men did not shoot. Instead, they turned and fled back through the unmarked door. Louis and Solesme stood watching the door. Renard and then Jean Marie came running up. Renard ran to the doors and stepped through, but the men were gone.

"Let's go quickly. Before they come back," said Renard. But they had to walk slowly because of Solesme. Renard had his car outside the terminal. The two passengers, and the mechanics and bus driver stood and watched as the strange little procession passed between them. Louis held Solesme by one arm while Renard supported the other. Louis stared at her in astonishment as they walked. Renard muttered under his breath. "That was a foolish thing to do, madame, for love or for any other reason. You placed us all in danger. You placed yourself in danger."

Solesme looked straight ahead as she walked. Then she turned to Louis. "Is it over?" she asked.

"I think it is," he said. Then: "But we will have to wait and see." Then: "I do not know."

"The card!" said Jean Marie and ran back to replace the new card with the old one and to lock the closet door. Nobody had come to investigate. Had anyone even understood? A few people had arrived from other parts of the terminal in search of what the announcements might have meant. A cleaning lady stopped to watch them pass. The receiver of the phone still dangled from its cord. The OUT OF ORDER sign lay on the floor.

XXV

*H*UGH BOWES REMAINED ALONE IN THE STATEROOM OF HIS PLANE for the rest of the flight home. The lights were out, but he did not sleep. The meal the steward had served him sat untouched on the table beside the bed. Hugh sat in the large leather chair by the window and looked out at the night sky. The moon above and behind them shone on the solid field of clouds below.

They were flying from London, where earlier in the day Hugh had met with the British and German foreign ministers. The airplane had been somewhere over Greenland when he had spoken by telephone with Louis in the Charles DeGaulle Airport. Hugh had been certain that he had arranged everything to afford himself complete protection. He could effectively deny that he had been anywhere near Paris at the time of the incident. Or that he knew anything about Louis's abduction and assassination, if it had come about. How had he underestimated Louis Morgon?

Hugh fought to restore his sense of equilibrium. What exactly had he said to Louis on the telephone? How much had been broadcast? It didn't matter what he had said. Simply the sound of his voice placed him in a compromising position. He had jeopardized everything to which he had devoted his life because of one ruinous lapse in his self discipline.

Hugh asked himself how he could best restore his advantage, how he could regain maneuvering room. By the time his plane landed at Andrews Air Force Base and he had been helicoptered to the Department of State, Hugh had composed his letter of resignation as secretary of state.

December 15

Mr. President,

It is with mixed feelings that I am tendering my resignation as secretary of state. My sense of satisfaction at all the things we have accomplished together is mixed with regret that I am leaving the job while so much remains to be done.

As you know, Ruth's sudden death not six months ago was devastating to me beyond description. I have fought to recover, but have finally come to the conclusion that her death is, and will remain, a distraction from my doing my best work for some time to come. I am sorry for not having recognized that fact sooner. I only hope I have not, in the meantime, brought harm to your vision for an enlightened and rational foreign policy.

Of course, I serve at your pleasure and will gladly stay in my current position until a new secretary of state has been chosen and confirmed by the Senate. Beyond that, I hope to be able to serve you and your administration in whatever advisory capacity you might require of me.

Thank you, Mister President, for your continued faith in me, and for your unwavering support, especially in these last months.

Sincerely,
Hugh Bowes
Secretary of State

The president was shocked when he read the letter which Hugh handed him. "Why, Hugh? Why now all of a sudden?"

"I am a slow study in some things, Mister President. I did not imagine how Ruth's loss would affect me. I was so preoccupied with various matters of state that it only dawned on me slowly to what extent I might have lost my edge and concentration."

"That is simply not true, Hugh. Isn't there any way I can persuade you to change your mind?" There was pleading in the president's voice and eyes. Hugh sipped from a glass of bourbon.

"It is time," said Hugh, "for a new generation to move into power. I am certain you will have no trouble at all finding many capable candidates. I will be only too happy to help you through the process. If you like, I can oversee the selection."

The president leaned back in his chair. "You have someone in mind."

"Several names come to mind," said Hugh. "James Dillworth, for instance. He was invaluable to me as undersecretary for European affairs. He has gained visibility and universal respect as ambassador to the United Nations."

"Who else," said the president.

Hugh named others. None of the people he suggested were

either too independent or too courageous. "And of course, Mister President, if you choose to keep me on as your personal advisor, I would have the capacity to act and to direct the further development of your foreign policy without the constraints that might encumber me as an official in your administration."

At his next press conference, the president announced that he was accepting Hugh's resignation with great regret, and that he was naming James Dillworth to be Hugh's successor. He praised Dillworth as a worthy successor, whose vision and belief in the power of diplomacy echoed Hugh Bowes's. "And let me add this personal note," said the president. He laid aside the pages of his statement and stepped to the side of the podium. "Hugh Bowes has served his country with courage and singular dedication throughout this and previous administrations. I knew, when I named him secretary of state, that I was getting an exceptionally capable man to direct my foreign policy. But I did not know his true mettle. In my studies of American political and diplomatic history, and you know I am a devoted student of these subjects, I have found no diplomat who has served his country better than Hugh Bowes has. He has been my most able counselor on matters, not only foreign, but also on prickly domestic matters. But he has also been a friend. And, goodness knows, a guy in my position can use a friend, especially when you folks in the press cut loose from time to time." The assembled reporters laughed along with the president.

Later that week, Hugh held a meeting with State Department officials assembled in the large auditorium to offer them his personal farewell. "You are the finest people there are," he told them. "It has been an honor serving with you as we all together serve this great democracy. It will be hard to go, but you know me: I won't be going far." There was laughter from the assembled diplomats. "Most of

you know how terrible Ruth's loss was for me. I am, I have been surprised to discover, a slow healer. At this time in my life, I want to
take some time to think. I want to write, memoirs perhaps, certainly
some thoughts about the conduct of foreign policy which, I fancy,
might be of some modest use to those that come after us. I might
teach. I will certainly offer advice, whether it is asked for or not."
Again there was laughter. "And now it is time to stop." Hugh
Bowes's voice suddenly choked with emotion. "It has been wonderful, to know you and to work with you. I will miss you all." The
assembly sprang to their feet and applauded enthusiastically and
with genuine affection.

Louis read the brief announcement of Hugh's resignation in the
International Herald Tribune. A few days later he received a note
from Sarah.

> *Dear Louis,*
> *I thought this might interest you. Is it good news for you, or*
> *bad? Does this mean he is finished with you, that whatever was*
> *going on is over?*
> *Jenny told me she is going back to school. She wants to be a*
> *nurse, she thinks. Her timing isn't great—health care here is a*
> *mess—but I think she'll be a very good nurse.*
> *I hope you're well.*
>
> *Sincerely,*
> *Sarah*

She had enclosed a story from the *Washington Post* about Hugh
Bowes's resignation, followed by an account of his long and illustri-
ous career. "Hugh Bowes is the consummate diplomat, the diplomat's diplomat. For, not only is he universally respected by the

international diplomatic community, he is liked and admired by the press corps as well. That is a test few Washington insiders are able to pass. For the press is susceptible to no amount of diplomatic skill. And political pressure counts for nought. 'Either the press likes you or they don't,' said Rusty Martinez, diplomatic correspondent for the *New York Times*. They like Hugh Bowes. From his earliest days in Washington, Hugh Bowes was a favorite of reporters. 'You could always count on Hugh to be straight with you,' said Stan Edmonson of ABC News."

Hugh Bowes was paid an enormous advance for his projected memoir, which he titled *All the World a Stage*. It appeared a year later to enthusiastic reviews. "It is filled with intelligent insight into the political process in the United States and in the world at large," wrote one reviewer. "Only a major actor on the world stage could have seen what Hugh Bowes has seen. And only a major actor could tell the stories Hugh Bowes has to tell. The immense value of this book is a measure of his success as a politician, diplomat, and human being. He is generous to his allies and magnanimous to his adversaries." Louis ordered the book and read it with interest.

The president continued to call on Hugh to help with ticklish situations no one else seemed able to deal with effectively, and Hugh helped where he could, with the enthusiasm, perspicacity, and generosity for which he was known. Hugh was invited to speak before prestigious groups, which he did with eloquence and humor. He continued to play a lively part in the highest echelons of Washington and New York society. He got quietly rich. He did not marry again.

Was it over? There was no way for Louis to tell. Had Hugh abandoned his desire for retribution, or had Louis's victory only redoubled his determination? Perhaps Hugh had resigned as secretary of state to devote himself more fully to his revenge. Or perhaps he had put it aside, was moving past it, just as he might move past any other small obstacle on the road to his renown. Neither possibility was unthinkable.

Louis only knew that he could not forget about what had happened, or let go of the fear that, if Hugh decided to commence their struggle anew, there was nothing Louis could do to prevent it. Whatever peace Louis had found in Saint Leon had been taken from him. Gnawing fear, which gradually faded to uneasiness, had been left in its place.

Louis was convinced that Hugh would not kill him outright. Louis had given taped copies of the broadcast conversation at Charles DeGaulle Airport which Jean Marie had lifted from the master tape to Renard for safekeeping in his police files. Jean Marie had also obtained a list of people on duty at the airport that night—ticket agents, security people, maintenance and janitorial people, freight and baggage handlers—who might have heard the broadcast conversation. There were seventy-six in all. Louis did not send a copy of the tape to Hugh Bowes since, he reasoned, Hugh's uncertain recollection of what he had said was probably far more powerful than the tape itself could ever be.

Isabelle Renard made a celebratory dinner and invited Louis and the Lefouriers. Jean Marie came from Paris with a young woman he had been seeing. Isabelle roasted two capons with onions, carrots, and potatoes. The crisp brown skin of the birds was studded with cloves of garlic. After the meal she served cheese and fruit. Solesme explained how she had hired a taxi and followed Louis to Le Mans, and that she was in the same train as he going to Paris, how she had followed him in the RER to the airport and then in the *navette*.

Suddenly, to everyone's astonishment, Pierre, the great pyramid, began singing to himself. He sang off-key. His voice was hoarse from more than sixty years of smoking black tobacco. Then, still singing, he rose from his chair and began dancing, circling slowly about the dining table. The others turned in their chairs, one by one, as he passed behind them. They watched in silent amazement.

Pierre held his right arm behind his imaginary partner's back and his left arm perpendicular to the floor. He turned small, careful circles, balancing on his toes, his great body swaying to the rhythm of his own singing. The song, a familiar one, croaked and wheezed out of him as though he were some ancient and decrepit instrument, which, in a sense, he was. After a few moments, Solesme stood and slipped into his arms. Her voice joined his, though he hardly seemed to notice. He danced with his eyes closed and his mouth smiling.

Louis and Isabelle stood at the same moment, and they too began singing and dancing, and then Jean Marie and Renard stood and began singing and dancing together, while Jean Marie's astonished girlfriend watched and laughed, her hand in front of her mouth in a state that alternated between amusement and shock.

It was a short winter. In late February, the grass began to grow and the jonquils and crocuses appeared. The wheat in the surrounding fields turned vivid green, buds appeared on the fruit trees. Louis and Solesme held each other as people do who are certain of their own deaths, wanting to obliterate forgetting and loss, hoping that the ferocity of their longing alone might accomplish that impossible feat.

They walked through the fields together. Once, taken by sudden desire, they made love in a barn in the straw. It was not the sort of thing people their age did, but they did it anyway. Their breath rose in hot puffs of steam. Their skin was covered with red dots where the straw had pricked it. They admired each other naked, gasping and laughing in the cold, then hurried back into their clothes.

Pierre died in March. His death was sudden, but not unexpected. How could it have been unexpected at his age? The hearse left the church in Saint Leon and moved up the hill to the cemetery on the edge of town. Solesme led the mourners. Her brother and a sister walked beside her. Louis walked with Renard and Isabelle in the crowd of townspeople. They walked through the square, past the Hotel de France, past the police station, the post office, the bakery. Outside the stationery store, a mother stooped to comfort her small daughter who had begun to cry at the sight of so many old people dressed in black.

Pierre was buried under a wrought-iron cross with his picture on it and his name and dates in gold leaf. Afterward, people shook Solesme's hand or embraced her. They stood about in small groups, talking about how the young were all moving to the city, and the government could do nothing to prevent it. Unemployment was epidemic. Village life was dying. Everyone nodded their heads in sad agreement.

XXVI

APRIL CAME, THEN MAY. LITTLE BY LITTLE, THE ROUTINE AND order of the day-to-day worked its way back into Louis's heart, until the chaos which had landed on his doorstep had been smoothed out and pushed into memory. The story of the dead man and Hugh Bowes became, like everything else that resides in memory, just another moment from his life, one more piece of experience. In his garden, Louis cut the small white heads of lettuce one by one. He pulled the radishes. He drew the earth up over the burgeoning asparagus stalks. He pinched off the tendrils from the strawberry plants. He hoed away the weeds. He planted and staked the tomatoes. He planted beans. He planted a row of zinnias. In the evening, he passed up and down with a large green watering can and carefully soaked each plant, each row, refilling the can from the spigot beside the garden.

Standing high on the wooden ladder, he cut back the Virginia creeper to keep it from growing under the roof of the barn. He cut the laurel hedge. He marveled, with Solesme, how everything had grown. He fertilized and pruned the roses. He stood below and watched as the Lagrande brothers clambered over the roof, replacing broken and missing slates. Guy Vivet hung the new oak shutters he had made for Louis. Guy had salvaged the hardware from the old pine shutters, which had not cost much, but had not lasted very long either. "Shutters," said Guy, "should be oak."

Renard came by for coffee. The people who had kidnapped Solesme seemed to have disappeared from the face of the earth. The search for them had gone nowhere, and once she had been released unharmed, the investigation had been shunted aside by more urgent matters. The resources of the police were stretched too thin. Louis showed Renard his newest painting, a still life of lettuces and radishes. "It looks good enough to eat," said Renard. He never knew what to say about Louis's paintings.

One morning in the middle of May, Louis was finishing a late and leisurely breakfast on the terrace. The weather was changeable: menacing clouds followed by brilliant sunshine. Charly Matrat arrived in his little yellow van with the mail. There was a letter from Jenny. Her handwriting was careful and round. All the periods were neat little circles.

May 10

Dear Dad,

I'm sorry it has taken me so long to write. I've been really busy.

Good news! I have been accepted by the nursing program at Marymount College in Arlington! Thanks for your encouragement in this. Mom has been encouraging too. Even Michael,

when I told him what I was going to do, said "Go for it, Jen."
So I guess I will, though I'm still scared about doing it. It's a
completely different direction for me, something I never even
thought about before. But somehow it really appeals to me.

Thanks too for your invitation to visit and your offer to pay
for my ticket. It is very nice of you. I have so much to do, so
much to figure out between now and the start of classes in
August, including a chemistry course I have to take this sum-
mer (a condition of my admission), that I just can't afford the
time away. I can't afford the time away, Dad, but I decided I'm
going to do it anyway! Michael told me you invited him too,
but he isn't coming this summer. He said to say that he'll write
you. As you can tell, now Michael and I talk from time to time.

As it happens, the dates you suggest are good ones for me.
But is it all right if I just stay for a week? Let me know how to
get from Paris to your house. I'll see you June 18! It's barely a
month away! Just this minute I realized I am really going to do
this and got very excited!

Jenny

On June 17, after tending and watering his garden, Louis drove to
Le Mans and once again took the train to Paris. He slept in a small
hotel, the Istria in Montparnasse, and early the following morning,
he took the RER to Charles DeGaulle. It was another sunny, crisp
day, just the sort of day Louis had hoped for.

Louis stood with his eyes fixed on the board announcing the
arriving flights. He almost expected to see Jenny's name appear on
the board. Jenny's plane arrived at eight o'clock. A half hour later she
pushed her luggage cart through the swinging doors that led from
customs. Her eyes searched the crowd and quickly found Louis. To

her surprise and his, she threw herself into his arms, and he held her for a long time, caressing her hair and kissing her forehead.

Jenny was tired, of course, so Louis suggested they go straight home and save Paris for the last day of her trip. To see Paris thoroughly, she would have to come back again and stay longer. In the train, Jenny fell asleep against his shoulder. Louis looked at their reflection in the window, afraid that if he turned to look at her directly, she might vanish altogether.

When they drove up the driveway, Jenny wanted to go straight to her room and sleep. "Just a nap, Jenny, or you won't be able to sleep tonight." Louis sat on the terrace and gazed out over the garden at the wheat swaying tall and green, showing the first hint of gold. While she slept he went shopping. He made a salad for lunch. He woke her after she had slept for two hours. "This is where I eat my breakfast every morning, all year round," he said and waved his hand to take in the landscape before them. "And lunch and dinner when the weather is good."

"You're a good cook, Dad," said Jenny.

"It's a salad, Jenny. But you're right: I am a good cook." He had invited the Renards and Solesme for dinner that evening. He made a roast pork loin with prunes, potatoes, and spinach. Jenny had had three years of French in high school. She had forgotten most of it and was shy about using what remained. Solesme and Isabelle knew very little English. Renard would not admit to knowing any. And yet, somehow, the dinner conversation was spirited. Renard would, from time to time, suddenly contribute a perfectly formed and horribly pronounced English sentence, which delighted everyone each time he did it. Solesme and the Renards were glad to finally meet someone from Louis's family. "She has your nose and mouth," said Solesme.

"She is very pretty, Louis," said Isabelle.

"I see no resemblance at all," said Renard.

"They seem like very nice people," said Jenny. "Solesme is quite beautiful. Are you in love with her?"

The next morning he and Jenny walked together through Saint Leon. Louis described the history of the town and of the region. He took Jenny into the church and showed her the traces of ancient frescoes that had recently been discovered. He told her about how, for centuries past, the pilgrims had found their way from all over Europe to Santiago, stopping in Saint Leon as they went. He pointed out the seashell carved in the stone above the church door, the symbol that meant pilgrims were welcome. He did not speak about his own pilgrimage of twenty years ago. After all, his pilgrimage had been her abandonment.

Louis introduced Jennifer to Madeleine Picard and to Madame Chalfont, who ran the Hotel de France by herself since Monsieur Chalfont's condition had deteriorated so badly. Each time he introduced Jenny to someone new, he tried to step back a bit and just watch. Jenny was tall and pretty, and though it was true she had a slightly stiff, slightly prudish air, she also seemed strong and sure of herself. When you were introduced to her, she looked into your eyes.

"What are all the decorations for, Dad, and the loudspeakers? Is there a fair or something?"

"It's the Festival of Music, Jenny," said Louis. "It's something quite remarkable. It's not just here, but it's in every town and village in France. The French celebrate the arrival of summer, and the longest day, by singing and dancing all night. They literally dance the night away. I'm glad you're here for the festival, Jenny." Louis stopped and looked around the square. It was suddenly as though he had just arrived, as though he had never been here before. "The first night I ever spent in Saint Leon was the night of the Festival of Music. It's somehow perfect that you're here now. I'm glad you're here."

The day of the twenty-first was, in contrast to all the previous days of Jenny's visit, rainy and chilly, with heavy clouds blowing in low over the hills from the west. Occasionally, the rain stopped and the clouds broke apart. But then they closed back up, and the rain would begin again. There was little hope that the weather would change. All of Europe was under the influence of a strong low pressure system over the Atlantic.

And yet the weather did change. At about nine o'clock, as Louis and Jenny were finishing their supper, the clouds suddenly broke up, and in a matter of minutes the sky was clear and blue. The sunlight poured through the window into the kitchen, and, unable to resist what seemed like an invitation, they took their plates and the fruit bowl and went out to sit at the battered metal table. The sun was low in the sky. The light had taken on that magical golden quality it sometimes assumes before sunset.

Over the last few days, the length and depth of Louis and Jenny's estrangement had become clear. They had come to understand how little they knew about one another, what a small part each of them had played, or, for that matter, could ever now play in the other's life. Some things simply could not, could never be replaced or made up for. They might perhaps come to like each other, might even love each other, might have lives that became intricately involved, might become friends, but they could never become father and daughter. That was lost to them forever. This knowledge filled Jenny with resentment and Louis with sorrow. That is why they had eaten their supper in silence, looking mostly at their plates. When Louis looked at Jenny, she chose not to meet his eyes.

Now, as the sun moved down toward the sharp blue horizon, their silence continued. In fact, it seemed to grow, to fill the landscape around them with a sullen, dead quality. "I'm not going tonight," said Jenny. "It's your Festival of Music. It's not mine." Louis had eventually told her all about his first day and night in Saint Leon, about meeting the gypsy Kadusco, Phillipe or Henri or who knew what his name had been. He had told her about hating to dance and yet dancing, dancing with Madame Chalfont, dancing with Solesme.

"Did you think of us, while you were dancing?" said Jenny. "Did you think of me?" This was the damage it seemed they would never get past. At ten thirty, the sun set behind the fields in front of them. They carried the dishes inside, and Louis put them in the dishwasher, while Jenny retreated to her room. Louis called to her that he was leaving for the festival, but she did not answer. He walked down the driveway and into town, not wanting to leave Jenny by herself, but not wanting to stay away from the festival either.

Children were dancing in the square to the recorded music coming from the loudspeakers. Some teenage boys were throwing firecrackers in the street. Louis greeted his friends. They inquired after Jenny. He found Solesme sitting with Madeleine Picard. "Where is Jenny?" she wanted to know.

"She isn't coming," said Louis. "I think she sees this as a celebration of my abandonment of her, something like that." He drew his hand across his eyes. Madeleine got up to visit with someone else. Solesme put her hand on his, a reckless gesture for her. It startled him. "She cannot forgive me," said Louis.

"Nor must she," said Solesme. "But why is it necessary? We all have a lot that is unforgivable about us, even someone as young as your daughter. If we were all without our unforgivable parts then love would mean nothing at all. Love happens despite the unforgivable. Loving someone unforgivable, now that is something. That is love." Now she took his hand in both of hers. "Come on, let's dance." They were playing the *musette*.

There was no live *musette* at the *fête de la musique* in Saint Leon any more. They had only tapes which they broadcast over the loudspeakers. Later, there would be a live rock duet with an electric piano and drums. But the gypsy accordionist had disappeared years ago. Other, apparently unmusical gypsies now camped above the cemetery for several weeks each summer and tried to sell the baskets they made to passersby on the streets of Saint Leon. Though the *musette* playing was a recording, it still drew everyone onto the square. And just as Louis and Solesme had bobbed and circled around the square that first time, and every year after that, they circled again with the tide of their friends and neighbors eddying about them.

They held each other gently. Solesme's steps were shorter still, and more delicate, than they had ever been. Louis sensed her fragility as he never had before. It was as if Pierre's death had taken some of her life too.